HAVOC MC: BOOK 1

UNCAGED

L.A. BOLES

ISBN: 978-1-7321970-0-8

Copyediting by:
EAL Editing Services

Cover Design by:
Natasha Snow Designs
www.natashasnowdesigns.com

Author's Photo by:
Yolanda Garcia Photography

Mom,
I wouldn't be who am today without you. Thank you and I love you.

GLOSSARY

1%er (One-Percenter) – Refers to the 1% of motorcycle riders that do not follow laws.

Bottom Rocker – Designates a geographic location or territory.

Brother – A fellow biker or close friend.

Burner – An untraceable prepaid cell phone usually used for confidential conversations.

Cage – A car, truck, or van.

Center Patch – Patch that sits in the center of a cut, showing the club logo.

Chapel – The meeting room where church is held.

Chapter – The local body of a larger club. Ex: Havoc Motorcycle Club, Sage Chapter.

Church – A club meeting where only fully patched member can attend.

Civilian or Citizen – Someone not associated with a Motorcycle Club.

Club Property – A sweetbutt or woman that has aligned herself with an MC.

Colors – The patches that identify a specific MC.

Cut – A vest that all club patches are sewn onto. They are worn as the outer-most layer of clothing.

Enforcer – Defends the clubs territory and collects debts owed to the MC.

Hang Around – Someone not affiliated with an MC that does small jobs for the club in the hopes of prospecting.

Ink – A tattoo.

Marker – A favor or IOU.

MC – A motorcycle club.

Mother Chapter – The original chapter of a Motorcycle Club.

Ol' Lady – A wife or long-time girlfriend. Does not refer to age and is not a derogatory term.

President - The leader of a chapter.

Property Of – Usually displayed on cut or tattoo to show who the woman "belongs to." Ex: "Property of Rock" means that woman has associated herself with Rock and Rock must answer for any rules the woman breaks.

Prospect – A prospective club member. Prospects must be voted into the MC by a unanimous vote. Wears a bottom rocker that reads "Prospect."

Road Name – A nickname usually earned during prospecting.

Rocker – A part of the MC colors. Designates geographic location or territory.

Run – A club sanctioned outing to a location in order to take care of club business. Can also refer to a club sanctioned party.

Sgt. at Arms – Enforces the bylaws of the club. In charge of managing the Enforcers.

Support Club - A smaller club that supports a 1%er MC.

Sweetbutt – A girl that hangs around the club for protection in exchange for sex or other duties, such as chores.

Sweetie – A club equivalent of a girlfriend.

Three Piece Patches – Consists of the top rocker, bottom rocker, and center patch.

Top Rocker – Designates the club's name.

VP - Vice President.

My soul is black. Darker than black. Stained with the sins of my past. I would give anything to step into the light.

PROLOGUE

Past

PAUL

SAVANNAH IS SINGING IN THE BACK SEAT AS WE MAKE OUR WAY OUT OF town and head to Atlanta. Today we are visiting Fernbank Natural History Museum. The museum is Savannah's favorite place in the world. She loves learning and seeing the dinosaur bones, and I love hearing her excited laugh as she runs from exhibit to exhibit.

Mary is singing along with Savannah to the song on the radio, and they are both giggling as they mess up the words. It is nice seeing Mary so vibrant again. Over the past few months, Mary has been drained from the radiation and chemotherapy. Most days she can hardly get out of bed, but somehow she does. She wants life to be as normal for our daughters as possible. Today I see a glimmer of the Mary I fell in love with.

"Oh, Mommy," Savannah screeches with excitement, "look at the water! It's so pretty!"

"Yes, baby, it is," she replies with sadness. "I want you to remember our time together. Anytime you look over the water, I will be with you."

"I will remember, Mommy. I will always remember."

The sadness in Mary's tone squeezes my heart. She is dying, and with grace she is preparing our baby for her death. How else do you explain to a child that their mother is dying? I don't know what I will do without her. She is the other half of my soul. How am I supposed to raise two little girls without their mother? I can't do this alone.

Smiling over at Mary, I try to hide the pain I feel. I glance at Savannah through the rearview mirror, her bright smile stretches across her face, and she is bouncing in her seat. I'm not sure she understands the magnitude of her mother's words, but someday she will. One day she will understand.

The open windows blow Savannah's long curls around her face, so much like her mother's. Suddenly, another car slams into us. My world is turned on its head for the second time in just a few short months. We plunge into the raging river water and I struggle to free myself from my seat belt. I'm losing air fast. I glance at Mary and she twists her body toward Savannah who has a look of terror sitting on her angelic face. Mary is desperately trying to free Savannah, but she is still buckled in her seat, and she cannot free our little girl from the front seat.

With an effort, I release my seat belt, and I begin to get my wife free, but she fights me. Her eyes are wide, and the panic I feel is written on her beautiful face. She flails her arms toward our daughter as much as she can in a sinking car. Instead of continuing to free Mary, I work on Savannah's seat belt as fast as I can in the murky raging river. I attempt to free her with my body leaning over the seats as much as possible. Once she is free from her constraints, I push her tiny body out of the open window and squeeze out of the window behind her. My heart plummets as my wife and the love of my life sinks to the bottom of the river with our car.

At the surface, Savannah gasps, her tiny lungs taking in air. Her cries pierce the sound of my blood rushing in my ears.

"Shh, baby," I coo. "I've got you."

"Mommy..." her unintelligible crying continues.

I wake up, still feeling the cold river water washing over my skin. Whenever I close my eyes, the darkness consumes me and the day my worst nightmare came true plays on a continuous loop.

Opening my eyes, I look over and see blonde hair fanned out over the pillow next to me, and it turns my stomach. All I want is the sweet scent of lavender and a soft brunette mane next to me, but she's dead, and it is all Savannah's fault.

CHAPTER ONE

SAVY

WITH THE CRASH OF THUNDER, I SHOOT STRAIGHT UP. MY BREATHING is heavy like I have been running. As my breathing calms, I look at the clock on my nightstand, 3:46 A.M., I need to sleep, but I know I won't.

So instead, I swing my legs off the edge of the bed as I sit up, though still slouching with sleep. This is the third time this week I have woken in the middle of the night, and I cannot figure out why. I lay in my bed and think of anything and everything that will help me understand what is wrong with me.

With another loud bang of thunder, I hear the soft patter of rain tap my bedroom window. Pushing myself to my feet, I walk to the bathroom mirror and stare. Looking back at me, I see myself. The real me, not the person I show to the world, but the scared, insecure girl I have always been.

But have I? Have I always been this way?

Big brown eyes with flecks of gold that curve downward stare back at me. It is almost like I'm staring at a stranger. My long, brown, naturally curly hair, and golden skin with light freckles dusting my nose are the only features I recognize. Huge bags under my eyes show the stress and worry I live with every day. Twisting the knob, water shoots out of the faucet and I splash it on my face, not waiting for the water to warm. Turning off the water, I return to my bed without drying my face.

I have to be up in just a few hours, as it's Ena's last day of school, and I want to make sure she's ready for her exams. I lay back down, the water cooling on my face and the sound of the rain dancing against the window panes. I toss and turn for a while, but mostly I stare at the ceiling for hours before I give up my attempt at sleep, and turn off the switch on my alarm clock before it goes off.

I head down the short, barren hallway to my tiny kitchen as I pull on my old ratty housecoat. The kitchen has a small two–person kitchen table, an old microwave that barely works, and a stove that is on its last leg. Starting coffee in my old coffee pot, I sit at the table and close my eyes while the coffee maker percolates.

I spend most mornings sitting in my little kitchen waiting for the dark elixir of life to finish. Today is no different, but my lack of sleep last night has me dragging this morning.

"Good morning, Savy!" Ena sings while strolling into the kitchen. "Can I have twenty dollars?"

"No," I groan. I'm barely awake and the first thing out of her mouth this morning is about money. I'm not awake enough for this shit.

"Aww, come on seester," Ena says, changing the word to the pronunciation she used as a child. "I know you have it. I'll love you forever."

McKena, Ena for short, is my baby sister. Being the baby of our duo, she usually gets her way. Typically after some whining or, often, arguing. She's laying it on thick this morning. She's smart too, asking for money before my coffee. As per her usual plan of attack, catch me when my defenses are down. The little shit.

Smiling to myself. *I love Ena to death, but she's too smart for her own damn good.* As soon as the coffee maker stops, I pour myself a cup, filling it to the rim. Today I drink it black. I hate black coffee, preferring it with lots of cream and sugar, but when you are struggling for money, these are luxuries you can't afford.

"Here," she says. "I swiped these from the cafeteria at school." She slides several packets of sugar and powdered coffee creamer across the table toward me, and my heart swells.

God. I love her so much.

"Thanks, baby girl." I add my creamer and sugar, and I close my eyes as I sip my coffee, letting its warmth seep into my tired body. "Ena, if you want to eat next week, I can't give you money." I give her a pointed look so she knows I'm on to her game.

"I hate being poor." She's only seventeen and hanging out with friends on a Saturday night is a rite of passage at that age. I know this, but I live paycheck to three days before paycheck most weeks. If it weren't for my tips down at the club, we would be screwed. Thankfully, the tips are decent, but not enough to pay all the bills and provide adequate meals and clothes for my sister. Teenage girls are expensive as hell. Who knew?

"Me too, kid," I reply.

It's true. I hate being poor just as much as Ena. Struggling to keep the lights on. Struggling to have enough food in the house. Sometimes I don't eat as making sure Ena has enough food means I'm often left without. I would never allow my sister to feel those stabbing, shooting pains deep in your stomach that feel as if you might die.

I, on the other hand, feel those hunger pains most days.

"Yeah, okay, Sav." The look on my sister's face devastates me and the vice in my chest constricts so tight that I can hardly breathe. "Maybe I'll just ask the girls to come hang out over here tonight." Ena turns to leave our tiny kitchen.

"Hey." The word barely makes it out of my constricted throat. I reach out and grab her hand stopping her progression out of the room. "I love you, kid. Go grab my purse."

"Really?" Excitement warms her eyes causing the vice to loosen, but only a smidge. She rushes out of the kitchen to get my purse from the chair in the living room.

"Yeah really," I whisper to myself, a small smile crossing my lips.

Seeing Ena so happy and excited for something as simple as twenty dollars reminds me why I stepped up as her full–time caregiver.

Though the police would say I kidnapped her. I had an excellent reason, and I would do it again without batting an eye. She's the only family I have left.

Everyone else is either dead or dead to me.

I'm happy I decided to give Ena the money, and I know it was the right decision. She's a good sister and never gives me trouble. I'll just have to work double shifts to make extra cash. I'll have to ask Donny for more shifts.

Fuck.

Ena comes rushing back into the kitchen with so much excitement that I can't help but give a full, toothy smile, her good mood pulling me from my thoughts. "You are crazy. You know that?"

"Duh! You love my craziness," she states while grinning. "I'm just excited I get to hang out with Ashleigh and Natalie tonight. It's been forever."

I love how much Ena enjoys life. She loves the small things that life has to offer. She's always been a sweet girl, and now she's growing into a sweet, mostly well–adjusted young woman. Thank goodness she hasn't picked up any of my bad habits. Except cursing. The girl can let them fly, but then so can I.

I often imagine that my mother is watching over us from wherever she is. I'm not sure I believe in heaven, but I hope she is beaming with pride at how Ena is turning out, minus the cursing of course. Me on the other hand, Mary Ann Riley is rolling over in her grave. I made promises to my mother before she died unexpectedly. Well, it wasn't unexpected, just sooner than we all had hoped, and more dramatic too. And I have done none of the things I promised to do. The thought of disappointing my mother causes the vice to tighten again.

I'll make you proud, Momma, I promise.

"I love you, McKena, so much." Despite our past, Ena and I have always been able to express our feelings to one another. We can show our love and devotion to each other without the worry of judgment or pain. That has not been the case with other people. It's easier to keep people at a distance. Distance prevents them from getting too close and hurting you. At least that's the case for me. McKena doesn't seem to struggle as much as I do, but I see her struggle. I see the shadows in her eyes, the pain underneath the surface, but we never talk about it. The past is the past, and nothing will ever change it, so we avoid it. It's not healthy, but most days we are just trying to survive and barely doing it. I plan to get us both counseling. We will go one day, but we can't afford it right now. Mental health is another luxury we cannot afford. "Where are you going tonight? Will there be an adult there?"

Rolling her eyes at my overprotectiveness, she says, "We are going to the movies. There is a new slasher movie out, and Ash and I want to scare Natalie. She's always jumping, even when nothing scary is happening," she says while shaking her head. "And, Ash's mom will drop us off and pick us up. Can I spend the night too?"

"You know I need to talk to Ashleigh's mom first, but I think that's a good idea. I'm working late tonight."

The joy from a minute ago is gone, replaced by a rumbling tension. Ena is now staring at the table in our small kitchen. "I'm sorry, Savannah." She whispers so low that I almost don't hear her, but I do hear her. *I always hear her.*

Setting my coffee mug down, I stand and round the table in a few short steps and stand next to her. I gently grip her chin, tilting her head up. She keeps her eyes on the table until she is forced to look me in the eyes. "What do you think you have to be sorry for, McKena? You haven't done anything wrong, have you?"

"No. It's just you have to work late because you are giving me money," she says. "I can just hang out here tonight, Sav. I don't have to go out." Hating that my sweet baby sister feels guilty about wanting to be a teenager almost kills me. The vice tightens even more. "Maybe I should get a job, Savy. I can help with bills, and we will have more money."

"No," I say.

"But–"

"McKena Marina Riley, I said no," I say, keeping my voice even. "You are not getting a job. You already have one, school. Or have you forgot? We have a plan, and I'll be damned if you get a dead end job and your grades start suffering because of it. Do you understand me?" I sound more like her mother than her sister, but I don't care. I made a promise to my mom, and I will kill myself to keep it. McKena will graduate high school and go to college. She has worked so hard at maintaining her grades and has already gotten letters from colleges offering full academic scholarships. Thank goodness for the scholarships because Lord knows I can't pay for college.

Staring at me for a long moment, she relents, and turns her eyes back to the table. "Okay, Sav. No job."

"Damn right no job." Satisfied that this crazy idea is out of her head, I say, "Now, just know I won't be able to give you any more money for a while okay, Pip?"

She looks up and smiles when I call her Pip. The childhood nickname I gave her when she was three or four. Short for pipsqueak, she had the cutest squeaky voice when she was little.

"I love that name."

"I know you do." Crisis averted, at least for now. A genuine smile flashes across my face. I'm thankful every day for the little moments I get to spend with Ena. Life has not been kind to us, but we keep pushing. *I keep pushing.* Without the determination to give Ena a better life, the darkness would consume my soul.

CHAPTER TWO

SAVY

WORKING AT THE JUNGLE ISN'T WHAT I PLANNED ON DOING WITH MY life, but it pays the bills. Not all of the bills, but most. I never imagined I'd be working in a club, let alone a strip club, but I do whatever my family needs and we need money to survive. I'm the only person my sister can count on, so the plans I had for my life are on hold. One day I'll do all the things I always dreamed of doing. College, career, who knows, but right now I need money, so The Jungle is my foreseeable future.

The Jungle is your typical strip club. It's dark, dank, and filled with girls willing to grind on a stage for money. The main room has several small stages surrounding one massive stage in the center, the large stage features three gold poles and neon lights, a lot of neon lights. There are several small private rooms along the left wall. Behind the main stage, mirrors stretch from the ceiling to the floor. The mirrors make the room look bigger, and many of the dancers use them to their advantage during their dances. Against the far right wall, there is a large bar with comfortable black leather stools lining one side.

Like any strip club, The Jungle is filled with horny men who will try to sweet talk the girls into sleeping with them. Most guys are decent enough, they just come to watch the girls dance, but some think they can treat all women like shit because they are paying to watch them take their clothes off. The bouncers at the club make sure the customers keep their hands to themselves unless they're paying. If someone is willing to pay enough, the owner will allow anything. It's one part of working at The Jungle that I hate.

The owner of the club, Donny, is a total asshole. With his buck teeth, large ears, and beady black eyes, he reminds me of an overgrown rat. His appearance is not lost on the dancers either. They often joke about his twitchy nose, and beady eyes. Despite his appearance, many of the dancers still choose to sleep with him. Donny is known for sleeping with the club girls. He often requires the dancers to have sex with him for extra hours or better shifts. Donny is a massive dickhead and someone I avoid as often as possible.

When I interviewed for the bartender position, Donny stared at my breasts for twenty minutes while I tried to persuade him to hire me. He asked me to be a dancer, but I told him no. I was thinking fuck no! I'm a bartender and nothing more. Despite his unapologetic lecherous stare, Donny seemed to be an all right guy in the beginning. I learned to never be in the same room with him alone. He follows me with his eyes. He's always watching, not like a boss, but like a pervert. So, like I always do, I protect myself by never being alone with him. I learned at a young age to trust my instincts. Because he makes my skin crawl, I limit the time I have to interact with him. Unfortunately, I need more hours, so I have to talk to Donny tonight. He has been in his office all night.

Shit.

"Donny, can I talk to you for a minute?" I knock on his office door.

"Wait a minute!" he yells through the door. Donny's office is down the back hall that runs behind the main stage. Positioning myself against the wall across from his office door, I feel the bass from the song playing vibrating through the plain white walls.

I love this song.

Waiting a few minutes until he lets me in, I let the beat of the song seep into me. The music lulls me into a more relaxed state, and I stare blankly at the closed door.

"Come in!" he says.

I push off the wall and open the door. Donny is not alone in his office. Leaning against the wall to the right of the desk is the sexiest man I have ever seen. He is everything Donny is not. Taller than Donny by a head, his long black hair that comes past his shoulders with the darkest eyes I've ever seen. They're almost black. They are also boring into me, seeing straight into my soul. A shiver runs down my spine, and his eyes intensify more. He is wearing well–worn, and faded jeans, black boots, and a black t–shirt that stretches across his muscular chest. His nipples show through his tight shirt, and his two thick tattoo covered arms cross over, covering his barrel of a chest.

A bolt shoots down my belly, right to my core. I lick my lips, but really I want to lick him.

Holy hell! Where did that come from?

Yum.

He is a badass for sure and in this moment, I want him to take me.

Now.

It's a feeling I have never experienced. I have to stop myself from drooling over this gorgeous man that is, from what I can tell, danger-ous. Over his shirt is a black vest. The diamond one–percent patch tells me everything I need to know. He's an outlaw biker, a dangerous man. I shiver as we stare at each other. This shiver is not of lust like the previous. Outlaw bikers are hardcore and ruthless, something I aim to always avoid. Bikers bring trouble, and I've been avoiding trouble for ten years.

I'm unable to move as my eyes sweep down his body and back up to his face. His chiseled jaw and sun–kissed skin are enticing, and I crave a taste. This biker is the type of man I often read about. Hell fantasize about even, but never the type of man I let into my life.

Remembering why I'm in Donny's office, I snap out of the trance I'm in and move toward the edge of the desk that Donny is sitting at. My steps falter, but I right myself before I do a full stumble and face plant on the dingy pile carpet. Embarrassment streaks across my cheeks as I right myself, and attempt to ignore the fact that I just tumbled through the door with a sex god standing right there.

Get your shit together, Savy.

"What the hell do you need, Diamond?" Donny is not happy to see me, but it seems he even unhappier at my open gawking at the man standing to my right. I've interrupted something.

Fuck.

With some effort, I turn my attention to the man behind the desk, "Sorry, Donny. I can come back later." Looking to my left, another man is leaning against the other wall. I didn't see him when I walked in because I couldn't take my eyes off on the dark eyed devil that captured my attention. I'm normally better at checking my surroundings. Survival usually depends on it. I shake my head to get my thoughts in order. I need to focus. I came in here for a reason.

The man to my left is dressed the same as the man to my right. He is wearing a vest with a matching one–percent patch.

Shit, what did I walk in on?

One foot on the floor and one against the wall, his arms are crossed over his massive chest. He's sexy too. Both men look alike, but the second man is shorter, he has sparkling gray eyes, and his hair is just kissing his shoulders. They must be brothers. Shaking my head, trying to get rid of the thoughts filtering through my head. I need to get out of here and behind the bar before I say or do something else stupid in front of these sexy men. I have never reacted like this before.

"You've already bothered me, what do you want?" Donny says. His face is a deep crimson. I'm not sure if it's from my interruption or if it has something to do with the two sex Gods standing on either side of me.

"Sorry." I glance at sexy man number one out of the corner of my eyes. "I, I was hoping to pick up some extra shifts. I can even work doubles. Do you think that would be all right?" Pleading with my eyes, *please just say yes so I can get the hell out of here.* The man to my right has been staring at me since I fell into the room and he is making me nervous as hell. The way he is looking at me has me feeling exposed. Like he knows all my secrets.

Some secrets can never be exposed.

Feeling his eyes on me, I turn my head to look at him. I arch an eyebrow, letting him know I'm not afraid and I know he's watching me. He doesn't move, but I see interest spark in his eyes. Does he like my challenge? Or is he pissed? I can't tell.

Donny hasn't answered my question. He has been watching the silent conversation I have been having with the biker. His jaw ticks like he's trying to stop the words from flying out of his mouth.

After a long, awkward pause, I say, "Sorry I interrupted, Donny. I'll just leave. Don't worry about the shifts. I'll figure something out." I turn to exit the office and notice that the man leaning against the other wall is smirking at me. My eyes narrow, and I walk toward the office door.

"Diamond." As soon as he calls my name, I stop. I turn slowly to face Donny again. "You know how you can get those extra shifts."

Yes, I know exactly how I can get those extra fucking shifts. The vice in my chest tightens even more. Fucking Donny is the only way I'm getting them. Well, he can forget that thought. The idea of letting Donny, or anyone, between my legs makes me sick to my stomach. I'd never sleep with Donny, let alone anyone for more shifts. I'm not that type of girl, no matter how desperate I am.

I raise my chin in defiance. "Like I said, forget about it," I say. The words are more forceful than I intended. I need this job, so I don't tell Donny how I really feel about his proposition. Donny can kiss my entire ass! No way will I sleep with him. I'll just have to figure something else out.

Shit.

The vice tightens again. I can't catch a break. There is always some creep or life circumstance that I have to overcome. I wish that I could be one of those girls that things seem to be easy for. Nothing has ever been easy for me. As I close the door behind me, I hear the combined chuckling of both mysterious men.

DIABLO

THE KNOCK AT THE DOOR PISSES ME OFF MORE THAN I ALREADY AM. I hate this son of a bitch sitting in front of me. Donny is a piece of shit. He's the type of man to take advantage of vulnerable people. And the girls working at his club are just that, vulnerable. I shouldn't even be here. Skull, usually handles deals like this, but I've heard a lot about Donny, and how he runs his business. I want to make myself clear that when you deal with Havoc, you play by our rules.

Who the fuck is interrupting us?

"Donny, can I talk to you for a minute?" A thick, raspy voice sounds, and my dick is standing at half–mast. It's a sweet sound.

"Wait a minute!"

"Who the fuck is that?" Skull sneers. He's leaning against the wall across from me. His posture indicates comfort, but I know better that to trust his faux–relaxed state. Skull is always ready to take action if it is needed.

"That's Diamond," the little shit whispers. "She's the bartender. I'll get rid of her." He stands, but I stop him. I want to see the body attached to that voice.

"No, let her in." He turns to look at me mid–rise, puckering his lips and his eyes dart between Skull and I. The creases in his forehead become more defined. I can tell he's afraid, unsure of what is coming.

Good.

"Okay, man." The worry on his face sets in more. "Come in!"

As the door handle twists, I'm not prepared for the girl that walks in the door. She doesn't look like she's old enough to be tending a bar in a shitty strip club. Hell, she looks like a teenager. She's the most beautiful woman I have ever encountered. She stands at about five nine with the curliest black hair I've ever seen. The shits unruly, but it suits her. Her golden skin looks smooth, but she's skinny, too fucking skinny. Just from looking at her, I know she doesn't eat enough. I don't like it and I don't even know the broad. I prefer my women with a little meat on their bones. Sex with skin and bones is no fun. I fuck a little rough, and I don't want to feel like she'll break. From across the room, I can't tell what color her eyes are. The light in here is too dim for that, but they appear to be dark. Probably brown.

"What the hell do you need, Diamond?"

All of the muscles in my body tense. I notice Skull tenses too. I don't want him talking to her that way. I don't know why, I just don't. I've always trusted my instincts, and I'll continue trusting them today. I ball my hands into tight fists, trying to control my anger. I don't know what the fuck is wrong with me, but there's something about this small woman standing in front of me. I have an urge to protect her.

What the fuck?

My gut twists when she asks about working more shifts. Why the fuck does she need more work? She doesn't take good care of herself, anyone can see that just by looking at her. I've never cared what some broad did. The instant attraction to this girl feels strange.

Strange, but right.

"Diamond, you know how you can get those extra shifts." His message is loud and clear. Donny will only give Diamond extra shifts if she fucks him. Donny boy is a real piece of shit. I guess the rumors I've heard are true. Manipulating his staff for sex doesn't sit right with me. That shit will change today.

Despite what people think about bikers and motorcycle clubs, most of us are decent people. We want to live by our own rules, without the judgment of society. In Havoc, we take care of our own, and we respect our women. Women may not have an equal say in the club's business, but all women in Havoc have a say in what happens to their lives.

"Forget about it." Her refusal makes my dick jump again. She's feisty, just like I like my women. I do a mental shake. She's not my woman. Hell, she's not even the reason I came to The Jungle tonight. I need to stay focused.

Watching her exit the office and quietly close the door, Skull and I chuckle at her refusal of Donny's offer. The tick of the door closing snaps me back to the reason we're here. We are here for a reason, but fuck, I couldn't take my eyes off her.

"Sorry man, the bitches here drive me crazy," he jokes.

Calling women bitches doesn't bother me, but I don't like him calling Diamond a bitch. I don't even know this girl, and I'm already feeling protective of her. I make a mental note to find out more about her.

Getting back to business, I turn my attention to the greasy man sitting behind the desk. He thinks we're friends. We're not. I'm his boss, but I prefer him to believe he runs shit. The truth is Havoc owns The Jungle and I run Havoc. Things are about to change at The Jungle, and soon.

Narrowing my eyes, I say, "As I said before the interruption. You better have the missing payment in one week. Seven days, Donny. Don't make me come back here." I pause, waiting while the mousy man squirms in the large chair behind the large oak desk. "And find out who the fuck is stealing. If you don't give me a name in a week, I'll assume it's you."

"No man! I swear. It's not me. I swear it. Believe me." His attempts to convince me are futile. Sweat beads on his brow, and his eyes shift between Skull and me. I know a liar when I see one and Donny is lying. He won't be owner of this club much longer.

Donny came to Havoc several months ago for a loan to keep The Jungle open. In exchange for the loan, he signed over ownership of the strip club to Havoc MC. If Donny can make his payments on time, and he pays all the interest due, he will get back full ownership. If he doesn't, Havoc keeps The Jungle. It's a win–win for Havoc, but when Donny came to ask for an extension on some payments because someone had been stealing from him, I came down here to make sure I was clear about the terms of our deal. You don't steal from Havoc and live to tell the tale. Donny is only alive now because we need his connections in Russia. Once we build our own relationship with the Russians, Donny is dead.

"Seven days. Understand?" My dark eyes squint with intensity. They are near black pools, and I'm used to people shifting their line of sight from mine. On a good day, a brave man shakes in my presence. A man like Donny is pissing his pants and I haven't moved from my position against the wall.

Donny is sitting in the black office chair, his posture straight and rigid. He's uncomfortable. Good. Dealing with Havoc is a dangerous business, and I have a feeling Donny will find out just how dangerous we are. I just hope he doesn't make me kill him before I get what I need from him.

"Yeah, man. I got you. I'll have it."

Just before leaving the office I lay out the final term of our deal. "And," I pause, "don't forget the extra twenty percent, Donny." His face pales. "And give Diamond those extra shifts, *without* fucking you."

We leave without Donny uttering a word. He just figured out just how fucked he is. Skull follows me down the back hallway into the main room of the club. I look to my right toward the bar to see if Diamond is there. She is, but instead of heading to the bar to see her up close, I change directions and I walk out the front door. I need to get back to the Compound. I'm drawn to this girl, but I can't have her. Meaningless sex is all I deserve. She deserves so much more, not the stench that being with someone like me will taint her with. I know nothing about her, but I know she deserves better than me. I need to find, Kris, she can soothe the need I'm feeling tonight.

CHAPTER THREE

DIABLO

SKULL RIDES NEXT TO ME ALL THE WAY BACK TO THE COMPOUND. THE
Havoc Compound is an old brick warehouse that my brother, Skull and
I own. Skull is my blood brother. He prospected for the club straight
after high school, following in my footsteps, something he's done since
we were kids. Pulling up to the Compound, Joker, who has been
prospecting for the club for a little over a year, is working the gate that
surrounds the property. He has worked hard this past year, and will
soon earn his bottom rocker.

Havoc has several acres in a rural part of Sage, California. It's a
small town about an hour off the northern coast. The land is covered in
trees, making it harder for the cops to spy on us. Hidden in the trees,
we have a couple dozen cameras, motion detectors, and other deter-
rents. No one is getting on Havoc property without every brother and
prospect running to the source of the intrusion with guns ready.

We pull into the parking lot and I pull to the front of the bikes lined
in a neat row. Skull parks next to me, and we both head inside. Upon
entering, I'm hit with the smell of weed, cigarettes, and pussy. It's a

scent I'm used to, and strangely comforted by. I don't partake in weed or cigarettes, but I get pussy as often as I can. Sweetbutts are willing and ready whenever I have the urge.

At the bar, Preacher is having a drink with Axel, Smoke, and Lexa. Axel and Lexa are twins. Axel has been a brother since he was twenty and Lexa has been around just as long.

"Yo' Prez."

"Preacher," I say to the older brother. Preacher is an old timer, someone that has been in the club since the beginning. He's been a member longer than I've been born and still serves as the club's Chaplin and resident psychologist. I nod to the others.

"Hey, baby," I hear Kris say. Turning my attention to the red head tottering toward me on her heels. "You gonna let me make you feel good tonight?"

"Yeah. Go to my room. Be naked when I get there," I say as I toss my room key to her.

"You got it, Daddy," Kris purrs as she slinks away. Normally the promise of pussy would have me hard and ready, but I haven't been able to get Diamond off my mind since seeing her at the club.

"Axel, I need you to dig up everything you can on the bartender at The Jungle. Her name is Diamond."

"I'm on it," he says and stands. He leans down to kiss his sister on the cheek, then he turns and walks away from the bar toward his room. Axel is our computer whiz. He has every piece of computer equipment you can imagine, and can hack anything. His skills have come in handy several times.

I see the question in Preacher's eyes, but I don't answer his unspoken question. I want to know more about Diamond for my own sick curiosity, and it's no one else's fucking business.

"Let me know what you find," I say. I turn to walk to my room.

Entering my room, Kris is kneeling on the floor by the bed naked, in the position I like. Her head is down and her small hands are resting gracefully on her thighs, palms up. She has learned well. I've been sleeping with Kris for months, but occasionally, we add Hazel, another sweetbutt to the mix.

"Good girl."

She shifts her head to look at me as I stand in front of her.

"Take my dick out," I instruct.

Kris scrambles to unbuckle my belt. Pulling out my cock, she sucks it into her mouth. The suction is right, just like I taught her, but as I run my hand through her hair, it's silky straight, not unruly and curly.

Although I've never touched Diamond's hair, I can imagine the texture, and it's nothing like Kris'. I try to enjoy the mouth engulfing me, but for once I don't. I wish it was the short knockout with defiance in her eyes blowing me instead.

"Mmm." Her moaning turns me off more.

I try to get my mind off Diamond, but those large dark eyes haunt me. Wrapping my hand around Kris' hair, I can't stand it any longer.

"Get out," I demand as I pull my shaft from her wet lips. A smacking sound rings out as I remove myself from her expert jaws.

"What?"

"I said get out!" I thunder.

She scrambles to get to her feet as I grab her dress and heels, tossing them to her in the hall where she is standing naked, and looking at me in disbelief. I don't respond to the hurt in her eyes. Instead, I close the door on her, bewilderment written all over her face. I stand in place, my chest heaving, and again attempting to forget the woman I'm so drawn to. I can't forget her so I decide to take a cold shower. Trying to wash Kris' scent off my dick, wishing it was Diamond's instead.

SAVY

I'VE BEEN WATCHING THE BACK HALLWAY SINCE LEAVING THE OFFICE. I want to get another look at the sexy biker. He is dangerous. I saw the danger in his eyes when we stared at each other in Donny's office. I can fantasize, right? I haven't had these feeling since Tyler.

I shake my head a little to clear my wayward thoughts. Memories of Tyler always make me anxious. Things ended badly, real fucking bad, and I vowed never to get involved with another man. I made that vow six months ago, and that went right out the window when I saw the sexy biker with the soulless eyes. I'm not sure why, but I have a need to see him again deep down in my gut.

"Jack straight up," a customer yells over the loud music, pulling me from my thoughts.

"Coming right up, darlin'." When I turn to grab the bottle of Jack Daniel's from the counter behind me, I almost miss him leaving the bar. I'm just in time to see him looking at the bar and continuing his powerful stride out the front door. I guess it was a good thing he didn't come over to the bar, but I'm disappointed. I'm drawn to him. Maybe it's the danger that pulses off of him, or maybe it's his looks. I'm not really sure why, but I want to see him again, I want to be near him.

I know better than to get involved with a biker. That type of man wouldn't be interested in me anyway, other than another notch on his bed post. And that's something I am not interested in. Men like him can't be trusted. They treat you bad and I've had enough bad to last ten lifetimes. I can't get involved and let it happen, again.

I enjoy working Saturday nights because of the fast pace. The club is always packed, and tonight is no different. As I'm counting my tips, I think about Ena and the money I gave her earlier today. I'm still not sure what I will do for the extra money I need, but I have to figure something out soon.

As I'm pulling off my apron for the night and making my way to the employee locker room, Donny approaches me. "Um, Diamond, you got a minute?"

"Sure," I say. I stop right outside of the entrance to the locker room, ensuring that if something goes wrong, the dancers will hear me scream. "What's up, Donny?"

"You got those extra shifts. You can work days right?"

My eyebrows shoot to my hairline, and I run my hand through my hair. I thought I made myself clear when I told Donny to forget about the extra shifts.

"Donny, I said forget about it. I'm not sleeping with you," I state in a chastising tone.

"I said you got the shifts. No sex required," he growls. Turning and moving further down the hall to his office, he slams the door closed behind him.

"What the fuck was that about?" I whisper to myself. Too tired to worry about why Donny had a change of heart, I move through the locker room door and get my purse.

I have a long bus ride home. My car hasn't worked in two weeks, and I can't afford to get it fixed. Something about the transmission, I'm not exactly sure what's wrong with it. All I know is it won't start. By the time I get home, it will be well after four in the morning. I'm glad Ena spent the night at a friend's house. I won't have the energy to get up early tomorrow.

Past

PAUL

I HATE COMING TO THESE BALLS WITH ALL THESE FUCKING PEOPLE pretending to care about the police. These rich bastards don't care about the police. They care about getting exposure for donating the most money at the Annual California Policeman's Ball. They are the same no matter which state you are in. Boring as hell.

Billionaire Mark Huntington is making his way around the room, shaking hands and smiling up a storm. I guess the schmoozing comes easily for him. I, on the contrary, hate blowing smoke up anyone's ass.

"Misty honey," I murmur, "go get us a drink and don't come back for fifteen minutes." Mark is heading toward me, and I don't want Misty talking to him. She's mine, at least for tonight, and won't be talking to any other men.

"Sure, babe." She slinks away in her tight red dress, catching the eye of several men on her way to the bar.

"Aww, Peter," Mark says while reaching out a hand and completing his progress toward me, "excellent seeing you again. What has it been, a year?"

"Paul," I say with annoyance. *How dare he forget my name!* "And yes, it has been a year."

"Sorry about that, Paul." He doesn't look sorry at all. "Lots of names to remember, you'll forgive me."

Not, will you forgive me? You *will* forgive me. Rich people always think they can get what they want, tell you what to do. The bastards.

"This is my son, Tyler Huntington," he changes the subject. "He will take over our new product division at Huntington Industries in a few months." The fake smile on Tyler's face looks uncomfortable, but well-practiced. I've been a cop long enough that I can see through the mask Tyler has put on tonight. He's attempting to hide his disdain for his father, but it simmers below the surface, trying to bubble over. He does a decent job hiding his hatred, but I still see it.

"Nice to meet you." I stretch my hand toward the younger man. I'm not ashamed to admit that Tyler is good looking. He is perfect for my plan. I just need to make sure he will play along.

"You too, sir," he says as he eyes his father, who is staring across the room at some other rich bastard.

"Well, it was nice seeing you again, Peter. I must go speak to someone else." He moves away, leaving me fuming at his blatant irreverence.

"Sorry about that, Paul," Tyler says.

His ready apology surprises me. Normally the rich bastards at these balls look down their noses at the lowly police officers that attend the ball, but it seems Tyler is different. He's perfect.

"No need to apologize for your father. I'm used to it," I say.

Misty returns to my side before Tyler can continue speaking. She is wearing a bright red, skin tight dress and Tyler's focus moves up and down her body, his eyes hooding with his desire.

Snaking my arm possessively around her waist, I say, "You'll excuse us."

"Sure," is all Tyler says as I move Misty and myself across the room where I can keep an eye on the room. The ball is the perfect place to put my plan into motion. I came tonight because I need to find a sorry bastard to do my bidding.

And I think I found him.

CHAPTER FOUR

Savy

THE PAST TWO WEEKS HAVE PROGRESSED THE SAME AS ALWAYS, constant fear, looking over my shoulder, time with Ena, and work. The usual. What's unusual is how many sexy bikers that have become regulars at The Jungle. Not just the two I saw a couple of weeks ago, but a lot of Havoc members frequent The Jungle now. I'm not sure what that's about, but the eye candy is much appreciated. The view is lovely, but the tips are better. Bikers are generous tippers.

Who knew?

"Hey, Cherry," I say to the dancer approaching the bar.

"Hey, Diamond," she replies as she plops down on the bar stool and rubs her sore foot.

"Can I get you some water?"

"Yes. It's hot as ball sweat in here," she says.

A peal of laughter shoots from my mouth. Slapping my hand over my mouth, my eyes bug out and Cherry joins in, while her shoulders shake uncontrollably. The temperature at the bar is fine, but being under the bright neon lights on stage can dehydrate the dancers.

"Hot as ball sweat?" I laugh again and pass her a glass of cold water. "Here you go."

"Thank you." Cherry smiles her lopsided smile. I see why she's so popular among the customers. She's beautiful. Red hair, big boobs, and an hourglass figure women pay thousands of dollars for. Sexy, smart, and nice, she's the total package. She's the closest thing I have to a friend at the club. Hell, Joss is my only other friend in Sage.

"How do you like all the sexy bikers we've had here lately?" she asks.

Smiling at Cherry I reply, "Hot scary bikers with tattoos and leather cuts hanging around all the time? I love it! But, I keep my distance."

Cherry gives me a perplexed look.

"What?" I ask confused.

"How do you know that their cuts are called cuts?"

"Um," I begin, "I read trashy romance novels. Bikers may be sort of my thing." I'm embarrassed that I told Cherry my secret.

"So why are you keeping your distance?" she asks with knitted brows.

"I like to read about bikers. I don't want to be with one," I say, trying not to sound suspicious.

Cherry raises one eyebrow and tilts her head to the side like she's trying to figure out if I'm lying or not. Of course I'm lying. Who wouldn't want to have hot sex with a biker? But I can't allow myself to lose focus. I need to remember why I keep men, all men, at a distance.

"Well, more for me because they are fine!" Her teasing eases the tension and questions dancing between us.

"Get 'em, girl!" I joke. Sometimes I wish I could be more like Cherry, but I have Ena to think about, so I can't let my guard down. I did that once, and it was an epic failure. I'm not letting it happen again. "Hey, you've been talking to some of the guys, right?"

"You know it!" she sings with a twinkle in her eye. Cherry has been hunting bikers, and from the looks of it, she's been catching her prey just fine. "Why do you ask?"

"I need to know someone's name. He's around a lot, but I don't know his name."

Her eyebrows snap to her hairline as surprise flashes across her face. Her cartoonish expression is hilarious, and a ball of laughter explodes from my body, my shoulders shaking.

"It's just a name Cherry, don't look at me like that."

"Diamond, you have to be careful. Don't go asking a bunch of questions about Havoc. They are a ruthless MC. And by ruthless, I mean all the dark, evil, horrible shit running through your mind right now, they are that and much more. You don't want to get involved with Havoc, girl."

"What? No! Cherry," I blush, "I just want to put a name to a face, that's all."

"Just be careful. They don't like people snooping around."

"Despite what you may think, Cherry, I can take care of myself. I just need a name, okay?"

With a heavy sigh she gives me what I've been craving since the moment my eyes landed on the dark eyed biker that looks like the very thing I should run far, far away from.

"Who is it?"

I nod my head toward my dangerous biker. He is sitting at a table across the room. His table is directly across the bar, and I've been keeping an eye on him all night. He's caught me a few times and each time, butterflies dance in my belly. I've dreamt about him almost every night since I first saw him. I know it's wrong, and creepy, and we can never be together or even speak, but I can dream, can't I? If I were a different girl with a different life, I'd try a life with this man, but I'm not. So I have to settle for fantasizing about what life would be like with a biker, *this* biker.

"That's Diablo. He's President of the mother chapter here in Sage." Looking nervous she continues, "Diamond, I'd stay away from him. They don't call him the devil for nothing. He *is* the fucking devil."

Her eyebrows knit and a look of worry is plastered across her face. She's the closest thing I have to a friend at the club, so I try to reassure her.

"Trust me, I have no plans to mess with him. I only want to know his name."

But that's not entirely true. I want Diablo, but I know I can never have him so I want to know the name of the man that visits me in my dreams. Cherry studies my face, trying to see the lies in my eyes, but I'm too good at hiding them. I learned early, your eyes give you away so I keep the mask in place.

She sees nothing in my eyes, and soon Cherry is gabbing like a school girl about anything and everything. She's interested in one of the bikers, but from what she has told me so far, he is only interested in casual sex. Cherry is looking for a long–term relationship. I'm not sure bikers are capable of relationships so I try to keep my opinions to myself. Cherry is my friend, but I don't want to become too close to her. I like her and if I let her get close, it will just be harder when I have to leave.

It is not a matter of if I will have to leave, it's when. The time will come, and again I will have to leave the people I have grown to care for. So to prevent that from happening, I am keeping my distance from the people I could care about. I try to be friendly with the girls at the club, but I never let them get too close. I don't want them to get hurt. If something ever happened to anyone because they associated them-selves with me, I would be devastated. I wouldn't be able to live with myself. I can't let that happen, so I keep a wall up to protect them.

The rest of my night at the bar goes easily. The customers are charming and the tips are good. That is until I am leaving for the night. After my shift, I walk out of the back door of the club, and a tight, clammy fist wraps around my upper arm, stopping my progress out of the building.

Panic clogs my throat and the scream I want to let out becomes stuck, unable to escape my tight airway. Turning my head, I see a black vest and one–percent patch much like the patch I see daily, but it differs from the one I've grown to recognize the past few weeks. The colors are different. The diamond is yellow, not red, and my throat tenses more.

"Where are you going, baby?" An alcohol coated voice groans into my ear. The heat of his breath hitting my neck, throws the panic I feel out the window. I thrash, attempting to fight his hold.

Not again.

Never again.

I fight harder.

Dropping my bag, I swing with a fist toward the face I've never seen before. The pale blue eyes are beady and lack warmth, or any emotion at all.

Soulless.

"Let go of me, you drunk bastard!" I scream. But it doesn't work.

He tightens his hold on my arm instead of releasing me. The feeling brings me back to when I was a child and suffered the same fate. I fight harder, throwing more punches. I thrash more and he slides his other hand up my body, squeezing my breast on his ascent to cover my mouth. He covers my nose, blocking my airway, but it doesn't stop me. I continue to battle the man who is assaulting me.

Tears are streaming down my face, and I do the only thing I can think of in this position. I bring up my knee as hard as I can, kneeing the son of a bitch in the balls. He grunts in pain, and for a moment, releases my arm and airway. As soon as he lets me go, I scramble backwards, falling on my ass, but I keep moving when I hit the hard ground. Trying to get as far away from him as possible, but feeling like I'm getting nowhere. As I get to my feet, I hear him recovering from my blow and I turn to run, but hit a wall that wraps its arms around me, halting my escape. I let out a frustrated, terrified cry. He has a friend to help him. There is no way I am getting away from him a second time.

"What the fuck is going on, Diamond?" At the sound of the unfamiliar voice I stop my struggle. Glancing up to the man holding me, Diablo's chiseled face shines like a beacon in the night. I take in a deep breath to steady me, bringing in his scent.

Oil and dirt.

I don't allow myself to bask in the scent of this magnificent man. I need to get the fuck away from him in case he is here to rape me too.

"Let me the fuck go," I scream. Tears are still falling, but my body is still. I'm paralyzed in place.

"I asked you a fuckin' question."

"Fuck you! I said let me go!" My words are strong, but I'm too afraid to pull away. I don't know Diablo, hell I only learned his name earlier today. Diablo doesn't let me go so I stay still in his arms, too afraid to piss him off. "That son of a bitch tried to rape me!" I continue to scream, my voice sounding more hysterical. "I kneed him in the balls and I'll cut his dick off if I get the chance. Now let me the fuck go!" Only my shoulders move because he is still holding me tight, but his grip is not rough. He is just holding me in place, not hurting me. It's crazy what your mind notices when it believes you will be raped and murdered.

Focus, Savy!

"Loco! Get the fuck over here," he bellows. The biker with the dead eyes, approaches, and my body gives me away. I shake uncontrollably as he approaches. My back is to him, but I can feel his stare boring into my body. Diablo continues to hold me, but he is looking at Loco.

"Yea, boss?" he asks. It's like he didn't just have my knee in his crotch. Like nothing ever happened.

I shiver more.

"Is what she said true?" he asks.

I freeze.

He doesn't believe me?

He doesn't fucking believe me!

They're bikers, they will always stick together. Just like cops, they stick together too.

"Nah, boss. She's fuckin' lyin'. She wanted to give me some pussy here in the ally, but freaked out when she heard someone coming. I'm guessin' she's trying to save face, ya' know?"

"Yeah, I know," he says.

I stare up into his handsome face. He is so powerful and dangerous, but I know I can't trust him. I know he heard my scream. Otherwise, why else would he come back here? But he believes everything this asshole just said to him. I have to get out of here.

"Get the fuck outta here, Loco."

Loco turns and leaves with a sick smirk on his face. It's just Diablo and I standing with his arms wrapped around my body. The shakes racking my body are getting stronger. My need to get away just minutes before was fueled by adrenaline, but that is now gone, and my body is struggling to stay standing. My legs feel heavy, my body lagging from my struggle with Loco and my shift behind the bar. Despite feeling like I will throw up and pass out, I move, pulling away from Diablo, and he releases me. It's strange, but I miss the warmth that his embrace provided just a moment before.

"Are you okay?" he asks with sincerity.

"No, Diablo. I am not all right! That piece of shit tried to rape me and you let him go!" My shrieking bounces off the walls, and he flinches as I stumble further from him. I don't want to be near him, despite my body's comfort in his arms.

"I'll deal with Loco."

"Yes, I'm sure you will. People like you stick together. I'm not stupid. I know that asshole will go on trying to rape someone else. I only hope she has a gun to blow his fucking brains out," I say without blinking an eye.

"He won't have the opportunity." His words are a vow.

I see the promise of revenge in his eyes, but I can't believe his words are true. "Yeah, well that's nice. I need to get going," I say while grabbing my discarded bag.

"Let me take you home."

"No!" I scream. "I got it. Just stay the fuck away from me. And you can tell your *brothers* to stay the fuck away from me too."

"Look, I'm trying to help you. I said I would deal with Loco." His jet black eyes bore into mine.

"The only help I want is for you and the rest of your gang, or club, or whatever the fuck you are, to leave me the hell alone. I'm not your property you can paw over and do whatever you please."

"I know you're freaked out, but you don't have to worry about anyone touching you again."

I leave the ally on shaky legs without saying another word. Diablo doesn't follow me and I'm thankful for that. I don't think I can deal with anything else right now. I walk to the nearest bus stop, and wait for the city bus to come. My car still isn't fixed, but I'll be damned if I let a biker take me home. They are all the same. Dangerous, abusive motherfuckers who don't give a shit about women.

The sun is just beginning to rise and I exit the bus and walk to my small house. I need to get my car fixed soon. It takes too much time to get home from work. Instead of going right to sleep, I make a modest breakfast for Ena, oatmeal with nuts and orange juice. She loves oatmeal, but I try to mix it up for her when I can.

I have to work later today so after breakfast I make my way to my bedroom where I don't sleep. I've been abused so much in my past that my near rape last night doesn't register. At least not the way it should. I should be shaking and traumatized, but I'm not. I feel numb to my experience with Loco. After laying down for several hours without falling to sleep, I get up and shower. Ena is in the living room reading a book when I come down the hall.

"Hey, Pip."

"Hey, Sav. Couldn't sleep?"

"I slept a little." I smile. My smile doesn't cover the lie.

"You've only been back there for a few hours and I heard you tossing. I'm sorry something is bothering you. Anything I can do to help?"

"Nope," I say, popping my p. "Just finish reading your book."

"Okay," she says with reluctance. Returning to the pages of her book, she glances in my direction every few minutes, worry wrinkling her beautiful face.

CHAPTER FIVE

SAVY

AT AROUND THREE THE NEXT AFTERNOON I GET A CALL FROM TYLER. He's my ex and thankfully we weren't together long. He showed his true colors pretty quickly. He cheated on me and tried to run my life by belittling the way I dressed, wore my hair, interacted with my sister. Every flaw I have was fair game. It was his comments about Ena that caused me to leave him, and he hit me. No one gets to tell me how to raise Ena, no one, and no one lays their hands on me, ever. Now he's my ex.

He asked me to meet him at La Petit, some fancy ass restaurant in the next town over. He wants to have dinner, but I'm not sure I should go. I'm not much for fancy, since I can't afford it. It also makes me uncomfortable to be around rich people who look down their noses at people like me. Instead of the restaurant that Tyler wanted to meet at, I suggested we meet at Jake's Pub in Sage. It's not too far from home, and whenever I have extra money, I take Ena there for a burger. They have best burger and fries in town. A bonus, Tyler hates the place.

Win-win.

When we were together, Tyler often looked down his nose at "those types of people." But the people that go to Jake's are like me. They are hardworking, everyday people who don't care if I'm wearing old ratty jean shorts and a tank top. I plan on wearing that to dinner because Tyler hates when I wear cheap clothes.

Asshole.

What did I ever see in him?

He was charming, intelligent, witty and rich.

"Oh yeah," I sigh. I was an idiot and desperate for someone to love me. Since we are no longer together, I'll wear whatever the hell I please. Screw Tyler's judgments of me and the way I dress.

Ena is spending another night at Ashleigh's house. I'm glad she's out of the house because she hated Tyler from the minute she met him. I introduced them once, and she hated him in less than five minutes. She has always been a good judge of character, something I lack. I should have known he was an asshole.

My phone rings on the kitchen counter and I tuck all thoughts of Tyler away.

"Hello?"

"Bitch! Where the fuck have you been?" Joss shrieks. A genuine smile breaks out on my face.

"Oh hey, Joss. What's up?"

"Don't you fucking 'oh hey Joss' me. Answer my question."

"I've been working, taking care of Ena, you know same shit like every other day of my life." It's true, since Tyler, I haven't had a life. I didn't have a life with Tyler either.

"Well, I have news, but I can't tell you until I see you. What are you doing tonight? I'm coming over."

"Uh…" I can't tell Joss I'm meeting Tyler. She will lose her mind. She hates him more than I do. And for good reason. She was there after the break up. I took it hard, but I tried to hide my pain from Ena, only expressing my pain and disappointment to Joss.

"Don't 'uh' me. Uh, what?" she says.

"I got a call from–"

"No! Oh god! No! Don't tell me the dick is back. I can't. I can't fucking deal with this shit again," she groans. I try to hide my laugh at her hysterics. "No, Savannah, fuck no! You are not going back down that road."

"Joss," I whine. Drawing out her name.

"Don't 'Joss' me," she mimics me. "Savannah Riley, he has taken you so low. You were sadder with him then you were when I met you." That is not altogether accurate. Despite Joss being my friend, she doesn't know about all of my demons. Some things you learn to keep to yourself. If I told her the truth about my past, she would look at me like the evil bitch I am. I vowed never to mention it to her, or anyone else. I love her too much, and it would kill me if our friendship were destroyed by my past.

It has done enough damage already.

"Don't you dare get back with that piece of shit! I swear Sav, I'll break your neck if you do!"

I hold my breath as water springs to my eyes, running down my cheeks and my chest becomes tight. I let out an audible breath, blowing the air from my lungs, and I smile. Joss' fierce defense of me warms something deep in my belly.

"I won't, Joss. Promise."

"Seriously, Savy. Please don't take that bastard back. You are just getting over him. Do you know what it is like when you are depressed? It is so hard to see you like that. You are so beautiful and full of life, please don't let him steal that from you, again."

"I won't, Joss." I feel terrible. I never want to be in that place again. I was a wreck when we broke up. I didn't realize how bad it was. "I'm over him, Joss. I even started checking out other men." I pause for emphasis. Sometimes you have to let things marinate for her. She doesn't say anything and I'm not sure if it's because she is shocked or she's letting me continue. "There was a sexy biker in the club a while back. I had a hard time keeping my mouth shut. I was drooling all over him. He is hot as hell and seriously wrong for me." I smile at my memories of my hot biker with the dark eyes. But my chest constricts when the events with Loco float to the surface. I tried to bury the events of that night, but they keep returning. If Diablo hadn't come, it would have been much worse. "I'm just going to hear what Tyler has to say. If I don't like what I hear, I'm leaving, okay?"

"No, it's not okay!" she says.

"Thank you for caring about me," I whisper. I choose to ignore Joss' stubbornness right now.

"You're welcome, babe. I love you. You know?"

"Yeah, I know," I say with another whisper.

"Okay enough of the sappy shit. Let's talk about this biker. What does he look like?"

Thankful for the change of subject, I spend the next hour telling my best friend about the man I cannot have, but desperately want.

SAVY

GETTING DRESSED FOR DINNER FEELS LIKE I'M PREPARING FOR BATTLE. I wear my favorite black jeans. They have cuts in the thighs, not because I bought them that way, but I've had them so long and wear them so often, they developed holes. Instead of throwing them out, I improvised and made them more fashionable. I also wear an old red and black lumberjack style shirt, and black boots, both of which I got from a thrift shop. Tyler always hated when I dressed casually. He thinks a woman should always be dolled up. On a normal day, I only wear eyeliner and a little mascara, but today, I take my time and apply almost a full face of makeup. As Ena would say, my face is *beat*.

Not too shabby, Sav.

I think I look good. The jeans hug my curves, but the shirt covers my flaws. Plus, my makeup is perfect. I put on just enough to enhance my features. Who says you can't get flawless makeup with drug store brands? I wear my hair flowing down my back in thick black waves. I hope Tyler regrets every hateful thing he has ever said, every lie he told, and most of all, I hope he regrets ever laying a hand on me.

He hit me once. Only once, but once was enough. I vowed ten

years ago to never allow a man to lay his hands on me again, and at the first sign of physical abuse, I left Tyler. I only wished I was smart enough to leave when he started the verbal abuse too.

I grab my matching faux–leather jacket and head out the door. I'm glad the pub is just a few blocks away from my house so I can walk there. My car still isn't fixed and I don't want to waste bus fare on Tyler. I'm on a mission to make it clear to Tyler that I'm done with him and I'm never coming back.

I spot Tyler as soon as I walk into the restaurant. He's easy to find in this crowd. Dressed in a button down shirt, khaki shorts and his blond tresses slicked back; he looks out of place in Jake's Pub. I have to admit, he looks amazing though. As always, the man knows how to dress, even if he sticks out like a sore thumb. I walk with confidence as I approach the table and Tyler stands to greet me. Taking a step toward me, he leans in and engulfs me in a tight hug, as I stand frozen in place until he releases me. He doesn't deserve the opportunity to touch me. Pulling out a chair, he motions for me to sit.

A thousand butterflies flap in my belly. My stomach rolls, and my mouth is dry. I never thought simply sitting across the table from Tyler would cause this reaction in me. I'm regretting my decision to meet him. He was such a sleazy, cheating, lying, abusive bastard when we dated. I don't understand how I could let his looks and money blind me.

Standing at 6'2", with gentle baby blues and thick blond hair he wears just a little too long, he is easy on the eyes. A knot forms in my stomach and I wipe my palms on my jeans to remove the moisture that is forming. Since I was a kid, I've been able to tell when something bad was coming. I knew when a beating was coming or when it would be a long night with Paul. I just knew.

Something bad is coming.

I trusted myself then, so I trust myself now. I put up the wall that I learned to build as a child to protect myself. The wall is for survival, mentally, physically, and emotionally. I focus on Tyler, he called me here for a reason, and so I want to hear what he has to say. Then I can get the hell out of here. I won't forget my promise to Joss. I am not going back to Tyler under any circumstance.

Ever!

"You look nice, Savy," Tyler says from across the table.

I know he's lying. It looks like that one compliment pained him to say. He ruined everything for skanky sluts and his inflated ego. His cheating was the reason we were fighting when he backhanded me across the face. I don't blame the women he cheated with. Tyler was the person that had the relationship, not those women. He is the one that committed himself to someone else. And he is the one that stuck his dick in other women, despite my feelings. He is the sole reason I left.

Forcing myself not to roll my eyes, I reply, "Thank you."

"I'm glad you could make it tonight. I wanted to see you after everything that happened." He has a confidence about him that puts me on edge. It's as if he thinks he knows what the outcome of this dinner will be.

"Well, I had to come and see why you wanted me to meet you. I couldn't miss this explanation," I say. This time I do roll my eyes not hiding my disdain for him.

"I wanted to see you, Sav. I haven't seen you since the incident, and you have accepted none of my calls. How the hell am I supposed to talk to you if you keep ignoring my phone calls? You're not even returning my voicemails!" he snaps. His chest is heaving, showing the anger the often tries to hide.

My defenses raise more. "The incident?" Disbelief clouds my features, one eyebrow twitching. "You mean when you *hit* me? Is that 'the incident' you are referring to, Tyler?"

"Of course, Savannah. Don't be so dense," he grits out.

One minute he was pleading with me to answer his calls and the next he is angry and insulting. The quickness of his mood change doesn't surprise me. The sad thing is he looked pitiful, right until he let his mask slip and his true face showed up to the table. That's when he showed me the man behind the facade he has been showing me for a year. The monster behind the handsome mask showed his face, *again*.

He was bound to show his true self, eventually. You can't hide your evil forever. He wants me to believe his bullshit excuses and to down play his actions. Then he chastises me in the same breath. I did that for too long. Listening to bullshit excuse after bullshit excuse and never standing up for myself. I'm done. And I won't take him back. I made a promise to my best friend.

I made a promise to myself.

All of this is running through my head as he is talking. I have to force myself to listen to what he was saying.

"Are you even listening, Savannah?" he says while snapping his fingers in my face. "See, this is what I mean. This is what you've always done. You've always ignored me when I talk to you, and you wonder why I cheated on you."

I cannot hide my hatred for the asshole sitting in front of me. Telling me that I was the reason he cheated. My not listening to him caused him to cheat?

Really?

I can no longer contain my composure. The pressure in my neck constricts, and I lose it. "Fuck you, Tyler!" I explode. "You cheated because you're a sorry ass excuse for a man who couldn't keep his dick in his pants! Don't you dare tell me I'm the reason you cheated on me. You know you cheated on me because you *wanted* to cheat on me. What? You couldn't pass up the titties she threw in your face? You cheated because you are worthless. You think sleeping around makes you a man? It doesn't. A man is someone who can treat *one* woman like she is the center of his universe." Not taking a breath, I continue, "He knows a happy woman means he won't have to worry about anything else. You think cheating makes you a man? Telling your buddies you 'hit that' and laughing about it while I sit at home, alone, building a life for us? It makes you nothing. You are *nothing*. You are not a man. A man can continuously please his woman. Mentally, physically *and* emotionally, asshole. He makes her feel safe and secure. He communicates. Do you think you did that? *No!*" I growl my last word, finally taking a breath. "You did none of that, none of it! I gave you the world when all I had to give was myself. You cheated on your own,

Tyler. Nothing in this world made you a cheater, except yourself!" I have to fight to calm myself. I am so angry that my chest is heaving. The sound of my blood rushing through my veins sounds in my ears.

Bewilderment sits on Tyler's handsome face.

Silence.

Well, that's a first.

I would have smirked at the look on Tyler's face, but I am too pissed. "I always just accepted all the nasty, mean things you said to me," lowering my voice so no one around us can hear, "You hit me, Tyler. Hit me! We aren't together, and I can give two shits about what you think of me." Because he says nothing, I keep on talking, "Why did you do it, Tyler? Was it because I was daydreaming and not listening to you? Or was it because you are a pig and a sorry excuse for a man? What was it, huh?"

I've never spoken to Tyler this way. His face is bright red. He is shaking and pissed that I caused a scene in the middle the bar. The people around us have stopped whatever they were doing and are watching the show. Embarrassment is an emotion I've never seen on him, and I get a sick satisfaction out of his embarrassment.

As if understanding just dawned on him, he says, "Lower your voice, Savannah! I can't believe you're bringing all this up now. You're making a scene. No, I didn't cheat on you because she was throwing her *boobs* in my face. I cheated on you because you didn't give me what I needed."

"You are a piece of shit. I hope I never see you again. Have a beautiful time with your secretary or whoever else you decide to fuck, I hope you use protection. Have a nice night and all that good shit," I say with as much sugar as I can muster. I'm frustrated and feeling sick to my stomach. If only I can keep my composure until I get out of here. Sliding my chair back, the screeching sound draws the attention of the remaining patrons who weren't already watching the show. I rise from my seat with a slight smile on my face and swiftly throw my water in his face. "How's that for a scene? Have a nice life, asshole," I say and turn to walk out of the bar.

My bravado is quickly fading, and I begin shaking. My legs feel like jelly and I move faster, trying to keep my face off the wood floor beneath my feet. I can't believe Tyler asked me here to tell me he cheated on me because I didn't give him enough attention.

What.

An.

Asshole.

I'm in a daze as I rush to the exit, but instead of walking outside to the cool evening air, I run right into a solid wall.

"Fuck!" Only trouble is this wall was not a wall at all, but a solidly built man. A delicious man. "Oh my goodness, excuse me. I didn't see you. I'm sorry," I apologize.

Then I make the mistake of looking up, into the face of the man wall. "Diablo."

CHAPTER SIX

Savy

"Nice to see you too, little bird."

Standing with my mouth hanging open, I can't get my brain to register that Diablo, President of Havoc MC, is standing in front of me, talking directly to me.

Me!

I have dreamt about this man since seeing him in Donny's office many weeks ago. Most nights are filled with nightmares, but when I have a moment of peace, it is Diablo's beautiful black eyes I see.

Diablo places his finger under my chin and slowly closes my gaping mouth.

"I–It's nice to see you again. I'm sorry I almost ran you over, but I have to get going." Trying to step around his massive frame, Diablo grabs my upper arm and stops my progress.

"Why are you running, little bird? I saw what you did in there. I'm impressed. And I have to tell you, I'm also proud."

Oh god, someone please shoot me.

Diablo, Hot Level 1000, just saw me go ape shit on my ex in the middle of a bar, albeit a laid–back bar, but we are in public for fuck's sakes! I'm sure I'll never step foot in Jake's again. Now that I'm thinking about it, I should have waited until after dinner to throw my drink at Tyler. I'll never be able to eat here again. I'm so embarrassed by what happened.

I should have–

"Ahem."

"Oh god! I'm sorry. I get lost in my head sometimes," I say blushing.

Diablo is staring at me like I'm amusing him. "That's okay, but it can be dangerous in there." He taps his temple indicating his head. "Be careful," he says with a raised eyebrow.

"Trust me, I know."

"Look who's the slut now!" Turning my head to see Tyler stalk over to where Diablo and I are standing just inside the door. "You throw a drink at me and walk away, and now you're chatting up some, some *biker*? I thought I knew you, Savy," he spits with venom like Diablo is beneath him.

The air in the room stills.

No one ever claimed that Tyler was the brightest. You would think the cut, would have been an indicator that you do not speak to Diablo this way. Tyler didn't get that memo. The entire bar knows you do not talk to or about Diablo, or any member of Havoc, this way, this is clear because the bar has become an eerie quiet. I hear the blood rushing in my ears, and feel my heart pounding in my chest, my fear taking over my mind and body. I'm rooted to the floor, unable to move from where I stand. I don't want to see what happens when you disrespect the President of Havoc.

"What?" I say. My face is burning with embarrassment, and fear. Fear for Tyler, fear for myself. This day couldn't get any worse.

"I asked you here so we can get back together, Lady Bu–"

"DON'T!" Forgetting my fear as my anger resurfaces.

A look of utter disbelief sits on Tyler's face. I glance at Diablo who is now leaning on the door looking like he hasn't got a care in the world. I lied, this is worse. I knew for sure Diablo would beat Tyler to a pulp for what he said, but no. He's completely relaxed.

What the fuck is going on?

I have to deal with this later. I don't have the energy to go for round two with Tyler while the man I have been lusting after for weeks is here watching me try to put Tyler and another fucked up piece of my life behind me.

"Don't you ever fucking call me Lady Bug again," I grit out. "You don't have that right. You lost that right the minute you fucked another woman. Call me Savy from now on."

"Lady Bug, I–"

"Tyler! Are you deaf? I said you could call me Savy. Not Lady Bug. You lost that right the moment you stuck your dick in another woman and put your hands on me."

Uh oh.

Diablo moves so fast I almost don't see it. One minute he was leaning against the door relaxed without a care on the world, and the next he has Tyler dangling in the air by his neck. A sick satisfaction slithers up my spine. Someone is finally teaching Tyler a lesson, though I don't want the lesson learned in front of so many witnesses.

"No," I say. Reaching out to grab Diablo's thick bicep. "Please, you might get in trouble. He's not worth it. I'm not worth it."

Diablo's face is a rage filled scowl. He continues to look the now purple Tyler in the eyes as Tyler claws at his neck, trying to get air.

"Don't you know, little bird? You *are* worth it." His dark eyes never leave Tyler. His message is clear. Tyler is an idiot for what he did, but so much more. Diablo is the first man to step into a situation on my behalf, ever. This is the second time he saved me in just a few weeks, and it makes me nervous. He is still a dangerous man who lives an unhealthy lifestyle. I have Ena to think about, and I would never put her in danger, no matter how much I want to be with Diablo.

"Please," I beg.

Diablo lets go of Tyler's neck just before he passes out.

When Tyler collapses to the ground, gasping for breath, I see fury flash across his face. He struggles to stand, but quickly gains his footing and his breathing begins to return to normal.

"Savy," he says. Sounding pained, Tyler tries to plead with his eyes. I've never seen him this way before. The Tyler I know would never grovel in public, especially with so many witnesses.

"That's enough, Tyler. We are over. Your choice, remember?"

"Ready to go, Lady Bug?"

With eyes the size of saucers, I turn to see Diablo extending his hand toward me. I can't believe he said that! What is he thinking? He is going to make this so much worse. Turning back toward Tyler, he is glaring at Diablo like he wants him dead. Pure rage and a promise of revenge is plastered across Tyler's face. He doesn't attempt to hide it.

The last thing I need is two grown men fighting in public, fighting over me no less. I can't deal with this right now. I don't want to deal with it as I feel a massive migraine coming on.

With a huff, Tyler rushes past Diablo, taking care not to touch him. He is moving faster than I've ever seen before. I guess he thought twice about taking on Diablo. Tyler is lean and agile, and no match for Diablo. Diablo is what I like to call the Double D. Dangerously Dark. He is 6'3" with long black hair and pure black eyes. It's obvious that he works out every day because his muscles are noticeable as they roll under his tattooed skin. He is yummy in every way, but I need to remember to keep away from him.

Turning to face Diablo, I say, "Why did you do that? Are you crazy? Or are you trying to start a fight?"

"Yes."

"Yes, you were trying to start a fight. Or yes you're crazy?"

The corner of his delightful mouth turns up, but he never answers the question.

I want to lick his mouth.

Geez!

I need to leave before I throw myself at him and embarrass myself even more.

"Well, it was nice running into you. Bye." Trying to step around him again, Diablo stops my exit by grabbing me by my upper arm once more. The way he's holding me isn't forceful or painful. His grip is just tight enough that I know I won't be getting away until he wants me to. But gentle nonetheless. Despite knowing the power simmering in his grip, I somehow know he would never hurt me.

Do I know that? Or am I just hopeful? Stupid Savannah, you can't let him in.

"There you go running away from me again."

"I'm not running."

"You are."

"I never ran before."

"You did, the first night I saw you. You ran to the bar, not because your shift was starting, but because you needed to get away from me."

The bastard is too smart for his own good. I know I won't be winning this argument, so I keep my mouth shut, mostly because he is right. I am running. Running from the man that visits me in my dreams each night. I can't get involved with Diablo. He's the President of a motorcycle club.

What the hell would he want with me? Other than sex.

I stand silently pleading with my eyes for him to let me go so I can go home and analyze this whole crazy night.

"Those doe eyes won't work on me, little bird. I want to see you again without the crazy ex–drama."

YES! God, I'd love to see him again.

"I don't think that's a good idea, Diablo. As you can see, I just got out of one crazy relationship. I won't be getting into another one any time soon."

"Little bird, I want you. I've wanted you since the moment I laid eyes on you. And you want me too." His black eyes roam my face. "You're the most beautiful woman I have ever seen."

"Yeah, sure. I bet you tell all the *sweetbutts* those same words," I say. My eyes never leave his. "Sorry, honey. I can't do this. Please let me go, Diablo."

I've been doing research on bikers and talking to Cherry and Joss, who oddly has a ton of knowledge on bikers. I wanted to learn every-thing I could about Havoc MC, so I Internet stalked them at Joss' house. There's not much online about the ins and outs of Havoc. I found a dictionary of biker terms, and some documentaries on other clubs, but the information on Havoc is pretty much non–existent. They have a two-sentence Wikipedia page. That's it.

"I don't tell the sweetbutts shit. They know their place in the club. They get passed around to all the brothers, why would I want them?" he asks.

His words cause the vice to tighten. I don't want those sluts touching Diablo, let alone, having sex with him. Too bad I have no claim on him. Hell, I shouldn't even be around him.

"I'll let you go right now, little bird, but you won't be running forever. I *will* see you again. I always get what I want."

Not this time, buddy.

He lets my arm go and I rush out of the door like the devil is hot on my heels. I guess he is.

Ha!

I almost trip on my semi-run down the street. "What the fuck just happened?"

SAVY

THE SCHOOL YEAR FOR ENA IS OVER, SO I HAVE MORE TIME WITH HER. I'm still tired from working last night, but I am happy to be spending time with my baby. I know she's not technically mine, but she *is* mine. I've been the only mother figure in her life and I raised her. I brought her from a certain hell and death, to the sweet bubbly girl I know today. I can't imagine what she would have been, had I left her to be raised by The Monster. The girl I know today wouldn't be living even if she still walked the Earth.

"Savannah, can I ask you a question."

My defenses go up. Ena only calls me Savannah when something is wrong.

Not one to bull shit, "What's wrong, McKena?" I ask. Throwing her full name back at her, she knows I know something's up.

"Do you have to act so suspicious?" she asks. Scooping a spoonful of oatmeal into her mouth, she chews and swallows.

"Yes."

"Can I spend the night at Ashleigh's tonight?" Biting her bottom lip and not looking me in the eye are my first signs that she is nervous.

Oh yeah, something's up.

"What's up?" I ask again, allowing more irritation to enter my voice. I don't like when Ena's sneaky. I'd rather her come right out and talk about whatever is going on.

"Nothing. I know you don't want me to work, but I got a job." She bites her bottom lip again. It's her nervous tick. Anytime Ena worries about something, she bites her lip.

"What?"

"Please don't be mad," she rushes to say. "It's just for the summer. Ashleigh and I will be babysitting kids in her neighborhood."

Taking several minutes to think about this news with a rational mind, I stare at Ena and she continues to bite her lip.

I pause for dramatic effect, but I'm not mad. "You should have talked to me first. It's just for the summer, McKena. Don't get any ideas, when school starts again you're done. I'm serious."

"Thank you, thank you, thank you, Savy. I can give you some money to help with bills too." She rushes over to wrap me in a tight embrace.

"No, Ena. Any money you make is yours. I want you to save for when you go to college, okay?"

"Okay. Thank you, Savy." She is bouncing in her seat, her oatmeal now forgotten.

"You're welcome, brat. Now, eat up." My heart warms. I love this girl more than I knew I could. A smile stretches across my face. With so much new in my life lately, I'm glad Ena is getting to do the things she loves.

Where the hell did this kid come from? I don't know what I did to deserve her, but I love her to pieces and I will do anything to protect her, even if it means sacrificing my own life.

"JACK AND COKE."

Turning around, Diablo is standing on the other side of the bar top, a sexy smirk on his face. I knew it wouldn't be that easy. Telling Diablo to leave me alone was like an invitation for him to speak to me whenever he gets the opportunity.

"Sure thing, sugar," I say. Turning my back to him as I grab the Jack Daniel's from the back counter.

After last night, Diablo is the last person I want to see, but here he is looking sexy as sin. Diablo has been coming to the club more, and the atmosphere of the club has been different. With Havoc around, Donny hasn't been harassing the girls as much. We are all thankful for that, but I'm embarrassed that Diablo saw me have an outburst on Tyler and he saw my encounter with Loco.

Perfect name too, the motherfucker is crazy.

Composing myself, I move to grab a glass and pour the amber liquid. I look to the man to his left. "What can I get you, darlin'?" I lay on the southern charm while working because it brings in higher tips. That's the only reason I work in this club.

Tips.

The Jungle may be a shit hole, but it's the only strip club on this side of town that pays well and has tipping customers. Horny men, and sometimes women, come here to get his or her fantasies fulfilled. The law says no touching the dancers in strip clubs, but the unwritten rule at The Jungle is, if you have enough money, then you can do whatever the fuck you want.

It's a disgusting rule written by Donny, but I learned at a young age not to ask questions, so I don't. I don't ask because I don't want to know. I don't judge either. The girls that fulfill those fantasies have to live with their decisions. Plus they are here for the same reason as me, money. Who am I to judge someone for doing what they think is right for themselves?

"Rum and coke."

"Sure thing." I add a little wink, and Diablo narrows his eyes at me. I don't think too much about it while I make the other man's drink.

Stepping further down the bar to help other customers, I keep an eye on Diablo. Uncontrollable feelings of possession overtake me whenever one of the dancers comes over and rubs her body on his arm, trying to get him to buy a dance. It's like I have an invisible string tying me to him, and I don't want other women to even look at him, let alone rub their body parts on him. It's strange because every instinct in my body tells me to run as fast as I can in the opposite direction, but I'm drawn to him.

I know it's crazy, but I never claimed to be sane.

As the night wears on, I check in on the two bikers who have been sitting at the bar for the entire evening. Several other bikers have stopped by to talk to Diablo and Skull, the other man in the office the night I first saw my hot, but untouchable biker. One person I don't see is Loco. Maybe Diablo kept his promise. Hopefully Loco never comes around again, but if he ever comes near me, I will put a bullet in his head.

I keep my gun on me since the night Loco grabbed me. The only exception is when I'm working. It's tucked away in my locker whenever I'm at The Jungle. Alcohol and guns don't mix.

At around midnight things take a turn for the worse.

Of course.

A couple of college kids have been harassing the waitresses for a while. Bo is head bouncer, and has already warned them once, but Donny has another dumb ass rule, warn rowdy customers and never kick them out straight away.

"Always give a warning first," he says. Now the group has parked themselves at the bar a few seats down from the bikers, and they are making a ruckus. They have had a little too much to drink and keep getting handsy with the waitresses and dancers that walk past. I decided to cut them off, and they didn't like it.

As I'm collecting the empty beer bottles in front of the group, the blond, a beach boy surfer type, who I presume is the leader of their little posse, grabs my wrist and squeezes while twisting it savagely.

"Give me another beer, fuckin' bitch." The sneer on his face would tell me he's pissed off if his death grip on my arm didn't.

What he doesn't know is, I've had to deal with a ton of assholes in this bar and the countless others I've worked at before The Jungle. His hold on my wrist is hard though. It will leave a bruise.

Before he can react, I reach up and grab his hair, gripping his blond tresses in a tight hold. With as much force as I can muster, I slam his head down on the bar.

Not once.

The fucker didn't let go until I slammed his head three times. After he lets go, I see both bikers have moved behind the group of kids, Diablo gripping the surfer tightly on the shoulder as Bo makes his way over to the bar.

"Didn't your mother teach you to keep your hands to yourself?" Blood is gushing from his nose. "Look at the mess you made." I toss him a towel. "You better fucking clean that up. And n*ever* touch me again. Or you will regret it."

Bo pulls the asshole off the bar stool and I give him a sharp look. I'm not happy about having to bust this asshole's nose. "What the fuck, Bo?"

"I'm sorry, Diamond." His ferocious eyes gentle as he looks at me and apologizes. He wanted these assholes out of here too, but he needs this job and kicking out paying customers without warning is a fireable offense.

Donny is a dick.

After the surfer cleans up his blood, Bo walks the entire group out of the club with instructions to never return. If they ever come back, they will know what real pain is. Not just a busted nose.

"Bo," Diablo's low grumble rings out like a shot and Bo stops in his tracks. "Wallet." Reaching into Blondie's pocket, Bo pulls out his wallet and hands it to Diablo who opens it and pulls out the surfer's driver's license.

"Samuel, it looks like you made a huge mistake tonight," Diablo taunts a now wide–eyed Samuel.

"I'm–"

"No," Diablo says while shaking his head and slipping the license into the pocket of his cut. "Your time to talk is over."

With one nod to Bo, the group is led out of the club, Samuel audibly sobbing. I kind of feel bad for Samuel, but he needs to learn to keep his hands to himself. Once they leave, I let my mask fall. My wrist is throbbing. I won't be able to keep pouring drinks for the rest of the night. But what choice do I have?

I need the money.

CHAPTER SEVEN

DIABLO

WORKING IN A BAR, YOU GET A FEW ASSHOLES. I'M GLAD TO KNOW Diamond can take care of herself. Her reaction was faster than I could move though. She had already slammed his head twice before I made it over to the little prick that grabbed her.

I got a sick satisfaction out of hearing his flesh hit the wood bar top. It's the same satisfaction I feel when my fists land against flesh. My dick twitched at her swift action, the combination of her sweet face twisted in anger and disgust. Plus knowing she can take care of herself fills me with pride and makes me hard.

Now that the assholes are gone, I see that his grip really hurt her. She's favoring her wrist even though she is trying to hide it.

"Are you okay?" Tipping my head down, indicating her wrist.

"Yep! I'm great. Can I get you another drink?" she says. Her fake happiness coupled with her avoiding my eyes pisses me off.

"Don't lie. I know you're hurting. You're babying that wrist." I know I look scary as fuck, but I want her to be honest with me. I want her to trust me.

"Yes. It's hurting," she concedes. Her reply pisses me off more. I want to go outside and find the bastard to deliver some real damage, much more than a broken nose. I took his ID so I have his address. I'll pay him a visit later this week. I'll wait a few days because I want him afraid and expecting me. Then I'll deliver the damage he deserves. Despite what people think about bikers, many of us have more respect for women than citizens. We protect women and shield them from the club's business, ensuring their protection. At least, in Havoc we do. I can't speak for other clubs, but we don't fuck over women.

That's why Loco is no longer breathing. I brought the rape allegation to church, and the brothers voted. It's against our charter. Rape is an offense that will get you snuffed out. Most brothers have enough pussy thrown at them every day that forcing someone to sleep with them is unnecessary. So after we cut the Devil's tattoo off of Loco's back, I burned him alive. His screams still fill my ears, but I don't care. He's been exterminated like the rabid animal he was.

"Come on, babe, let me take you home."

She freezes at my words. "No!" Her eyes are wide and wild, panic is rolling off her in droves. She wants me to leave her alone. She's had to deal with two assholes, a near rape, and here I am trying to get her on the back of my bike. I should be ashamed, but I'm not. It's too fucking bad, she's mine.

At least for now.

I don't like her reaction, but I ignore it. Turning to my brother, I say, "Skull, get someone back here to tend bar. I'm taking Diamond home."

With a slight nod of his head, Skull strides toward the back office.

"No, I have a ride. Thanks anyway, Diablo. And plus, I need to sanitize the bar, blood got everywhere," Diamond says. She is still clutching her wrist and has a grimace on her beautiful face. She catches her bottom lip between her teeth. She's trying to put on a brave face, but she's terrified. "I got it. You don't have to worry about me. I'm sure you have something, anything better to do than dealing with me, and taking me home."

"What could be more important than taking you home, Diamond?"

"Savy."

"What?"

"Uh, please call me Savy. Diamond is my club name." The look on her face tells me she didn't mean to give me permission to use her real name.

A ghost of a grin crosses my lips. Savy doesn't realize how much we have in common. I know she has demons. I see the shadows in her eyes. I have demons too. Hell, my road name is a testament to my past. I *am* the fucking devil. I earned the name, but I don't tell her that. I want to keep her safe. I want to soothe her past hurts. And it's a feeling I've never experienced before.

"Well, Savy, you ever been on the back of a bike?"

"No, but look, I'm fine. Thanks anyway. I'm just going to clean the bar, then I'll tell Donny I'm leaving for the night and I'll get home. Don't worry about me." Flashing a nervous smile at me while she rounds the bar. She pulls off her apron and tucks it underneath her arm.

In a stern voice I say, "Savy, don't make me haul your ass out of here. Get your shit and get on the back of my bike." My tone is even, but firm. She's getting a ride home, from me. I know she's been taking the bus, and that shit ends today.

Her entire body tenses, and I don't like it. There is something about her. Something causing her to hesitate, and I don't know what it is. I'd never hurt her, but she doesn't know that.

Her reaction pisses me off.

She only knows what she sees. A scary as fuck biker and most days that suits me fine, but with Savy, I don't want her afraid of me. I don't know what is so alluring about her, but I want her, even if I'm aware I can never have her.

I'd just fuck her life up too.

I quickly shake off the thought. I haven't thought about Katie in years, no sense in living in the past now.

"Come on, *darlin'*. Let me take you home. I just want to make sure you're all right." I smile, trying to ease her worry. I don't want her to think I'm the devil I'm named after.

One.

Two.

Three beats pass before she answers, "Fine."

She sounds defeated, but I don't care. She'll be on the back of my bike. And something inside of me settles.

She rushes off to the employee section of the club to grab her bag from her locker. I don't follow her even though I want to. And I could. I can go into any area of the club I want, but I don't. I'm giving her space, even if it is just for a minute. Havoc owns this club until Donny pays us back, and from the look of it, those payments won't be coming anytime soon. That little fucker only paid part of the missing money. Wolf paid him a little visit and made it clear that we are not joking about the missing money. Just two days after Wolf beat the shit out of him, Donny paid all the missing money. So far, he has been on time with the payments, but I don't have faith that he will stay on track.

As Savy dawdles back to the front of the club, I see her wince when she moves her purse over her shoulder. I don't know if she will be able to hold on while on my bike.

"Little bird, are you going to be able to hang on?"

"Of course, it only hurts a little. And please, call me Savy."

Fuck that! I'll call her whatever the hell I want.

I know she's lying about her pain, but I say nothing because I want her on the back of my bike. The muscles around her eyes are constricted with pain. She's tough as shit and I'm impressed with her pain tolerance. I've seen grown men cry for less.

"Come on, little bird. Let's go."

She narrows her eyes with irritation, and then she walks in front of me toward the exit. Placing my hand on the small of her back, I guide her out the front door toward my parked bike. I feel a tingle when I touch her back where her shirt exposes her skin.

Fuck.

I know she felt it too. I need to get her home and get the fuck away from her before I get too caught up in her. I can't have her, even though she is mine. I want to make sure she gets home, and that's it.

Stop lying to yourself.

Sitting on my bike, I look over my shoulder and watch as Savy looks at my large metal beast like it will eat her. She's fearful, but I see a hint of defiance sparkling in her eyes.

That's my girl.

"Come on, just throw your leg over."

She does as she's told and it pleases me more than it should.

"Now, wrap your arms around me."

Not saying a word, she moves to wrap her arms around my waist, but her grip is weak. If she plans to hold on like that, she'll fall right off the back. Grabbing her arms, I tighten her hold, but take care to be gentle with her injured wrist. The moment our hands touch, a current rolls through me, and I pause, unsure of what to say. I recover and decide to ignore the current running between us both.

"Hold on tight, baby. I don't want to see that lovely ass of yours hit the ground."

She maintains her hold and shakes her head.

"Give me your address, little bird." I should already know her address, but Axel wasn't able to find one. It seems she doesn't want to be found. She lives in one of the worse parts of town. There isn't much in the neighborhood, other than drugs and gangs. I don't like where she lives, but I'll take her home and make sure she gets inside safe. I keep telling myself that I just want to make sure she is all right, but the little voice in my head keeps saying, "That's a lie." I know I want her. I've been drawn to her since she walked into the office.

"All right," I say. Kicking up the stand I take off, and Savy tightens her grip, holding on for dear life. She squeezes my waist as I shoot off from The Jungle parking lot.

More like it.

It has been a long time since I've had the desire to have a woman on the back of my bike. Savy is the first since Katie. Riding down the highway, I think about the girl holding me from behind. After I cranked up my bike, the tension I've felt over the last few hours fades. Being on the road calms me. The rumble of the pipes and the breeze in my face puts me at peace. But the brown-eyed beauty I've thought about since the day I saw her brings me more peace. It makes no sense.

I drop Savy off at her small house. It isn't much, but you can tell she's done work on the property. The flowers out front are the only beauty on the whole street. She takes pride in her surroundings, and I like it.

"Thanks, Diablo," she says. She gets off my bike, unbuckles the helmet she's wearing and runs her delicate fingers through her wild hair.

"Careful. You'll have shaky legs for a few minutes," I say.

She stumbles with her hands still in her hair. Reaching out to catch her before she falls, I wrap her into a strong embrace.

"Shit." Once she's steadier, she pulls from my arms and says, "Thank you for the ride."

"Let me get the door for you." I slip the keys from her unsteady hand and walk up the path to her small porch.

"Thank you. Again."

"You're welcome, again." She gives me a puzzled look.

"What?" I say giving her a smile. "I do have manners, Savy. Despite what I look like."

"Sorry," she says. Embarrassment flashes across her face, and she looks away from me. She looks back at me as if to speak, but I take this opportunity to slam my mouth down on hers. At first, she doesn't open to me, but when I tangle my fingers in her thick hair, she allows me entrance into her sweet mouth, and a moan escapes her lips. The raspy sound caresses my ears, and my shaft stirs.

Her hands snake up my back, and she clings to my cut. The fact that I'm allowing her to touch my cut means something. I like this girl a lot. My cut is my most prized possession, and I never allow women to touch it. It's sacred.

She tears her mouth from mine, and a growl escapes my lips. I don't want this kiss to end. I look down into her beautifully flushed face with hooded eyes.

"Um," she starts, while shifting from foot to foot, still clinging to me.

"Shh. It's okay, baby." I want to reassure her. She's perfect, and I can see the doubt in her eyes.

"Uh, okay. I should get inside."

"You should."

She lets go, and I unlock her front door, moving out of the way so she can get inside.

"Lock the door, baby," I say, and hand her the keys.

"Goodnight, Diablo."

"Caleb."

She looks at me with startled eyes.

"You call me Caleb."

"Goodnight, Caleb."

"Get inside and ice that wrist."

She turns to close the door, her head peeking out until the closing door blocks her view. I stand on her tiny porch until I hear the locks engage. Two locks, a dead bolt and a latch on the handle. I'll have a prospect install better locks and a better door in the morning. I adjust my hard dick before getting on my bike to ride back to the Compound, where I sleep alone and dream about the curly haired beauty with the dark, haunted eyes.

SAVY

FOR THE LIFE OF ME, I DO NOT UNDERSTAND WHY I AGREED TO LET Diablo take me home. I mean his name is the devil for goodness sakes! What the hell is wrong with me? Diablo is the type of man I need to stay away from. He reminds me so much of Tyler, and everything I've been running from, but he's different. Where Diablo is rough and rugged, Tyler is refined and well-manicured. But Tyler is dangerous too. He is the proverbial wolf in sheep's clothing. And I fell for his tricks.

Because I'm an idiot. I can't let that happen again.

But there is something about Diablo that puts me at ease. If I'm honest with myself, I know he's different from the rest of the men I've known. Different, but I still need to protect Ena so I need to stay away from anything or anyone that can put us at risk.

I hate thinking about Tyler because I let him in and it backfired on me. That was one of the lowest points in my life, other than my childhood. *Nothing* can compare to the fucked up childhood I had. That's another side of myself that I try to hide. The scared, little abused girl, who just wants to be loved. So I put up walls around me and I let no one in. The only time I tried to let someone in, backfired in my face. So I can't let Diablo in now. What if it fails again? What if he hurts me? Or worse, what if he hurts Ena?

These thoughts are dangerous on the back of a bike. Tightening my hold, Diablo gently pats my tense hands as we make our way toward my street. His touch is reassuring, and I feel a spark whenever our flesh meets. I don't live in the greatest neighborhood, but it could be worse. My neighbors are friendly, and we look out for each other. When I gave Diablo my address, his eyes flashed. I wasn't sure what it was, but there was something there for a split second.

As we turn onto my street, I loosen the death grip I've had the entire ride, point to my little house at the end of the drive, and he pulls into the small driveway. It's not much, but I love my house. I don't own it, but it's mine.

As I dismount from the bike, I stumble, and Diablo is there to catch me, "Careful. You'll have shaky legs for a few minutes."

With a rueful look, I say, "Thanks." My heart beats faster as he holds me, making sure I don't fall. Taking care of me without being asked.

How can someone like this be the devil?

After a minute, I feel steadier and pull away from him, not realizing I was holding my breath. "Thank you for the ride." Turning to walk away, I grab my keys out of my purse, trying not to wince from the pain in my wrist. Of course, he sees the small show of pain and is immediately at my side.

He sees everything.

Slipping the keys from my hand, he says, "Let me get the door opened for you."

"Thank you. Again," I say and Diablo grins a sexy little grin.

Sexy bastard.

At the top of my porch steps, Diablo unlocks my door. "Thank you. *Again.*"

"You're welcome, *again.*" His politeness catches me off guard. I never expected it from a biker.

"What? I do have manners, Savy."

His chastisement embarrasses the hell out of me. Of course, he does. I guess I let my expectations and prejudices override what I know about Diablo.

"Sorry."

Then Diablo's thick, soft and oh so delicious lips are on mine. I'm stunned and wishing I didn't smell like stale liquor, but a moan escapes my lips, and I allow Diablo entrance. My core pools with my need for this sexy man who has taken control of my head and has deepened our kiss. I realize I'm holding onto him for dear life, but I don't care. It's the most amazing kiss I've ever experienced.

I tear his lips from mine and shuffle from foot to foot. The wetness in my black jeans is uncomfortable. I need friction to alleviate the ache his kiss has caused.

"Um."

"Shh, it's okay, baby."

Letting Diablo go, he unlocks my door.

"Goodnight, Diablo."

"Caleb."

My breath stills.

Did he just tell me his real name?

"You call me Caleb."

Yep. He told me his real name.

HE TOLD ME HIS REAL NAME!

From what I've learned about bikers, and that is not much, bikers rarely allow people to call them by their given name. And in one night, this sexy biker that I wish I could have, even on a small level, went from Diablo, the big bad devil, to Caleb, a sweet and caring man that helped me home.

WHAT. THE. FUCK?

"Goodnight, Caleb."

"Get inside."

I move into my small foyer and close the door, keeping my eyes on Caleb until the door closes, blocking my view. I engage the lock and deadbolt. Then turn my back to the door, sliding down until my butt hits the floor, my hand touching my lips. I still feel the tingle of his kiss.

Then I get into bed and touch myself, imagining it's Caleb's fingers instead of my own giving me a much needed release. I fall asleep, and for the first time in a long time, I don't have a nightmare, but sweet dreams of a black-eyed biker.

CHAPTER EIGHT

SAVY

THE NEXT MORNING, THERE IS A LOUD KNOCK AT MY FRONT DOOR.

At seven thirty.

Seven–fuckin'–thirty!

Needless to say, I'm not happy to see a big scary biker standing on my porch. He's a prospect, someone who wants to be a fully patched member of Havoc MC, as indicated by his prospect patch.

"What do you want?"

"Prez wants your doors and locks changed."

"Prez?" I ask.

"Diablo?" The prospect states, looking at me like I'm crazy.

"No shit," I growl. "I know who he is. What the hell?" Whirling around, I stomp back down the hall to my modest bedroom, leaving the front door open. My room has cute purple and light blue curtains, but not much else. Snatching up my phone, I let out a small angry scream.

I don't have Diablo's phone number.

In my haste to answer the door, I didn't put on my robe so I angrily put it on and stomp back into the living room where I left the bored looking prospect standing.

How dare Diablo send someone I don't know to my house at seven in the morning and change my locks, without asking me first? What the fuck?

"Can you call Diablo? I don't have his number, and I need to yell at him," I ask. Thrusting my phone toward him.

"I have strict orders."

"No disrespect, big guy, but I don't give a shit about your orders. Either call him or leave right now."

He smirks at me while pulling out his own phone, and calls Diablo.

"Stupid biker. Kiss me once and get all bossy. Fuck that," I say to myself and pace back and forth. In my haste to yell at Caleb, I didn't realize that I let a stranger in my house at seven–fucking–thirty in the morning!

"Uh, Prez? Your girl wants to talk to you," he says with some apprehension. "She's uh...she's getting, uh–"

"Just give me the damn phone." He hands me the phone.

"Diablo, what the fuck?"

"What's wrong, little bird?" There is no annoyance, only patience in his voice.

"What's wrong?" I shriek. "You sent a fucking scary giant to my door at seven–fucking–thirty in the morning. I opened the damn door without a robe. I left the stranger in my living room when I realized I didn't have a robe on and I needed to yell at you. Oh! And I can't afford new doors and locks!"

"You opened the door without a robe on?"

A groan is my only reply.

Silence on the other end has me gritting out, "Diablo!"

"Look, babe, your door is shit. I'm willing to bet your back door is too." He's right, but still, I can't afford it. "So I'm fixing it. And I didn't ask you to pay for it."

"It's too much."

"It's not."

"You should have told me you were sending someone."

"I know."

"Fine," I give in. "I don't even have your number."

"You'll have it as soon as we hang up."

"Oh, all right."

"Good. Now go put some clothes on. While Joker finishes your doors, I'm taking you for a ride."

"What?"

"I'm taking you for a ride, little bird. Be ready."

"I can't go."

"You can. You have the night off," he says.

"What?"

"Little bird," he growls. The timber of his voice has me wetting my panties and I cave.

"Fine, but just know my wrist is still a little tinder. Where are we going?"

"I'll take care of your wrist. And it's a surprise. Give Joker his phone back."

"Okay," I say. Then hand the phone back to Joker.

"She has a robe on now, Prez," Joker says into the phone. He looks embarrassed and I feel bad. I'm sure he is here because Diablo told him to be.

Hanging up, he grunts, "I'll just get this done."

"Sure."

I get a text from Diablo as soon as Joker hangs up the phone.

Go put on clothes.

I save his number under Caleb and realize I don't know his last name. I shoot off a quick text to Ena and let her know that the locks are being changed and that I will give her a new key once she gets home. After getting dressed in a pair of blue jeans, a red tank top, and a pair of black and white Chuck Taylors, I go to the kitchen and make coffee.

As the coffee is finishing, I hear the rumble of motorcycles coming down the street. I'm not sure how many, but there are several. Diablo and two other Havoc members enter the house as I stick my head out of the kitchen entry.

Trying to ignore Diablo I ask, "Joker honey, would you like some coffee?"

"Uh, no thanks, Savy."

"Of course you want some. You were sent over here at the ass crack of dawn," I say, ignoring his initial response. "I'll get you some."

"He can get it, Savy."

"I'll get it," I grit out. "He's a guest in my house, *Diablo.*" Using his club name.

His eyes narrow, but he doesn't try to stop me.

I move back into the kitchen, praying that my earlier irritation with Caleb goes away. Taking a few breaths, I make Joker's coffee. I also make a cup for Diablo. I hope they like it black because I don't have any creamer.

"Thanks, Savy," Joker says as I hand him the steaming cup.

"You're welcome."

"Here you go, honey," I say to Diablo as I had him a cup as well.

"Thanks, babe."

"I'll just go finish getting ready. The rest of you can help yourselves," I say. I move down the hall to escape the men that have taken over my living room and kitchen. I am ready to go, but I also need a minute to make sure I am perfect. This is my first date with Caleb, and I want it to be perfect.

This is a date right?

"You ready, babe?"

I let out a little scream and whirl around to glare at Caleb. He is standing in my tiny bedroom, looking like a Greek God or something. He's seriously hot, and my sex gushes just looking at him.

"You scared the shit out of me, Caleb."

"Glad to see I'm Caleb again."

"Oh shut up," I grumble while moving toward Caleb. Once I'm close, I push up on my tiptoes and give him a chaste kiss. For some unknown reason, I'm comfortable being myself around him. It's just been a few days, but it's nice to let the long hidden part of myself out. I've always trusted my instincts, and I am doing that with Caleb too.

We spend the day exploring a little sleepy coastal town about an hour west of Sage. It has a southern charm I long for. It's amazing, and I love it instantly. The smells, breeze and best of all the ocean. We sit on the shore and I stare into the water, thinking of my mom. I know she's still with me, but the ocean helps me feel connected to her in a way I don't feel at any other time. While we're at the beach, I don't talk much, and Caleb doesn't push me. I'm thankful for that because I'm not comfortable talking about my past.

I never imagined I would love having the wind in my face as we sped down the highway, but I did. While I was behind Caleb on his bike, I took the time to explore his abs. They are rock solid and again, I gushed. I didn't continue my exploration further down his body because we were on the highway and I didn't want to die. Honestly, I don't think I'm ready to go there with Diablo, *yet*.

We window shop at the little vintage shop in town and have lunch at a small café. I laugh harder with Caleb than I have since I was a kid.

"Thank you for this. It's been a long time since I laughed this much." Sincerity is crisp in my voice.

"Even with your ex?"

"Even with my ex," I admit.

"He's a rich prick anyway," Caleb says.

"Wait! How do you know Tyler's rich?"

"I did some research on you and Tyler Huntington."

"Research? Why did you do that? No, he'll..." I say. Panic inches up my spine, I reach up to rub my stiff neck. Fear creeps into my voice and I feel the tension increase in my body.

"He'll what?"

I keep my mouth shut. I've said too much already and I can't get Caleb involved.

"Just forget it." I can't even blame Caleb. How would he have known I was running from someone? He wouldn't and most employers do background checks. I guess he assumed I was a normal employee. I'm not. I persuaded Donny to bypass the background check so my father wouldn't know where we are. He's found us several times before and each time I was able to get away with Ena, but I know I can't run forever. I just have to keep trying.

"Savy, are you in trouble? What are you running from?"

"No of course not, silly." My attempt to avoid the situation doesn't work. Caleb is too smart for his own good.

"Don't lie to me, little bird. I can help you, but you have to trust me."

"I can't trust anyone," I whisper.

"You can trust me."

"I can't. And it has nothing to do with you. It's all me, but I need to get back. I'm getting tired."

"It's only six. Don't let this shit ruin the rest of our day. I'll drop it for now, but I will prove to you that you can trust me." His declaration rings in my ears, but my heart is shielded from his words.

Then Caleb does the one thing I need most at the moment, he changes the subject, and I'm grateful for his kindness when I shut him out.

"I'm glad you've been having fun today, baby. You deserve it," he says with an intensity that steals my breath. "I plan on making sure you laugh this much every day."

Maybe I wasn't quite ready for this declaration.

"I won't be around much longer, so every day until I'm gone sounds good."

"Every day. Period."

That's what you think, honey.

"I have to tell you, I don't believe we should be together."

Caleb doesn't understand the danger he inadvertently put Ena and me in. Not to mention the danger he has put himself in. We will leave soon, but I want to enjoy my time with Caleb until I'm gone.

"I don't deserve someone like you and to be honest, you scare the shit out of me."

"I'd never hurt you, Savannah." It's the first time Caleb has used my full name. And for the first time in a decade, I don't cringe when a man says my name.

"Somehow I know that. I'm not sure how, but I know you'd never hurt me." I pause, not sure if I want to reveal too much about myself so soon. "I've had rough relationships in the past, and I'm careful about who I let in." Giving him a little, but not disclosing the depths of my past.

"As you should be," he says. "But, I will prove it to you, baby. We are destined for each other and to be honest, I never believed in love at first sight and I'm not sure I do now, but I knew the minute I saw you that I wanted you."

I think I knew too.

A shiver runs down my back. I say nothing.

"I can live with you not responding."

"Me too."

Caleb steers the topic to easier territory. And I'm thankful because I don't want to get attached to him. I know that we cannot be together and I have to find a new safe place for Ena and I to live. I'm sure Paul knows where we are and is on his way to end me.

During our date, I learn that Skull and Caleb are brothers and they had a rough childhood too. He didn't need to tell me that to know. There is something about a person who had a shitty childhood. It marks them for life. And the scars are often easy to see.

I have the same scars.

Around nine o'clock, Caleb and I head back to my house. I want to ask him to stay for a while, but I'm afraid it's too soon. I just don't want this day to end. Having a regular, healthy date with no worries was nice, especially when it's with a handsome biker.

CHAPTER NINE

P<small>AUL</small>

"H<small>URRY THE FUCK UP</small>!"

"I am. I can't see shit in here. Turn on a light," Tyler whines. He sounds just like the little bitch I knew he always was. He fucked up my plan and now I need to hurry before Savannah takes off again with my baby girl.

"No, dipshit. Do you want someone to see us?"

"Oh yeah."

"Just trash her bedroom. I'll take care of the rest."

"Right, boss," Tyler replies as he rushes down the small hall.

"And make it look good! Try to find any money or weapons she has." I know Savannah deals in cash. I've been tracking her since she took Ena. And I've had alerts on her social security number so I would know if she had a bank account, which she doesn't. No bank accounts, no credit cards, nothing. It has been difficult keeping up with her.

I walk to open the front door just a crack. I want Savannah to know I was here as soon as she steps foot on the porch. I hope terror slips down her spine and engulfs her whole. It's a part of my plan. A plan she keeps fucking up. I'm surprised she's been so elusive since she's a fucking idiot. The bitch is worthless so I'm shocked she's been able to stay hidden all this time. She didn't even change their names. Rule one when you want to stay hidden, change your name. What she doesn't know, is her last boyfriend, Tyler Huntington, was planted in her life by me. He had one job, make her fall in love with him, propose and marry her. Then he would hand her over to me to keep in a safe place. A place where she will never see the light of day again. I need to make sure she pays for what she did to my Mary.

But he fucked it up. And Savannah left him. She has only spoken to him once since they broke up and now he has to help me get Savannah and Ena.

Savannah to kill.

Ena to bring home where she belongs.

"I couldn't find anything. She doesn't have much. Just some old clothes and a few shoe boxes."

"Fine–" The sound of a motorcycle pulling into the driveway draws my attention away from Tyler.

"What is that?" he asks.

"Shut the fuck up!" I whisper. "Go out the back door."

Tyler moves through the kitchen to the sliding door and I follow him out, turning on a light before exiting. I watch as Savannah, looking too much like my wife who she murdered, and a big fucking biker move up the small walkway.

The soft glow of the streetlight illuminates the back of the biker's cut. Savannah is with a member of the Havoc Motorcycle Gang. And I fucking hate that it has changed all my plans, *again*.

SAVY

JUST WHEN MY PRESENT AND FUTURE BEGIN TO LOOK BRIGHT, MY PAST slams back into my life reminding me of who I truly am. Walking up the walkway to the door, I notice that the lights in my living room are on. Slowing my pace, I nervously look around; maybe the guys left them on by mistake. The front door is open.

What the hell?

Panic sets in as I advance to the door knowing Caleb's brothers would never leave it open. Ena is at her friend's house tonight, so there shouldn't be anyone inside. Ena would have called or sent a text if she came home early. It's just after ten thirty, and the pace of my heart is insane, the sound of my blood is rushing in my ears. I'm afraid of what I will find.

Has he found me again?

Reaching out to grab Caleb's arm is of no use, he's already on alert. He motions for me to stop where I am, so I do immediately, letting Caleb take over. I wouldn't listen to anyone else, but I trust him. He sensed that something was wrong and is helping me without me having to ask, again. Stepping up the two porch steps on silent legs, he pushes the door open and slips inside. What if someone is in there?

God, please don't let Caleb get hurt.

He walks back out the front door, returning to his previous demeanor, but not one hundred percent normal. He's still aware of his surroundings. His eyes sweep over the neighbor's yards to make sure everything is normal.

"It's okay, Savy, no one is in there, but your back window was smashed. New doors won't stop a rock. It looks like someone went out the back door and trashed the place."

The color drains from my face. He's found me. This I already know and we need to get out of Sage right now.

"Oh my god," I say.

"Come inside, Savy. I don't want you outside." Climbing the steps takes forever. My legs feel like they are made of lead. I enter the house, and the vice in my chest tightens. It's so tight this time I can't breathe.

All the pictures of Ena and I are littering the floor. Sweeping my eyes from one end of the living room to the next, glass and paper are strewn about the floor. And my heart aches at the life we've built that has been destroyed. Violated. It's worse than I thought. I walk to the single picture frame on the mantle. The thick silver frame usually holds a picture of my mother, but the photo it holds is not my mother. It's a picture of The Monster.

It is much worse than I thought. Deep down, I hoped it was kids who broke in for some fun or maybe Tyler, still pissed about our fight. Instead, The Monster that has haunted and tortured me since I was a little girl is back. The blood in my veins turns to ice, and I shake. I'm in more danger than I thought.

The Monster has haunted me since I was fourteen. And he is back to continue his torture. This monster is so much worse than Diablo, much worse than outlaw bikers who may or may not have rapists and murderers among them. I have to get to Ena and get away, from this house, this town, and although it hurts my heart, from Caleb too.

Why do thoughts of leaving Caleb hurt so much?

"I need to go. Now!" Turning to run back out of the house, Caleb catches me around the waist. I struggle to loosen his grip, but I'm no match for his easy hold. Despite the futility of my effort, I keep fighting and screaming for him to let me go. I need to get Ena, and we need to leave, right now. I have little money, but I have enough to get away. I always have an escape plan. I save a little money every week in case he finds us. And it will be put to use tonight.

He has found us before, but we were able to leave town before he got too close. I saw him on a busy street in the last town we called home. The minute I saw him, we ran. I got Ena in the car, and we drove west then north and back east. Continually changing directions until we got out west and as far away as we could get. That time, we didn't take any clothes or belongings. I keep a grab bag for Ena and myself in the trunk of the car that contains the essentials. That was four years ago, and he's found us again. This can't be happening.

"Wait, baby. Talk to me."

"Please, please. Let me go. I need to get Ena!" I beg. Pleading with Caleb while still fighting him. Tears sting my eyes as I fight to be freed from the arms of the man I am falling for.

"Stop!" Hollering his command, I still. "You need to tell me what the fuck is going on, Savannah. What are you running from and where is Ena?"

"Paul." The blood in my veins runs colder as I utter his name. I shiver. Caleb keeps his arms wrapped around my waist, but his warmth does nothing to warm my coolness. "Ena is at a friend's house."

If I were another girl, at another time, I would enjoy his embrace. But I am not another girl, and this is not another time. I am Savannah Mae Riley, a broken girl, a weak woman, who has been running from a monster and trying to keep her baby sister safe.

I hate that Caleb is seeing me this way. I can't control the fear as it inches down my spine, and wraps around my heart. My only worry is Ena and making sure Paul doesn't get to her. I won't ever let him take her. I can't let him hurt her the way he hurt me.

"Who is Paul?" Confusion and sincerity written across his face, but his eyes hold an intensity that steals my breath. No one has ever looked at me this way. No one has ever cared for me this way.

I pause as I glance up into his chiseled face. So handsome, and concerned. For *me*. Concern for me is not an emotion I'm used to seeing on someone else's face. I cannot understand why he cares about what I'm running from. Why would someone like Caleb care about what happens to someone like me? His black eyes hold an intensity I'm unfamiliar with. He doesn't understand my reaction, and he wants to know what is going on. He's probably wondering why I'm reacting this way to a break in. He probably thinks I'm crazy. He certainly thinks I've gone off the deep end. He does not understand the demons in my past.

"My father."

SAVY

"GET WHAT YOU NEED. I'LL CALL SOME PROSPECTS AND HAVE THEM come clean this up," he says in a hushed tone. He's trying to keep me calm. I'm thankful he's here with me, and taking control of the situation. I don't know how I would have reacted if I were alone. But his presence does not stop my need to flee.

"No, I need to leave. Just leave it all. We can't come back here. I need to get Ena. Please, you don't understand," I plead.

My answer pisses him off. "You will get the shit you need, and we are going to the Compound." The look on his face tells me I'm going to the Compound, even if I think it's a terrible idea. I can't bring this kind of trouble to Havoc's doorstep. They don't know what kind of man Paul is. He won't stop until he kills me and gets his hands on Ena.

"Caleb, you don't understand. I can't let you do this. You cannot get involved. Paul will kill you. Don't you understand that?"

"Savannah, don't you understand that I'm already involved?" His admission is like a declaration. He's in this even though he does not understand what he is getting himself into. "You don't have to run. You think I'm afraid of some pussy that threatens his own fucking daughter?"

"No, of course not!" How can he think that? I know he is not afraid of Paul, but he doesn't understand the type of man Paul is and what kind of power he has.

"Good because, baby, you have a choice. You like a life on the run? You want that for Ena?"

"No! I only want the best for Ena." The ferocity of my reply vibrates off the walls of my tiny living room.

"Then you need to be brave, baby."

Standing among the littered memories of my mother, tears fill my eyes. I love Ena more that I love myself and I want the absolute best for her. I know we can't keep running, but I'm afraid. How can I protect Ena when I wasn't even capable of protecting myself? This is something I struggle with daily, but never say out loud. I have always been the strong one and I need to remain strong for Ena.

"Shh, baby. Don't cry," he says as he strokes my back and I let the years of pent up frustration flow. I haven't cried in front of anyone since my mother's funeral, not even when I got the worst from Paul. He always wanted me to cry, but I was too stubborn to give him the satisfaction. As my tears ease, Caleb runs his calloused fingers through my curly hair. His rough pads stroking my scalp in the process.

Once my tears have stopped, he asks, "Okay baby, what will it be? I will respect your decision, but you need to be the one that makes it."

Pulling out of Caleb's arms, I say, "I will pack some things for Ena and I."

"Good choice," he says with a sexy grin.

I smile to myself as I move to the back room, causing the vice to tighten more. Everything I own is ruined. I run down the small hall to the first door to see Ena's room is mostly untouched. The drawers are all open, but nothing is broken.

Thank God for small favors.

I already know what I'll see once I step into my room. Everything is destroyed. I stride to the closet, my heart beating faster than a minute ago. The initial shock wearing off allows me to assess the situation more carefully. Paul didn't pull down the shoeboxes. Reaching for the first one, I pull out my thirty–eight revolver.

Hopefully, I'll never have to kill anyone, again.

I will kill though. If it comes between Ena and Paul, he's a dead man. My vow from years ago still firmly seated in my heart. Ena and I come first, the way it always should have been.

Pulling down the next box, I grab the stash of money I've been saving. Just in case we needed to disappear, again. Which we need to do now, but Caleb, the hardheaded biker, won't let me. I want to cry and scream and plead, but I know Caleb won't let me go, so I don't. I don't want to go either. I'm tired of running.

"You ready, little bird? We need to go."

"Fuck!" Whipping around to face Caleb with wide eyes. "You scared me."

Narrowing his eyes, he says, "Let's go. You can tell me about Paul once we get to the club."

"Te–tell you about him?" Clearing the huge rock in my throat, I say, "There's nothing to say. He's a monster, and I'll die before I let him get his hands on Ena."

"You ain't dyin'. You hear me?" His voice raising, he says, "I will help you, Savy. You just have to trust me."

I know he's frustrated with me, but I haven't had to trust anyone except Ena in years. Last time I tried to trust a man, he turned out to be a jerk. Tyler was an asshole, but Paul is the beast who has been haunting me since I was a child.

"The prospects are on their way, leave them your bag by the door, and they will bring it to you once they finish here. Hurry and pack a bag for your sister too. She's not coming back here. I'll send someone to get her."

"I should be the one to get her, Caleb. She will be afraid when I tell her what happened."

"Savy," he sighs. He's trying not to lose his patience and slowly losing the battle, "Listen, go pack two bags. I'll deal with getting your sister. Stop fighting me and just listen so I can get you the hell out of here. I won't let anything happen to her."

Searching his eyes, I see the truth of his words. He won't let anyone or anything harm Ena. I rush to grab the escape bags I already have packed and send Ena a text message letting her know she can't come home.

He found us. I'm sending someone to get you.

I'm not surprised when I get a series of texts back immediately.

What!?
How'd he find us?
I'm scared.
Can they get me now?

Walking into the living room to meet Caleb, I say, "I need to be the one to go get Ena. She's scared." My emotions are running high. I want to trust Caleb, but last time I trusted a man...I shake my head to rid myself of those thoughts. Caleb isn't Tyler. I turn my attention back to Caleb.

"You're with me, babe. I'm sending Skull." Pulling out his phone to make a call to Skull. I respond to Ena's text.

I'm sending someone to get you. His name is Skull. Go with him, Pip. He'll bring you to me.

Skull? Why can't you get me, Sav? I'm scared.

I know. Pip, just do it. He will protect you.

Okay. I love you.

Love you too. See you soon.

"I need you to go pick up a package. Yeah. Ena. Let me know. I'll text you the address," Caleb says.

Hanging up the phone and looking at me, he asks, "Address?"

I rattle it off, my voice quivering.

"Come on, babe. We've been here too long."

That kicks me into gear. I don't want to be here if Paul comes back.

"Okay," I whisper. I feel the vice tighten. You would think the way I left things would be enough for Paul to leave us alone forever, but no, not Paul. He's back, and he's gunning for Ena. I'll be damned if he hurts her how he hurt me. He will have to kill me before I let that happen.

Six Months Ago

PAUL

I'VE BEEN IN CALIFORNIA FOR SIX MONTHS FOLLOWING SAVY AND ENA. I have known where they have lived the whole time, but I haven't tried to make contact because the last time I did, Savy ran and I had to track her down again. She's careful, never using a credit card and working at shitty bars that pay in cash. She's not as smart as she thinks though. She didn't change their names. That would have made it harder to track them, so I'm glad she didn't. With my police resources and connections, I found her in a few days of her running.

I never contacted her because I didn't want her to know I knew where she was. I wanted her to feel safe before I turn her life into a nightmare, like she did mine.

After the Policeman's Ball, I did a background check on Tyler Huntington. He's the perfect candidate for my plan. I need someone to woo Savy so I can exact my revenge. She's the reason my Mary is dead, and she took my Ena from me too. It's time I end her life, but I need to make sure my pawn is in place. I need to make sure there is someone that can take the fall if things go south.

"Nice of you to meet me, Tyler."

"It's not like you gave me a choice, man," he fumes.

"Now, now. No need to be angry," I say. "I just want to talk to you. I have a proposition for you, and if you decide what I'm offering isn't worth your trouble, that is fine. You can walk away."

He doesn't reply, just gives a blank look, so I continue.

"I know you have some financial trouble, Tyler, and if your father finds out you blew your trust fund on whores, he won't be too happy, will he?"

He raises one eyebrow, and clenches his teeth, but he doesn't say a word. We both know I'm right.

"I need you to date, my daughter," I say. "You must get her to fall in love with you and then you will help me get her out of the picture. She took something precious to me, and I want it back."

He finally speaks, "You expect me to get rid of her? You mean, kill your daughter?" he asks.

"Yes."

"No."

"Before you make your final decision," I draw out, "I want you to consider the other information I came across." Sliding a thick envelope across the table, Tyler reaches out and opens the envelope.

His sharp inhale of breath tells me I hit my mark. Inside the envelope are several contracts, emails and text messages between Tyler and his father's biggest competitor. Tyler has been making deals behind his father's back to outbid Huntington Industries.

Tyler will do everything I tell him to do. He doesn't want his daddy to know he's been a bad boy. He is my puppet now, and as long as I am controlling the strings, he will do whatever I tell him.

"I'll do it, but only on one condition," he says.

"You're in no position to make demands, Tyler." My muscles tighten in annoyance.

"Please," he says with a distressed reply. "You can't let this get out. Please," he continues to beg, "I will lose everything."

"I know," I say with a devilish smile.

Tyler blanches at my words. He knows I control his future. He will do anything I tell him, or he will suffer his fate.

CHAPTER TEN

Savy

The Havoc MC Compound is in a deserted area of the city, surrounded by a barbwire fence. There's another cut wearing prospect guarding the entrance of the chain link gate. His dark eyes pierce mine when Caleb and I ride through the gates of Havoc. I shiver despite the warm temperature. I feel like I've just entered the gates of hell.

We pull up to an old brick warehouse that has a large reinforced steel door. After dismounting, Caleb grabs my hand and leads me to the entrance of the Compound. I step into the brick building and I'm afraid for a wholly different reason. I trust Caleb, but I have stepped into a room full of the type of men I vowed to stay away from. But here I am letting the President of Havoc, lead me into the devil's playground.

There's a bar to the right with several men wearing the same cuts I've come to know. As soon as we enter the Compound, the room goes quiet except for the rock music blaring from speakers somewhere in the room.

All eyes are on me.

Caleb gives my hand a reassuring squeeze. I'm crushing his massive hand in my clinched fist. I'm freaking out and ready to run out of the Compound never to return. He continues to pull me through the Compound to a back room.

"Church in one hour," Caleb roars. The atmosphere in the room changes. All the men stop staring at me and stare at Caleb as he pulls me the rest of the way into the room, slamming the door behind us.

"Start talking. Why are you running from Paul?" Caleb's change in demeanor rocks me.

He is tense and his eyes are piercing though I'm not afraid. He asked me to trust him, so I am. I'm thankful that Caleb called him Paul, not my father because he is anything but a father.

"Where's Skull with Ena? Did he get her? I need to make sure she's okay." My attempt at deflection doesn't work.

"Savy, she's fine. They are on the way here. Now talk."

"You don't understand. I can't tell you," I say with a hitch in my voice. "The less you know, the better for everyone."

What will he think of me once he knows what I've done?

"No, you look," he states in return, "I'm involved whether you want me to be or not. I don't give a fuck what you say. I don't know why, but you have a pull on me, baby. I can't explain it, but I'm involved and to help you, I need to know what you're running from. You already made your choice. There's no turning back."

And the dam broke.

I cry like a baby in front of a man. But he's not just a man. He's the man I'm attracted to. I don't understand why, but I cry without the fear of showing my weakness. He wraps me in his arms and rocks me back and forth. The motion soothes something inside me that has been broken for over ten years. It's not completely healed, but it's fusing together like new calcium on a broken bone.

As the tears ease, Caleb continues to hold me and I want to cry more. The tenderness he is showing me makes no sense. How can he be so gentle? This large rough man, my gentle biker. Finally, Caleb lets me go and I pace back and forth along the side of the long oblong table with the Havoc emblem embedded in the wood. I have to move or I'll break down again, and honestly, I'm sick of crying. Now is not the time for tears. I need to make sure Ena is safe and if I'm being honest with myself, it's time to tell someone my story. But I don't want to be honest with myself, denial is the only thing getting me through this right now.

"You don't even know me that well, how can I have a pull on you?" I say to myself. My brows are furrowed in confusion as I look toward Caleb. He's leaning against the wall with an amused look on his face. But it's not just an amused look. It's something else, possibly love?

Don't be stupid, Savannah! It's not love. That sounds crazy.

But I feel it too. I can't explain it, but I'm drawn to Caleb. It was instant. From the first time I laid eyes on him I felt it in my heart, but how is that possible?

He's just being nice to you. Don't be an idiot.

Caleb lives a life of danger, and I have a driving need to disappear because a bigger threat is back. That threat is hell bent on getting to my sister, but something is pushing me to trust Caleb. I've always trusted my instincts before, they haven't steered me wrong.

Hard pounding on the large wood door, stops me in my tracks and I look to Caleb with wide eyes. He flashes an easy smile. Whoever is on the other side of the door isn't a threat. My suspicions are confirmed as Skull walks in before Caleb can tell him to enter. He's pulling Ena into the room by the hand. As soon as I see her, I lunge toward her to wrap her in a tight embrace. Ena looks terrified, but when she sees me, she rushes toward me too. She returns the hug with the same intensity.

"Are you okay?" Rubbing my hands over her head, face, shoulders and arms, I need to make sure she's all right. There hasn't been a threat to her directly, but the return of Paul has unnerved me. Seeing the fear on Ena's face has revealed just how afraid I am and it reaffirms my driving need to leave. But I told Caleb I would be brave. I want to be brave. I just hope my bravery doesn't get anyone killed.

Turning to Skull I say, "Thank you. Thank you so much." Tears glisten in my eyes.

Again.

The shit is getting annoying.

I take a deep breath to stop my tears from falling.

"You're welcome." His eyes never leave Ena. Ena, shifts from one foot to the other, she looks uncomfortable, but she's staring right back at Skull.

Oh hell no! Snapping my fingers in his face, I say, "Hey! She's seventeen. Stop that!"

"Savy!" Ena says.

I ignore Ena as I stare Skull straight in the eyes. He needs to know I never back down, especially when it comes to Ena.

That was the wrong thing to say as Skull narrows his eyes at me. "Look, I don–"

"Skull! Get the fuck out. We got church as soon as I know what the fuck we are dealing with here. Make sure everyone is ready." Diablo booms and Skull snaps his mouth shut. Skull keeps staring me down with his teeth clenched. He's obviously not used to someone challenging him. As he turns to leave, he catches Ena's eyes again, and she blushes.

Fuck.

No way am I letting that happen. She's seventeen.

Once the door closes, Diablo turns his attention to Ena. "You okay, kid?"

"Yes," she states. Worry plain in her eyes.

"Sit down, sweetheart." He pulls out a chair for Ena and she sits in it stiffly.

For the first time since entering the room, I look around. The room is large and has a large table in the center, pictures of what look to be the past and present members of the club line the walls. Some pictures are mug shots while others are more candid photos taken at large gatherings. On the center of one wall hangs a Havoc MC flag with a giant skull with horns like the devil, its mouth open as if screaming. Red, orange, and yellow flames shoot up around the skull.

It is the same as the center patch on the back of all the club members' cuts.

"Savy." His gentle timber draws my attention away from the fiery skull and back to Ena and Diablo.

"Is there somewhere Ena can go? I don't want her to hear this."

"What? Hear what, Savannah? Stop hiding shit from me." Tears begin streaming down her face, but her determination is clear.

Moving to the seat next to her I try to explain. "I know you're upset and scared, but I can't do that to you, McKena. There are just some things I can't tell you, I won't tell you." The vice in my chest tightens. Her beautiful face is sullen and the tears running down her face break my heart. Havoc will protect us, but some things even Havoc can't protect us from. "Ena we aren't going anywhere. Havoc has agreed to protect us."

Ena's tears dry immediately, and she has a huge smile on her face, despite the danger we are now facing. I know we should go, but Ena loves it in Sage and I want her to be happy. She cannot be happy while running across the country hiding from a mad man.

"Thank you, Savy!" She clutches my hand a little too tight, and I cringe. The pain inflicted by the surfer the night before, forgotten. At my grimace, Ena freezes. "What happened?" A look of horror crosses her features, and her eyes snap to Diablo.

"It's fine. I had an asshole at the club last night. I took care of it."

Whispering so Diablo cannot hear her, "Are you sure?"

Diablo heard her too because the tension in the room ramps up. "Yes I'm sure, Ena. Diablo has been a gentleman, despite his name." Giving a small smile to my sister, I try to calm her fears. I know Diablo wouldn't hurt me, but Ena doesn't know that.

At least I think I know.

So far he has done nothing but help me. He's a dangerous man and Ena doesn't know we can trust him, yet, though my words seem to ease the tension. Deep down, I'm hoping I didn't just drag Ena to the depths of hell with me.

"Savy, I need you to talk to me. I can take Ena to my room if you want."

"No!" At her cry, Skull comes barreling back into the room. As I'm about to demand he leaves again, Ena asks, "Please, Savy, can he stay?"

Narrowing my eyes, I say, "Fine." I never could deny her.

"Thank you. I love you, Savy, but you have been holding this secret too long. I know there's more that you haven't told me, but I need to know too. Please." Her pleading does it.

With a long pause, I finally say, "McKena, once I tell you, you can never forget. I don't want that for you. I never said anything because I don't want that on your soul."

"Savannah, I love you. I'd do anything for you. Don't you know that?" she says with sadness. "You can trust me, and by the looks of it, you can trust Havoc too."

The accuracy of her words strike me. I guess I knew all along. From the moment I laid eyes on Caleb. I knew I could trust him, despite not even knowing his name.

Sighing, I give in. I have been holding this secret for too long. And it's time Ena knows the full truth. It's ugly, but she deserves to know. She's been on the run with me all this time. I look into Caleb's beautiful black eyes. "As I told you before, Paul is my father. He has been looking for us ever since I kidnapped Ena about ten years ago." I pause to gauge Caleb's reaction, but he doesn't look disgusted or surprised. He has a perfectly blank face and isn't giving anything away. I cannot tell what he is thinking, so I continue.

"My mother, Mary, and Paul met when they were in college. They fell madly in love and planned to spend the rest of their lives together. They had the typical boy meets girl romance, you know? After my parents graduated from college, I was born. Back in those times, life was good. It was incredible even. Paul was a cop, and Mom was an elementary school teacher. We had the perfect family." Tears begin to stream down my face, but I continue with my hands clutched together in my lap. I'm too afraid that if I let go, I'll stop and never continue my story.

"I wanted a sister or brother so bad that I asked my mom for a baby every day. And I finally got one. McKena was born and life got even sweeter. At least I thought so. I was just a kid, what the hell did I know about my parents' marriage other than, they were the best parents in the world?"

Ena reaches out and grabs my hand, gently forcing my grip to loosen.

"My mom was diagnosed with advanced stage cervical cancer before Ena was born. She refused treatment because she was pregnant. She said she wanted to give her baby a chance at life. So she sacrificed her own."

Ena tightens her grasp on my hand. It's almost painful, but not as painful as the past. "Mom was given six months to live. Her odds would have been better, but she refused treatment for my sister." I turn to look at Ena and I see she is silently crying. Skull is gripping her shoulder. It's sweet that he is comforting her, but she's only seventeen, and I don't like it. For now, I say nothing.

"After Ena was born, Mom started aggressive chemotherapy and radiation, but nothing seemed to work. The chemo just made her sick, and so she stopped treatment. Ena was just a baby so she has no memories of Momma, only what I've told her over the years. I remember the sound of her throwing up in the middle of the night only to have her attempt to be the same happy school teacher the next morning. She wasn't. She was dying, and I was angry."

Caleb moves to sit on my other side, grabbing my free hand. The strength in his hold grounds me. "One day, she wanted to cheer me up. I had been having a hard time. You know my mom was dying and all, and my new sister was taking all the attention." Shaking my head, I can't believe I was so angry at my mom for being sick, and I was pissed at Ena for being born. I'm disgusted at myself.

"One day we were going to the museum. It was one of Mom's and my favorite places to go. Dad loaded us into the car, and we dropped Ena off at the babysitter's house. It was supposed to be my special day with Mom and Dad like we used to have. They were trying to make lasting memories."

I pause as my voice cracks. Taking a deep breath, I continue while the vice in my chest tightens. It becomes harder and harder to breathe. I pause again, and a reassuring squeeze on my shoulder allows me to continue. It's Caleb's hand on me. I know without looking.

"We never made it to the museum that day. We had a car accident on a bridge. The car went over the edge, and we sank. Paul was able to free himself from his seatbelt, but I was strapped in the back, and I couldn't breathe. I remember Mom looking back at me, and the panic in her eyes told me everything I needed to know. I would never see her again. Paul attempted to save Momma first, but she fought him. She pushed him away and frantically pointed. She pointed at me! She died for me!"

"Paul squeezed in the back of the car, and he saved me. He saved me, and Mom died. She died because he chose me." I push out the words, unable to stop myself from crying.

This is the first time I ever talked about what happened in the car that day, and just speaking the words hurt. The pain in my chest is immense and I'm struggling to take in air. I remember the burning in my chest and back from not being able to breath under the water, the rush of sweet cold air as our bodies finally reached the surface, and my pained cries as I realized my mother was sinking to the bottom of the river still strapped into her seat. "I knew. I knew Mom wouldn't make it. She was fragile already. She couldn't breathe, and he saved me. She died, and I lived, and I killed her," I cry. "I was so angry that she was dying, and I wanted to go to the museum that day. We would have never been on the bridge that day if I hadn't asked to go."

"No! Savy, it's not your fault." Hysterically crying, Ena tries to make me see reason, but no matter what she says, I know it was my fault. My mom was dying, but she died sooner than expected because of my actions.

I will never forgive myself.

"Yes Ena, it is my fault."

"No!" She sounds defeated, but she knows it's true. They all do. I'm afraid to look at Caleb. I can't handle the judgment I'll see in his eyes.

"Yes! It's my fault. Can't you understand that?" I scream.

"No it's not! Why can't you fucking understand what I'm saying?" she screams back.

"Babe. It's not your fault. How old were you?" Diablo asks before I can reprimand Ena for cussing.

"Eight."

"You were a fuckin' kid who was losing her mom to cancer. Of course you were angry, but did you crash that car? Were you driving? No. It's not your fault, little bird." The steel in his voice doesn't change my mind.

It's your fault she's dead.

I continue my story so they can stop trying to convince me of my innocence. "After the funeral, Paul treated me different. I was no longer his precious little girl. He blamed me, too. And he was right, but he was terrible to me. He beat me almost every day. No matter how small the offense, he doled out beatings, and I took them because I never knew if he would lash out at McKena. It was my penance to pay. So I took each fist, each kick. I knew every day I would be beat so badly that I wouldn't be able to lay down. The bruises and open wounds were so bad that I slept leaning against my bedroom wall several times a week."

"I remember. I remember that you were sleeping while standing, but I didn't know why. I asked you all the time, but you always had an excuse. You said it was from sports, or you tripped, or some other accident from being clumsy. I never realized you didn't even play sports until I was much older. I'm so sorry, Savy. I should have done something," Ena sobs.

I release my grip on Ena and Caleb's hands and place my shaking palms on each of Ena's cheeks. "Baby, I didn't *want* you to see it. I don't want you to remember. You know that?"

All she does is nod her head. I release her face and look down at the wood table. I avoid the stares of the only three people I've confided in. The humiliation is too much to bear. "Between beatings, Paul let his friends rape me. Every day there was someone new. He was a cop so telling someone about what was happening wouldn't have stopped them from coming around. I learned to keep my mouth shut."

"Fuck," Ena says.

"Shit," both Caleb and Skull say at the same time. The vehemence in their voices causes me to jump, but I continue. I can't stop now.

"It lasted for three years until I killed Paul's best friend Jon. He was a cop too. I shot him between the eyes as he entered Ena's room one night. I was already dead inside, but I couldn't allow them to hurt Ena too."

The anguish on Ena's face gives me pause, but I don't stop. I've opened the dam and can't control the flow of words or emotions that I feel.

Looking up to meet Ena's eyes, I say, "I overheard Jon and Paul talking about letting Jon rape Ena so I waited in her bedroom for him to come in. I made her stay hidden in the backyard until I came for her." Her sharp intake of breath almost stops me, but I have to get it all out. "I couldn't let him do that. It killed me every time someone raped me. I felt like less of a person and would have rather been dead. I couldn't let him kill the sweet little girl I loved, so I killed him. I shot him between the eyes as he pulled back the covers to her bed, and I don't feel bad about it. The bastard took my innocence, but I would not let that happen to Ena so I shot him and I ran out of the house into the backyard. Then I bundled up Ena and we left."

My hands are shaking, despite each of them again being held by Ena and Caleb, and my voice is quivering, but I must continue because after today, I don't want to talk about my abuse again.

"Where did you go?" Caleb asks.

"I was sixteen by then, and Ena was just eight, but looked much younger. I pretended to be her mom and caught a bus out west. I checked the papers frequently, but he never reported us missing. I saw a news story about Jon's murder one day. They blamed it on an unknown suspect. They covered it up to hide the horrible shit he did, but I didn't care. The bastard got what he deserved and I've never missed a wink of sleep for the life I took."

I pause to slow my breathing. "We moved occasionally, never settling down anywhere because there was always a chance he would find us. We were free for a while, but then he found us and again we took off. A few years ago I saw him again. That time on the street in Oklahoma, and we ran again, and now he has found us *again*."

The vice in my chest loosens. In fact, the weight has lifted. For the first time in what seems like forever, I can breathe freely. I love Ena with my whole heart. And I would do anything to take care of her. Anything, but I fear telling her the truth will ruin her.

The way she is looking at me tells me, I just shattered her world.

CHAPTER ELEVEN

DIABLO

"OH, SAVY! I'M SORRY. I'M SO SORRY, SAVANNAH. I DIDN'T KNOW. I didn't know," Ena cries while throwing herself at her sister.

"Of course you didn't know! I didn't tell you because I didn't want to lay that on you, Ena. It's just been us for years and I would never lay that at your feet. You are a kid. I wanted you to live like one."

Ena's anger rises to match her sister's. "You were a kid too! Don't you get it? Fuck Savannah! You were a child too!"

"Watch your damn mouth, McKena Marina." A sharp reprimand is delivered with a stern look.

"Sorry." The look on Ena's face shows she's not sorry at all. Her scowl is still firmly in place.

The pride I feel for Savy is immense. It's clear she raised Ena right. She is strong willed just like her sister and from the way she keeps stealing glances at Skull, she is a handful too. I need to talk to Skull about it before Savy cuts his dick off.

"Babe, you were so strong and so fucking brave. You don't have to be anymore. I will protect you."

"You don't understand. Paul will kill you, all of you." She looks around the room, with an exasperated look. It would have made me laugh if I wasn't so pissed off.

"*You* don't understand. Savannah, I'm the President of Havoc. Just because I'm nice to you, doesn't mean I'm a nice guy. I *will* kill him because he has come after you again. I promise you. Hell, I've done it once and I'll do it again," I reveal.

"What?" Savy breathes out.

"I told you I would take care of Loco, and I did just that. No one touches you, babe, I cut the Havoc tattoo off his back and burned him alive." I pause and allow Savy to comprehend my words. "I told you I would take care of him, and I did."

"Why would you do that?" she asks. Her eyes are wide and she's running her small hand through her curly hair roughly. "Caleb, I don't understand."

"I keep my promises, baby. I told you I would deal with it and I did. You were mine since the day we first saw each other and I'm protective of what's mine," I growl out.

"But, but you don't even know me that well," she mutters her lame reply.

"No shit, babe. I told you I don't understand it, but I'm drawn to you. You've been running all these years, and you're dying. You don't live, Ena doesn't live, and you're dying every day. When are you going to stop suffocating, stop running, and live?"

She intakes a sharp breath, and I know my words landed right where I intended. Looking around the room with tears in her eyes, she nods her head once. Then she breaks down. Pulling her into my lap, I tuck her head under my chin and allow her to release all the tears she's been holding in over the years.

Stroking her back as the soul deep sobs wrack her body. "Shh, I've got you."

Looking over her head, I tell Skull it's all right to leave the room with Ena. He'll take care of her. Despite what Savy thinks, Skull won't touch her since she's under eighteen. That shit's not allowed in Havoc.

Savy's crying stops, and her hiccupping slows. She's gradually returning to normal. Pulling away from me, she leans her head back and looks up to my eyes. "Thank you."

"I told you I would take care of you."

"I believe you."

I lay a sweet kiss on her, trying to show her my level of devotion in this one kiss.

———

DIABLO

STILL HOLDING SAVY IN MY LAP, I CONTINUE TO STROKE HER BACK. I've never had an instant attraction to a woman or the need to comfort as I have with Savy. I mean I've been attracted to women, but not like this. I want to wrap her in cotton and keep her safe. Hearing her story almost killed me. And I want to be the one to take out the lunatic that has terrorized her since she was eight years old.

Her mother dies, and he acts like it's her fault. He's a sick son of a bitch! It makes me sick to my stomach to think about the life Savy has been living. The hell she endured at such a young age shows me she's a fighter. She has suffered in silence for eighteen years, and I intend to make the rest of her life sweeter than heaven. I can't believe I feel this way, but I know deep down it's true. I want to be with this girl for the rest of my life. She's my ol' lady, even if she doesn't know it yet.

"I'm better now. Thank you," Savy says. The sobs of a few minutes ago have subsided.

"No thanks necessary, little bird," I say. I hope Savy is ready for the bomb I'm about to drop on her because I'm not letting Savy go.

Not now.

Not ever.

"Babe, I need to talk to you."

She goes rigid at my words. Before she pulls away, I tighten my hold and keep her tucked under my chin where our eyes can't meet.

Our position makes it easier on both of us. I'm about to drop a bomb I'm not sure either of us is ready for.

"I want to talk about us. I know you're scared, but I can't let you go. I don't know why, but I can't. You are mine. My girl. My responsibility."

She tries to pull away from me, but I don't let her. "Stop pulling away."

At my words, she goes limp in my arms.

"I know you feel it. Why are you fighting this attraction?"

"Um, let's see," she says. She is still tucked under my chin, and I can feel her lips move on the skin of my neck. "I met you like six weeks ago, my disgusting boss propositioned me for sex in front of you, a biker almost raped me, my wrist was almost broken, my house was broken into, my life is in danger, my *sister's* life is in danger, I have a driving need to move from the first place I've been comfortable at in years, I met a super-hot, super sexy man I'm *really* attracted to, but I can't be attracted to because my taste in men sucks." She sucks in a breath and continues, "My mom died in front of me. I saw her panic, and I couldn't do anything, and it's my fault, and I want to be with you, I'm staying, but I can't be with you. I have to be strong for Ena. I have to protect her because no one was there to protect me. And I keep replaying the accident over and over in my head. It's my living nightmare, and it won't stop. And my taste in men sucks. Did I already say that? It's true. So you see, I can't be with you because I'm a black hole. Everything around me is sucked in and turned into nothingness. I destroy all the surrounding light, and despite what you think you are and what you think you represent, I see the good in you, Caleb. I feel it in my soul, but I would never bring that kind of darkness around you. You know what I'm saying?" She finishes on a heave. I feel the rise and fall of her chest as she struggles to catch her breath.

"You think I'm super sexy?" I ask. My smile is beaming. My chest warms at the thought that this beautiful creature sees who I am deep down inside.

"Caleb!" she admonishes. "Is that all you heard me say?"

"I heard what you said, but that's all that matters."

"It is not all that matters!"

"It is," I say. "All that matters is we like each other. That's half the battle, babe. You like me, and I like you. Fuck. I see the light in you too, Savy. You think you're a black hole. I know how that feels. We all have our demons, but you don't have to fight them alone. You don't have to worry about your shitty taste in men because it doesn't matter. None of it matters anymore. You hear me?"

"Obviously, you don't understand," she grumbles.

"I understand. You think I have light in me, but you don't? Baby, you have no idea how black my heart is. I'm going straight to hell when I die. I'll meet my namesake when I leave this Earth. I am not light. I have a dark soul. I've done horrible things to men who deserved them, but the acts were still awful. And you know what? I don't feel guilty. But you see the light in me. You see something good. Something I don't recognize in myself. Why can't you accept that I see the light in you too?"

SAVY

I HATE BEING WRONG, BUT I'M SO WRONG RIGHT NOW. I'VE BEEN running from Paul for a long time, but I always knew he would find me one day. I mean, he is a cop and cops have resources not available to the average person. I'm sure he has known where we were for a while. Now that he has made a move and presents a danger to Ena and myself, I have realized that I am still running, even though Caleb hasn't allowed me to physically run anywhere. I'm running from Paul. I'm running from my past. I'm running from my future. And now I'm trying to run from Caleb, too.

And I hate it. I'm running from the man I want to stand alongside forever. I'm running from happiness. But how can I be happy with so much emotional baggage? I don't deserve happiness. I know it's irrational, but I can't help thinking about the life I took. I killed a man and ran like his life didn't matter. And I don't feel guilty for killing Jon. What I feel guilty about is the family he left behind. I feel terrible for taking a man away from his daughter. A girl who was my best friend. We were once inseparable.

The sick part about Jon and Paul's friendship was that Jon would bring his daughter to play with me. I loved Hope. She was like a sister to me before Ena was born, but she stopped coming over after a while. Unfortunately, Jon kept coming. He never stopped showing up to my house, my room, my bed. Not until the night I shot him.

I've always known that Paul was molesting Hope, just as Jon was molesting me. I believe that was the reason she stopped coming over. I've never been able to prove it, but I know deep down that Paul abused Hope, too. How can a once loving father and well–respected member of the community become a child molester and abuser in what seemed like overnight?

And how can Caleb see the light in me? I can't wrap my head around what he is saying. These thoughts and feelings of guilt are something I cannot deal with tonight. I'm exhausted from the crying and fear, I just want to check on Ena and go to sleep.

"I can't deal with this right now. Can you take me to Ena? I need to make sure she's okay." I look to Caleb with pleading eyes.

"We will talk about this tomorrow morning." He returns a look that tells me there is no getting out of this conversation. Hopefully, I can delay it as long as possible, at least until I can wrap my head around it.

"Thanks," I say. He strolls across the room to the large door and opens it. Stepping aside to allow me to lead our exit.

My throat clogs as we walk out of the room. Every single person in the Compound is gawking at us. The music is off and the large room is eerily quiet. The tension in the room is so thick I can hardly breathe. They are staring at me. I'm uncomfortable with their stares, the beautiful girls and bikers alike. I hate being the center of attention, but more so, I hate that they are judging and wondering why I'm here. I didn't use to be this way, but life on the run teaches you how to fade into the background.

Caleb steps to my side and engulfs my hand in a tight embrace.

Lessening the pressure to a reassuring grip, he leads me down a well–lit hall lined with more pictures of the brothers and club decorations. The hall is long, with several closed doors on each side. We stop at the end, and Caleb unlocks the door with a key. Stepping inside, he closes the door and engages the lock.

"What are you doing? I need to check on Ena." I square my shoulders, ready to take on his enormous frame to find Ena.

"Skull will bring her here in a minute, but I want you here, in my room. Got me?"

"In your room?" I breathe.

"Yes. You got a problem with that?" He furrows his thick brows.

I cannot tell if it is confusion or frustration, but the look doesn't last long.

Refusing to acknowledge his question I ask, "Are you staying here too?"

"Yep," he states. He can be so frustrating sometimes.

"Yep?" I ask. "We can't sleep together, Caleb." The heat in his gaze intensifies.

"I don't know how else to tell you, babe, but let me tell you straight." The steel in his words set me on edge. "You are mine. *Mine.* You hear me? I don't care about your past. You did what you had to do to survive. I can't explain this attraction, hell, I don't even want to explain it. But I know you feel it too. Stop fighting me. Stop fighting us. You're sleeping here in my bed, with me. Good?"

Unable to speak, I nod.

Yes, I got him.

I *so* got him.

And I feel it. He's right, but there is a little voice in my head that tells me I cannot be with him.

I don't deserve love. Is this even love?

"Good. I'll send Ena in." With a heated glance, he walks out of the room. Staring at the door for several minutes after Caleb's departure, my pounding heart finally slows. There's something I'm attracted to, but something else is holding me back. Shaking off these thoughts, I take in my surroundings.

The room is barren except for a bed made with black sheets, across from the entrance. There are doors on both sides of the bed. The door on the left is ajar so I walk to the two doors and test the door that is open and find it's the bathroom. Although dingy, I can smell that it had been cleaned recently. Thank goodness. I hate using a dirty bathroom.

Opening the second door reveals a small closet with a simple dresser. Opening the first drawer, I find several old t–shirts. I pick a Havoc shirt and close the dresser drawer. Not wanting to invade Caleb's space more than necessary, I stop snooping.

There are clean towels under the bathroom sink, so I wash the filth this day has brought away. Turning on the shower, I let the water heat as I pull off all my clothes. Stepping into the shower and plunging my head under the spray, I let teardrops fall again. I've been hiding for years and tonight was the first time I told anyone my story, but I didn't tell the full story. I couldn't. It isn't my story to tell, and truthfully, I'm not sure I know the whole truth, anyway. I said nothing to Caleb, Skull, and Ena about Hope because I'm not entirely sure Paul molested her. Deep down in the pit of my soul, I know. Paul raped Hope, and he traded me to Jon as payment for his sins, but I have a small hint of doubt. I never saw anything with my own eyes and Hope never told me about it.

As the water continues to assault my body and mixes with my salty tears, I cry for my mother. The woman I loved who spent her life married to a monster. I sometimes wonder if he ever unveiled who he truly was, but I know he never did. My mom would have left him. The real Paul was born the day she died.

I cry for McKena. The little girl who lost her mother before she had time to know her. I cry for the memories she never got the opportunity to make. I grieve for the life she never got to live. I cry because I forced her to live on the run with me.

I cry for Hope. The little girl who endured the pain and betrayal of molestation at the hands of someone you should be able to trust. I cry for the beautiful person who was ripped apart by my father.

I cry for myself. The little girl that was betrayed by her father. I cry for the little girl that prayed for death every day. I cry for the little girl whose life was stolen from her.

After crying for what seemed like an hour, my tears slow, and I continue my shower. Stepping out of my warm cocoon into the air of the dank bathroom, I wrap a towel around my hair, attempting to dry it as much as possible. Drying my body, I pull the Havoc shirt over my head. It's much too big for me, coming down below my knees, but it's soft and comfortable and holds a hint of Caleb's essence, earthy with a hint of oil.

Yum.

Hanging my towel on the thin rail, I move to the bed and pull back the covers. I'm just going to lay down until Ena comes to the room with me. At least that's what I tell myself. I'm asleep before I crawl in the sheets.

CHAPTER TWELVE

DIABLO

HEADING DOWN THE HALL TOWARD THE MAIN ROOM OF THE Compound, I can tell the brothers are anxious and want to know what the fuck is going on. I'd like to know exactly what is happening too, but all I know right now is Paul is back, and Savy thinks he will kill her to get to Ena. That shit will not happen. Savy told me her story, and it almost killed me to hear her talk about her molestation at the hands of her father and his friends. The matter–of–fact way she talked and her constant blaming of herself gutted me. The bastard is a dead man, I vow. I will kill him.

As I enter the chapel, I say to Skull, "Send Ena into my room to see Savy."

"Can't brother, she's out cold." Looking at my brother's face, I see the old signs resurfacing. Hearing Savy's story affected Skull more than he would ever admit. It brings up bad memories of our childhood. The demons that were long buried are resurfacing and I can't let him spin out of control. We had a shitty childhood, but it seems Savy got it worse than we did and that's saying a lot.

Despite the mini standoff he had with Savy earlier, Skull likes my girl. He told me a while ago. Skull is a hard motherfucker to get along with, but when he likes you, you have his loyalty forever.

With a nod of my head, I say, "She's worried about her?"

"No shit." Skull runs his hands through his hair.

"That bad?"

"Yep," he says.

The last brothers file into the room and a prospect closes the door from the outside. Church is only for fully patched brothers. "All right. I'm laying claim to Savy. She's off limits." I stare at each brother in the eyes. My black orbs sweep around the room. Each brother nods, acknowledging my claim.

"It's about fuckin' time your evil ass settles down," Shadow says. He has a smirk on his face.

"Yeah, fuck you," I say deadpan.

Laughter filters around the room. These assholes are getting a kick out of this shit. I have always been the brother that was too evil to settle down. No woman would put up with me, they said.

"God bless her, she's going to need it," Axel says.

"Fuck you too," I say and the laughter increases.

"That's Savy's job now, brother." At his words, I crack a smile.

Fuck yeah it is.

I can't wait to get between her luscious thighs. Shaking off the thought, I get back to the reason for church.

"I have some real shit doing down. I need to know if my brothers have my back." The tension in the room intensifies. I fill them in on what happened at Savy's house and a little of her background. Not willing to reveal too many details, I tell them only the basics. I want my brothers to know what they are getting into, but this is too personal, and it's Savy's story to tell. I want to make sure my brothers know what they are signing up for, and what kind of sick son of a bitch we are going after, but I can't bring myself to tell them everything. I can't break the trust Savy put in me by telling me about her past. I don't want them blindsided. But I don't want her pissed that I told so many people. They need to know as much as possible if they are going to help me protect her and her kid sister. But some things need to be kept a secret.

"Motherfucker," Preacher says with a rolling thunder. He's an old timer and has a soft spot for the vulnerable. He's the brother everyone goes to for council, including myself. Preacher is our resident psychologist. He's licensed in the state of California and provides counseling when we need it. The shit's unethical, but what the fuck do a bunch of bikers care about ethics? Preacher makes sure we have our heads on straight. I nod my head toward him and we exchange a glance. He will make sure my woman and her sister are all right psychologically. He nods his head at my silent request.

"What do you need from us, Prez?" Axel asks.

I turn my attention to my brothers.

"We need to find this fucker before he comes after Savy and Ena again. I don't want them going anywhere by themselves." Again, I see nods around the room. "We can have a prospect go with them if they need to go anywhere."

Wolf, our Sergeant at Arms, is scowling. "Wolf? Now is the time to voice any objections."

"No objections, but this is shit timing, Prez. We just took over The Jungle, and we are making contact with the Russians. We are already spread thin."

"I know." Running my hand through my hair, I agree, "I fuckin' know. Savy works at the club. She'll be taking time off until we catch this asshole. Neither of them are to leave the Compound for any reason unless there is heavy artillery with them."

Again, nods all around.

"Let's vote on this shit," I say. I'm ready to end this bastard. We just have to catch him first. "All opposed to sending a child abuser to hell?"

Silence.

"All for –"

"Ay!" they roar in unison before I can finish.

Pride fills my chest as my brothers take my back. This is why I joined Havoc.

They always have my back.

And I always have theirs.

"Go finish what you were doing. Tomorrow we hunt a pedo."

"Before we head out, I'm laying claim to Ena. She's off limits."

I go rigid at Skull's words, and my eyes bore into his. His blue eyes stare back into my gray.

"You know what you're doing? Savy'll kill you herself," I say with a straight face. We both know my words are true.

A small, tight nod is all he gives.

"Fine, it's your funeral," I say shaking my head. The poor bastard doesn't know what's coming to him.

"All right, head out." The brothers file out, but Skull stays behind.

"Don't fuck this up, Nathanial." I use my brother's given name. "She's only seventeen."

"I'm not a fuckin' pervert. Jesus, Caleb!" Disbelief flashes across his face. "I want to make sure she's protected."

"I know you're not," I reassure. "I think I love her, Nate. I can't lose her now so don't fuck this up for me."

"Love, huh?" he asks with a hint of humor. His eyes sparkle with the same mischief that he had when we were kids. "Are you sure you're the devil or just a pussy?"

"Look who's talking, dickhead," I laugh. "You claimed a seventeen–year–old in front of the entire club." Mirth dances in my eyes.

"I know," he sighs. "I can't explain it, but I'm drawn to her. When I first saw her, she was so fuckin' afraid, but she tried to hide it. Her fearlessness had my dick hard in an instant."

"Sounds like the Riley sisters have a lot in common."

SAVY

WHEN ARE YOU GOING TO LIVE?

Caleb's words keep ringing in my head.

Live.

That sounds so simple, but for the fact that a psycho is after me. I know Caleb's words are true. And the crying session in the shower was cathartic in a way. I'm not sure how long I cried, but crying in his shower, in his room, in his club, I have never felt safer.

It's crazy that a man, who has killed before and wouldn't hesitate to kill again, is the source of my comfort. I'm not comfortable around men and haven't been since my mother died. Not even with Tyler.

I shiver at the thought.

I've got you.

My heart feels lighter than before. I'm not sure how I know, but I know Caleb and I are destined for each other. I never believed in fairy tales, but I'm beginning to.

SAVY

THE NEXT MORNING, CALEB GOES TO CHURCH WITHOUT SAYING A WORD to me, other than giving me instructions to stay in his room and get some rest.

Bossy asshole.

I'm wrecked emotionally and I'm having a hard time keeping my eyes open, even after sleeping for the entire night. But I don't like being ordered around. I want to stay in bed. I just don't want Caleb telling me to do it. Even if it is nice to have someone care about my wellbeing for once.

I decide to shower and venture into the main room of the Compound, despite Caleb's instructions. There's no sense in me hiding away in his room for an entire day. Before going to the main room, I head to the bathroom to take a shower.

I walk out of the room, making sure the door closes behind me as I exit and tread down the long hallway. I get an eerie feeling and the hairs on my arms stand on end. I'm not sure why I have this feeling. I glance over my shoulder, but I don't see anyone so I keep walking until I reach the end of the hall. I look around the open space, taking in my surroundings. Several old couches are littering the large, open room and a pool table sits in the back corner.

I make my way toward the bar as a skinny blonde with a pixie cut walks toward me.

"You're Savy," she says.

"Yep. And you are?"

"I'm Lexa. Axel's sister."

I'm not sure who Axel is, but I don't tell her that. "Nice to meet you, Lexa."

"You too." She sweeps her eyes up and down my body. "I see why Diablo chose you. Hell, if I weren't straight I'd pick you too."

I blush at her words. "Uh, thank you I think," I say.

"So where you from?" she asks.

"All over."

"You can tell me, sweets. We're on the same side."

"No disrespect, Lexa, but I don't know you. So forgive me if I don't want to tell you my life story right away," I say.

A beat of silence passes, and then Lexa lets out a belt of laughter causing heads to turn in our direction. "I like you, Savy." Her dazzling white smile stretches from ear to ear. This girl is crazy, but there is something charming about her. I'm glad she didn't take my remarks the wrong way, but I've been careful all this time and I won't be revealing anything about myself to strangers, again.

"Um, I'm gonna go look for my sister, Ena. Have you seen her?"

"She's with Skull. He doesn't like people interrupting him when he's busy."

"Well he can fuck off too. She's my baby sister and he can keep his fucking hands to himself."

"I do like you," she says while smiling. "I'll be right here. I need to make sure you know what you are getting yourself into. I'll give you the low down on the club and the rules."

My stomach feels like it's tied in knots. *What the hell have I gotten myself into?*

"Thanks."

I go back down the hall, and feel the same eerie feeling as before, it's like someone is watching me, but I ignore it. My mind is only focused on one thing, checking on Ena. I stop at an unfamiliar door, but I know it's Skull's because the outside reads, VP. With three firm knocks, I hear, "What?"

"Is Ena in there?"

"Savy!" Ena replies on the other side of the door. A few seconds later, the door swings open and I see my sister's angelic face.

"Ena," I breathe with a sigh of relief. "Are you okay?"

"Yes, Savy, I'm good."

"Why don't you shower and get dressed and we can talk." Looking over Ena's shoulder, I see Skull sitting in a lone chair where I suspect he slept, as evidenced by the blanket and pillow now discarded on the floor.

"Okay, sissy," she says.

I go back out to the bar to wait for Ena, ignoring what Caleb told me to do earlier. He needs to learn that he can't order me around. I appreciate his help, but I don't need him trying to run my life. I take a seat at the bar. It's early morning, and there are women in the main room and bar area. There is not much drinking going on although there are some prospects and hang arounds partaking. I wonder where Caleb is since Skull is still in his room. I thought he was at church.

"Well, look what we have here, girls," a voice interrupts my thoughts.

I turn my head to see who is speaking, and tense. The woman walking toward me is staring at me like she wants me dead. I have no idea what I've done, but I will not give her a chance to make good on the threat in her eyes. I ignore her and the two other girls with her.

"You see this shit, Hazel?" she asks a girl who barely looks older than Ena.

Hazel is beautiful. Even I can give a compliment when it's due. She's gorgeous. She has long straight, black hair and the bluest eyes I've ever seen. Her skin is a pale luminescence. And her sharp features give her a modelesque quality.

I tear my eyes from her. "Are you talking to me?" I ask. Of course, she's talking to me. Fortunately, while we were on our date, Caleb told me all about the sweetbutts. I wasn't sure why he told me so much about life inside Havoc, but right now, I'm sure thankful for his openness. I didn't know his lesson would come in handy so fast. Being with the president of Havoc is a position the sweetbutts would kill for. For me, it has put a target on my back.

What else is new?

"Yes, bitch. I'm talking to you," she snarls. "Who else would I be talking to?"

Standing, I rise to my full height. With her heels, she towers over me, but I've only been afraid of a fight when my opponent was my father.

"I suggest you get out of my face. You don't want trouble."

"And *you're* trouble? I've been watching you walk around here like you own the place," she accuses. Well I guess I know who has been watching me.

"Savy, what's going on?" I don't look to see who is speaking.

"Ena, go chill over there," I say. I point across the room with my left hand.

"You're about to kick some ass. No way am I missing this." Her teasing makes me smile. My sister is a dork, but she has my back. Even at seventeen, I know she will always have my back. God, I love her.

"I didn't catch your name," I say.

"Because I didn't throw it, bitch."

"Original."

"Who the fuck are you callin' a bitch?" Ena asks.

"Ena, I don't need help," I say. The calm in my voice does little to ease the tension rolling off my protective sister. Working in the club has taught me how to deal with catty bitches. I've laid out a few girls in my time behind the bar, but after a few run–ins, the girls don't fuck with me too much. Guess I need to make a point at Havoc, too.

"What's your name, honey?" I question again.

"I don't have to tell you shit, bitch," she shrieks. "I want you to stay away from Diablo. He's been in my pussy every night. Then you come along, and I haven't had his thick dick in weeks."

My heart clenches at the thought of this girl with Caleb.

"Yuck," Ena grumbles. "He's going to be my brother for god's sake. I don't want to hear about his dick, lady."

How the hell does she know he will be like a brother to her? This kid is too smart for her own good. I chuckle at her words. I love that Ena already sees Caleb as family because we're not going anywhere. I made a promise to Ena and Caleb, and I intend to keep it. This bitch needs to get over it.

"Well, Red," emphasizing the color of her hair, "You can stay away from Diablo and his dick. His dick is mine now. Be a good little girl and go away. Okay?"

"You fucking bitch!" she screams as she reaches out to slap me. But she never connects the blow. I've dodged enough fists in my life to know how to avoid a punch. I twist my body and dip low, grabbing her elbow as she misses my head. Squeezing her elbow, I push her away from me. She stumbles into the stool in front of the bar, and catches herself before she falls in her stilettos.

"Now, is the time to walk away, *Red.*"

Instead of following my advice, she throws another fist, this time I step to the side and allow her momentum to throw her body past me. Turning around, I catch her by her red mane and wrap my fist around her hair, pulling it taut to increase the pressure in her neck.

"I see you have trouble hearing." I tighten my hold more until she whimpers.

Looking over to Hazel, I ask, "Do you want to help your friend, Hazel?"

She shakes her head no. I thought so. These bitches just wanted to test me. Well they have no idea who I am or what I'm capable of. Caleb was right. Well, I'm going to finish it.

"I'll give you one more chance because I can tell you're kinda slow." Giving her head a rough shake I continue, "Are you going to leave me the fuck alone?"

"Yes," she whimpers.

"Good." Releasing her hair with a push, I send her stumbling several feet away from me. "Now get the fuck away from me."

She scampers away in her too high heels, almost falling on her way out of the room.

"Who the fuck wears six inch heels at ten in the morning?" I ask as I retake my seat at the bar.

"Aw shit, Savy. You should've pounded her."

"Ena, stop cussing," I say. With an exasperated sigh, I shake my head at my sister. The girl is never going to stop cussing. "I can't just beat her up. She's a sweetbutt, a club girl, and I don't want to hear Diablo's mouth about beating the shit out of their beloved property."

I still feel weird calling her property though. I mean, what the hell? This isn't ancient times, but Caleb assured me that all sweetbutts are here of their own free will. It's a mutual agreement between her and the club. She provides entertainment, sex, does chores, or anything else the club needs and the club provides protection and a place to live. To each their own I guess.

"I would have paid to see it." I jump with a small scream as Caleb walks up behind me.

"Shit me too," Skull says.

"You two need bells or something. You almost gave me a fuckin' heart attack," I say clutching my chest.

"Savy, stop cussing," Ena teases.

"Oh shut up."

Standing behind me, Caleb leans over. "You did good, babe."

Twisting my neck, I touch my mouth to his. "I wanted to pound her," I whisper into his lips.

His chuckling fills my ears as he plants a juicy kiss on me, right in the middle of the Havoc Compound.

CHAPTER THIRTEEN

SAVY

I AM STANDING IN A KITCHEN THOUGH NOT JUST ANY KITCHEN. IT'S THE kitchen I saw every day for sixteen years. My heart pounds so hard that I can feel it in my head. I'm standing in the house where I grew up.

How the hell did I get here?

The blood is rushing to my head, and I'm feeling light headed. Pure terror takes hold. I need to get out of here before Paul sees me, but my feet are rooted to the floor. I'm stuck, and the familiar feeling of dread takes over my body. I still hear the cries of what sounds like a child. The sounds are coming from the living room, but I can't move. A howl of frustration rips from my chest, the sound of a banshee, foreign to my ears. At my cry, I tear myself away from the kitchen where I was previously rooted, as the memories assault me...

SAVY

"DIDN'T I TELL YOU TO CLEAN THE FUCKING KITCHEN?"

A small, uncontrollable whimper escapes me.

"Get your fucking ass in here and clean up this mess."

I hurry past Paul as quickly as possible, knowing no matter how fast I move the blows are coming. And they do, they always do. The pain radiates through the muscles in my neck and back. I almost lose balance and hit my head on the corner of the countertop.

"Didn't I tell you to clean this goddamn house!" he starts. The rage rolling off of him is clear in the force of the fists he rains down on me. My only defense against the larger man is to drop to the floor and curl into a ball, stretching my arms up to protect my head.

"I fucking hate you!" he screams. "You are a piece of shit. You little bitch. It's all your fault."

These are words I hear during each beating. I already know it's my fault, but Paul reminds me during each punishment, as if to rub my guilt in the still fresh wound. I used to apologize and plead for leniency, for forgiveness, but that made the beatings worse. So I stay silent now, letting no sound escape when Paul decides I need discipline. Whatever infraction he deems punishable, I remain silent. No matter how hard he hits me. Nothing he does to me can hurt me more than I'm hurting myself.

The beating lasts for what seems like an eternity when I hear a whimper at the entrance of the kitchen. It pulls me from the place I go inside my head to survive, even when surviving means more beatings, more rape. Ena, with her brown eyes so wide and brimming with tears, is standing just outside the kitchen. She is watching as a ranting Paul continues to punch me, continues to kick me.

Ena is terrified, but I see something in her eyes, the same something I see during each beating. She wants to help me. She is dying to step in, but I can see the hesitation in her eyes, too. I shake my head as much as possible while protecting it with my arms, begging her with my eyes, to let it be. I don't want her to interfere. If she tries to help me, his wrath will be directed at her instead, and I can't live with that. He's never hurt Ena. She has always been spared. Not exactly daddy's little girl, but off limits to the abuse I'm so accustomed to. Unless you count the mental abuse he inflicts every day. Having her watch while he punishes me effects Ena, whether he knows it or not. I won't allow Paul to hurt Ena. So I take each beating. Today will not be her first.

The fists stop as abruptly as they started, but Paul ends it with a swift kick to my side, cracking my ribs. I feel them break and it takes everything out of me to keep the scream inside. It hurts so badly, but I will not cry. He thrives off the cries. Although I won't make a sound, nothing can stop the tears from streaming down my face.

"Now, get the fuck up!"

I try to stand, but a shooting pain in my left arm has me collapsing back down. Again, I don't make a sound. He will never again have the satisfaction of hearing my screams.

"I said, GET THE FUCK UP!" he says. And with an immense effort, I stand on shaking legs.

"Clean this fucking kitchen and don't make me tell you again." He grabs his keys from the hook next to the sink and leaves the house with a slam of the front door.

I clean the single cup in the sink. He beat me for one cup. The bright pink and purple princess design mocks me. I'll never be as happy as the princesses smiling at me. It's a life of darkness and pain for me.

I want to die.

SAVY

I FEEL SOMETHING TOUCH MY FACE. JUST A GENTLE STROKE, BUT I SEE nothing.

"Savannah, baby, wake up."

The voice washes over me, calming my previous fear.

"Savannah, WAKE UP!" The voice sounds angry now. What was once gentle and soothing is now angry and terrifying.

"Savy! Baby, get the fuck up!"

I jump up and scramble out of the black sheets on the soft bed. My natural instincts of fight or flight kick in. I've been choosing flight for years, this moment no different.

Before my feet touch the floor, I'm engulfed in a firm embrace. My mind is still stuck in the haze of the nightmare, and before I can think, I start to thrash, "No!" I choke out.

"Shh. Baby, I got you. It was just a dream," Caleb whispers in my ear. "I've got you. It's over now."

But it wasn't just a dream. It was real. *Very real.* I'd lived that nightmare daily until I packed Ena up and ran.

The dam bursts and I sob against Caleb's hard chest, all my weight collapsing into his arms. He turns me around, so I'm pressed against his front, while gently stroking my back. I cling to Caleb like he is a life preserver in a sea of my painful memories. After some time, I calm. In a span of days, I have cried more than I have in the last ten years.

What the fuck is wrong with me?

"Thank you, Caleb. I'm good now," I say. Embarrassed by my behavior.

"Damn it, Savy, you are not good. Stop saying that shit!" he barks and I jump out of instinct.

I can see the pain in his eyes, I know he won't hurt me, but life has taught me that men cannot be trusted. Caleb has proved otherwise. He cares about me, and I don't understand why. I'm damaged. He deserves someone whole.

"I'm sorry."

"Don't be. I care about you, Savy, let me take care of you."

"You already have. I haven't cried in ten years, and I've cried three times since being here. You make me feel safe enough to let it out."

His face goes blank.

Uh oh.

I shouldn't have told him that.

"You were crying before?"

Yep, shouldn't have said anything.

"Yes," I murmur.

"Since you're up, we are going to talk. Want to tell me what the dream was about?" He changes the subject to a topic I don't want to discuss.

"No."

Sighing at my quick response, he says, "You can tell me anything. I'd never hurt you."

"I know that. I don't know how I know, but I know." Caleb wouldn't hurt me.

"So you can tell me."

"Fine," I say a little annoyed at his persistence. I describe my nightmare. His body goes taut as I describe the day in the kitchen. It was a dream today, but that is a day I will never forget.

"Babe," he chokes out and hugs me. His embrace is tight. It's like he's afraid to let go. "I'm going to kill him." It's all he says. And I believe him.

Diablo is going to kill Paul. I just hope I'm there to see the life slip from his eyes.

DIABLO

"I CAN'T PROMISE THAT, BABE, BUT I'LL DO MY BEST."

"Oh shit. Did I say that out loud?" she asks.

I chuckle and pull her up against my hard body, my back to the mattress and her on top of my muscular frame. I feel her nipples through the t–shirt she's wearing as she slides over my bare chest and abs, and my dick gets hard... I do my best to think about other things. Now is not the time to lay her bare and ravish her sexy body.

"Yes, you did, and I don't blame you for wanting to see him suffer."

"You don't think that makes me a bad person?" I ask warily.

"Hell no. That makes you human. Wanting revenge is normal."

After Savy revealed her dream, I held her until she slipped back into a restless sleep. Every time she rolled away from me, I pulled her back into my embrace, and she settled. Her scent calmed my racing heart and rising anger. Each time I think about her childhood and the pain she endured, it pisses me off, so I inhale and I settle. She smells like a mixture of me and scent all her own. And I love it. I can't explain this strange attraction we have to each other, but I'm not going to fight it. I know I want her and I'll do anything to make sure she is mine. I always take care of my property.

Loud knocking draws me from my sleep. "Prez, we got a problem," Wolf says.

"Shit," I whisper. "Give me a minute."

Sliding from under Savy's sleeping form, I move to grab some jeans and a black tee.

"Where are you going?" Savy grumbles.

"I gotta go, babe. Go back to sleep."

"Can you send Ena in here to lay with me?" she asks. Pushing herself up on one elbow, her long hair is curly and wild from sleep. She looks sexy as hell and I want to slide into her sweet pussy, but there never seems to be the right time. It's hard to believe that I'm considering the timing of sleeping with a woman. In my past, the right time was whenever I wanted, but with Savy it's different. I need this to be different.

"She's sleeping. It's only six thirty. Rest," I command.

"Fine," she grumbles. "Stupid, bossy man." Her words are muffled as she snuggles back into the covers.

Shaking my head with a smirk on my face, I leave my room. Skull is standing just down the hall, and his scowl wipes the grin right off my face.

"What's going on?"

"Some guy was sneaking around Savy's house." My body tenses and I wait to hear the rest of Wolf's report. "Smoke gave chase, but the fucker got away."

"Who the fuck was it?"

"Dunno man, but we got a plate number and Joker got a good look at him. I have Axel on it now."

"We got a description?"

"Yeah," he says. "I was waiting for your go, but I wanted to see if Savy or Ena can identify this guy."

"Let me go get her up. You get the kid. Church, now," I growl. I want to give Savy time to rest. She woke up with that fucking nightmare and tossed and turned the rest of the night, but now that's over. She needs to help find out who the fuck this was because her nightmares may have just gotten real.

CHAPTER FOURTEEN

Savy

Caleb left the room early this morning. It was too early for me to be awake, but after he left, I laid in the soft bed, unable to go back to sleep. He held me all night. I felt it. Each time I felt myself slipping into a dream, I jerked awake, and Caleb pulled me into the crook of his arm. He held me and protected me from my dreams.

Minutes after leaving, Caleb comes back into the room and tells me I need to wake up.

"Okay," I say, still half asleep.

"Hurry." Then he leaves again.

I'm not a morning person so as soon as Caleb leaves the room, I close my eyes and try to fall back to sleep. Just as I'm dozing, a loud knock sounds on the heavy wood door, "Savy, Diablo wants you in the chapel, now."

"Well tell him he's gonna have to wait!" I yell back.

"Come on, Savy," the voice half pleads.

I recognize it as Joker's. I would know his voice anywhere. "Fine,

Joker. I'm coming, but can I get dressed first? Or do I need to come in my robe?" I tease.

"Hurry up," is his only reply.

I snicker to myself.

Minutes later, I'm sitting in the same room I sat in the night I first stepped foot into the Havoc Compound. I'm starting to get concerned because we're waiting for the other brothers to get here. Women are never allowed in church, but here I am, sitting in church. All Caleb will tell me is that someone was outside my house.

"All right," Caleb says after the door is sealed and Joker takes his position against the wall. Although I'm not sure why I'm allowed here, I sit and wait to see what the hell is going on. Asking this silent question to Caleb with my eyes. His only response is one jerk of his head, indicating no.

Jackass.

"Prospects, you're in church today because this is potentially larger than we thought. Keep your fucking mouths shut unless asked a question. We all agreed to protect Savy and Ena. This morning there was someone outside their house. We have Axel on it, but..." he turns his dark eyes to mine, "Savy we need to know who else is after you."

"I don't know." The vice in my chest has tightened so much, I can barely breathe. Who the hell else would want to hurt me? I don't know. Tears start forming and roll down my cheek before I can stop them. What did I do to deserve two people trying to hurt me?

"Think, baby," he says in a gentler tone. "I need to know what we're up against."

"I don't know," I insist. My body shakes uncontrollably. Tears keep wetting my face. "Why is this happening? What the fuck is happening?" I say hysterically.

"Babe, rein it in!" Diablo snaps.

It takes me a few minutes, but I control the tears and wipe my face roughly with the back of my hand.

I know Diablo is president of this club, but I'm pissed that he snapped at me. I mean, what the fuck? Someone is after me, but I'm supposed to keep a straight face about it?

Stupid biker.

"Joker saw him. Who do you know that has blond hair and is about six–two with a slim build?"

"Oh my God," I say and turn my eyes to Ena. My throat feels like it's on fire as I push the words out of my throat. "It's Tyler."

"Fuck!" Diablo says. "I've seen this little fucker. I didn't consider him."

"I don't think he wants to hurt me, Diablo. Maybe he was just coming to see me." The words sound lame even to me. I'm sure Tyler is up to no good. We didn't end things well, and Diablo embarrassed him the last time I saw him. His intentions can't be good.

"Bullshit! That asshole was pissed. Don't be naïve, Savy. You're smarter than that."

I wince at his words.

Diablo's tone hurt, but his words hurt worse.

"Give me his address. We're gonna pay a little visit to Tyler."

I rattle off the address, defeated by the way Diablo spoke to me in front of his brothers. I'm not naïve. I'm scared. God forbid I believe that the man I dated for months not want to hurt me.

Stupid me.

"We need to show force. Everyone rolls on this one." As I look around the room, all the brothers nod in agreement. And it makes me feel worse. They have no reason to help me. They don't know me, and they're putting themselves in danger. But I keep quiet. I don't want Diablo thinking I'm a stupid little girl who crumbles at the slightest sign of trouble, even though that's how I feel. So I keep my damn mouth shut.

When I leave church, I head back to Diablo's room and sit on the bed, staring at the grimy carpet. He really should run a vacuum in here once in a while. A short time later, Diablo enters the room and closes the door without a sound.

I don't look at Diablo, but I see his black boots as I continue to stare silently at the floor. He stands in front of me in silence too. He just stands there, staring at me I assume. I still refuse to acknowledge his presence so I can't be sure.

"You're pissed," he finally says.

I don't say anything in return.

"Look, babe, I don't know what you're pissed off about, but I have to go. We need to catch this asshole before he's onto us."

I give no response.

Diablo reaches out to cup my chin and tilts my head up, forcing me to look at his face. His touch is gentler than I expected. "What's wrong, little bird?"

I stare at the black orbs that I've fallen in love with.

Holy shit! I'm in love with Caleb.

Even with this realization, I continue my silence, though my heart is beating like the little drummer boy.

"I gotta go, babe, but I need to make sure you're okay."

"I'm fine," I finally say.

"You're not." Impatience seeps into his tone. "What's wrong?"

"I said I'm fine, Diablo. Just do what you need to do. I'm going to check on Ena." I stand.

Diablo doesn't move an inch. His hand is still cupping my chin, but now I'm pressed against his chest. Attempting to walk around his massive frame, he snakes his arm around my back and squeezes my body closer to his. My breath hitches. His scent invades my nose, and I breathe in, his essence coating my soul, soothing my anger.

Slightly.

Diablo slams his mouth down on mine. I fight his kiss. I don't want to let go of my anger, but the fight quickly leaves me. His kiss is demanding and passionate, and I open to him. Snaking his tongue into my mouth, exploring its depths, a moan escapes me as I reach up to pull his head closer to me, eager to taste him more.

Diablo rips his lips from mine, and in–between breaths says, "Fuck, Savannah." Staring at each other, the only sound in the room is our audible breathing, both of us attempting to catch our breath.

"Little bird, I have to go," he groans. "I'm sorry."

His apology shocks me. Diablo apologizing is a rare gift I never expected to receive. I accept it eagerly. "It's okay, babe. It was stupid anyway."

"It wasn't. Savannah, what you feel is valid. Got me?"

"Yes," I say with a small nod. But the truth is, I don't have him. It *was* stupid. I was naïve. Of course, Tyler could want to hurt me. Hell, my dad is trying to hurt me. Why not the ex I've only known for a short time?

"I gotta go, babe," he says again, as he leans in and gives me another sweet kiss.

"Fine," I whine. "Hurry back, honey. And be safe."

I love you.

This unspoken declaration scares me even if I only thought it. It scares me because it's true. I'm in love with Caleb, but not just Caleb. I'm in love with Diablo, too.

Shit!

DIABLO

A WEEK HAS PASSED SINCE THE RILEY SISTERS MOVED INTO HAVOC AND the drama is just beginning to settle. We went looking for Tyler, but he wasn't at home and his neighbors haven't seen him in weeks. It's odd that he disappeared so suddenly, but we have a lot of connections around town and if he is spotted, I'll be the first person to know. We have been out every night, looking for Paul and now Tyler, while also keeping our deal with Donny and working with the Russians. Havoc has their hands in a lot of deals right now, but it's not anything that's too much for us to handle.

When I made it back to the room the previous night from meeting with our Russian connection, Savy was asleep. I sat on the edge of the bed and watched her sleep for several minutes.

She snores a little. I smile at the thought.

I take a shower and get dressed in the bathroom because I didn't want to disturb her. It's crazy how much I want to protect this sassy, sexy woman with the smart mouth. I haven't felt this way since Katie.

And even then, it wasn't this intense. She's had a lot to deal with the last week, so I want her to sleep as much as possible. She looks sexy as hell in my shirt, but instead of climbing into bed with her, I leave her to rest and go out to the main room to grab a drink with my brothers.

As I'm sitting at the bar, I sense Savy as she enters the room. I turn on my stool and see she's dressed in tight black jeans with rips at the thighs and one of my old Havoc t–shirts. This one is smaller, but still a little too large for her. She's tied the bottom into a knot at her belly, and it is hanging off one shoulder. My dick hardens at the sight of her. She looks sexy as hell.

When she's within reaching distance, I snag her around the waist and pull her between my legs. She puts her hands around my neck and rises on her toes to plant a kiss on my lips. This kiss is so sweet and tastes like mint. Pulling back I look over her face, my eyes roaming all her features. I need to make sure she's all right because she has been through a lot, and Tyler showing up at her house is a shitty coincidence. The thing about me is, I don't believe in coincidences. My gut is telling me Tyler has something to do with Savy's house being broken into. I have no proof, but I always trust my instincts.

"You should be resting," I say.

"I'm not tired."

"You good?" I ask. Keeping my voice low so no one else hears me.

"Hmm. Hm," she replies.

"Come with me. I want to take you somewhere."

"But, Paul and Tyler. I shouldn't–"

"It's fine. We aren't leaving the grounds. Trust me."

"I do," she says. No hesitation. The look on her face shows complete trust and admiration, and it shakes me to my core. No one has ever looked at me this way before. Not even Katie.

"Come on," I say. I grab her soft hand and we walk toward the front door.

We walk around the brick building toward the grass that runs for miles along the backside of the Compound. Havoc owns the land, so we are safe here. We run regular patrols, and there are cameras hidden in the tree line.

Her audible intake of breath draws my attention back to Savy.

"What is it?"

"I never expected there to be a swing set out here."

There is a playground along one side of the grassy area for the club kids. It's not uncommon for children to be present at the club. Several brothers have kids, but I've banned all family from the premises until things with Savy and Ena are straight. I'm responsible for all brothers and their families. There is no sense putting others in danger.

"We may be evil motherfuckers, but some of us have kids we want around."

Her flinch is immediate. Shit, I didn't mean it like that.

"I didn't mean that," I say.

"I know, Caleb. I'm not going to breakdown on every word you say, despite what you think of me. I'm a big girl. I can handle it."

I stop walking and turn her toward me. Looking straight into her big brown eyes, I say, "I know you are a big girl, baby. You are so fuckin' strong."

With a nod of her head, she begins walking again, not knowing where we are going.

"Come this way." I lead her down a small hill, and she sucks in a breath.

"What is all this?"

"It's a picnic." I shrug. "What? You've never been on a picnic before?"

"No," she says.

I see the sadness in her eyes. I'm pleased, despite her sadness. This means I'm her first. And it's going to be special.

I see her shake off her moment of morose and say, "You did all this?"

"Well, I had help, but it was my idea."

She nods and sits on the red and white blanket lying on the grass. She opens the wicker picnic basket and starts pulling out containers. "Ena," she whispers.

"She helped me a little. How'd you know?"

"Zebra cakes."

"She said they were your favorite."

"They are. Thank you, Caleb."

"You're welcome, little bird."

We dig into the feast before us, but not before Savy unwraps a zebra cake and takes a huge bite. The sight of her eating has my dick standing on end, painfully pressed against my jeans. Once we finish eating, we lay back, her tucked into the crevice of my arm, and talk for hours. She asks a lot of questions about my childhood. I tell her about the fucked up childhood Nate, and I had. What I don't reveal is Katie. That is a part of my life I want to forget forever. I know I need to tell her, but this is not the right time. And she may finally see me for the sick fuck that I am if I tell her. I want this day to be special. So I decide to tell her after all this shit with Paul is over.

We take turns cuddling and fondling each other just as it starts to rain, but we don't stop what we are doing. Savy is lying under me, her shirt pulled up, exposing her simple black bra. She moans as I roll her nipples between my fingers, above the material, adding pressure and releasing it gradually. I work her into a frenzy before I cup her large mounds in my bare hands. Then I slide them under the cups of her bra, feeling the weight of her large breasts.

I slide my hands down her body and unbutton her tight jeans, made tighter by the rain. I want to feel the heat of her pussy against my hand. Just as I'm running my fingers down her belly, into her black panties, my phone chirps.

Savy responds with a frustrated growl, "No!"

Pulling my phone out of my pocket, "What!" I bark. "Fuck. Yeah, I'm coming," I say.

"Please no," she whines.

"I know, baby, I want that sweet pussy too, but we gotta go."

"Fine," she grumbles as she is pulling her bra down, her shirt quickly following.

I stand and adjust my dick; trying to hide the stiff state our roll in the grass left me in. Reaching out to help her up, I say, "Let's go, babe."

"What's going on?"

"Club business," I say.

"Fuck that! Does it have to do with Paul?"

"Little bird, there will be times I can't tell you shit. You have to trust me to keep you protected. Part of that protection is keeping shit from you. Get me?"

"Yeah, I fucking get you," she says. She begins walking toward the Compound. I shake my head as I follow a pissed off Savannah back inside.

"I'm just gonna go take a shower, and get some dry clothes on," she says.

The frown on her face is cute as hell, but I don't tell her that because I don't want her pissed at me more than she already is.

"Okay, babe." I watch her stomp down the hall, leaving water droplets in her wake.

"Kris!" I bellow. "Come clean this water up."

"Sure thing, Diablo. Is there anything else you need me to clean up?" she asks while pushing her tits on my arm.

"No."

"Ten minutes," I say over my shoulder. I go to my room for dry clothes. I need to change too.

CHAPTER FIFTEEN

PAUL

I'VE BEEN SITTING IN THE WOODS SURROUNDING THE PROPERTY OF THE biker gang Savy has been staying with for days. The club members do patrols of the woods, so I'm always on the move, making sure to never leave a trace of my being here. I can't let them catch me before I complete my plan. They already found out about Tyler, but they haven't caught him yet. The little shit head hasn't reached out to me either. He better not be on the run. If he is, I'll just add him to my list of people to kill, right after Savannah.

Havoc is a ruthless gang that doesn't care about the destruction they leave in their wake. I need to make sure I'm not next. I should have done this alone, but I couldn't get close to Savy without help. So, I picked Tyler. I should have known better. He's a spoiled rich son of a bitch that is used to getting anything he wants. Too bad he won't be getting his way this time. I run my dirty hands through my dirty hair.

I'm going to kill Tyler as soon as I get the chance.

It's midday, and the bikers are having a get together. I'm surprised to see so many children running and playing in the open field that sits adjacent to the backside of the brick building. I never imagined these animals would care for their children. I figured they would beat them and neglect them, but the children look happy. I'm surprised at the normality that I'm seeing.

I've been in the same position for two hours. I need to move before one of the biker trash comes by, so I move. That's when I see her. I have my .300 Win Mag Sniper Rifle with me although this mission is reconnaissance only. I get my rifle ready with Savannah in my cross hairs, and I watch her turn and smile in my scope. She looks like my Mary. It almost takes my breath away, almost. Her wild curly hair is flying around her face, much like Mary. My breath stalls as she looks into the trees, looking straight at me. I know she cannot see me, but I feel like she has looked right through to my soul, my dark soul.

Savy turns around, a massive grin plastered across her face, and she wraps her arms around a girl almost the same height, and I lower my gun. They look exactly alike. Ena, my sweet Ena comes into view with her hair wild, just like her sister's. It's been over ten years since I last saw my baby girl. I aim my rifle again, ready to exact the revenge I swore, all I need to do is pull the trigger, but I can't. Ena will see, and I promised Mary I would always take care of Ena. I lower my gun again, just as I hear someone approaching from my left. On silent legs, I move to a new location as a big biker with broad shoulders, patrols this section of the woods.

I will get her in time.

SAVY

SEVERAL WEEKS HAVE GONE BY WITH NO WORD FROM PAUL OR TYLER. I'm pretty sure Tyler is dead, but whenever I ask Caleb, he only says, "Club business." The shit is annoying. He's keeping secrets about my father and my ex. I don't push too much because I'm thankful Caleb took care of the problem for me. Today we are having a family picnic.

So the danger must have passed. Caleb would never let children be around if there was something that could harm them.

All the brothers are bringing their families during the day and then the brothers are having a party tonight. Ena, Lexa and I are setting up a long table behind the building with food and drinks, mostly beer, but we have sodas and juice for the kids, too. The spread is pretty impressive. It's more food than I've ever seen outside of a grocery store.

Lexa and I have gotten close over the past few weeks. She's Axel's little sister, he handles all of the tech for the club, and she's grown up around the club life. From what she tells me, she and her brother had a rough childhood, and Axel started prospecting for the club when he turned eighteen years old. He was young, but did well and was patched in just over a year later. Since Axel and Lexa are twins, she has been around Havoc ever since.

I asked Lexa about her dating life, but she didn't answer me. Her eyes got glassy, and she looked over at Wolf. I dropped the subject. I didn't mean to upset her. There's something between her and Wolf, but she hasn't told me. You can't exactly miss the way they look at each other or the way they fight, but I don't press. I haven't told her about my past either. Maybe one day we will both feel close enough to reveal a little more about ourselves, but we haven't gotten there yet.

"Your friend is coming to the party tonight right?"

"Yep. Joss will be here later." I'm excited to bring my only friend, other than Lexa, into my new life with Havoc and Caleb. I've talked to her a handful of times, but Caleb always limits the calls to just a few minutes, and I can only call her on one of the burner phones. He's paranoid that Paul has my phone, or Joss' phone tapped. He probably does, being a cop and all, but I get pissed every time. I shouldn't have to change my life because Paul is a psycho. I did that for too long.

Across the lawn, I see Caleb, Skull, and Shadow talking together in a group. Soon after, Red and Hazel join them. Red, I later found out, is named Kris. She's been pissed since I started dating Caleb. There are rumors that Caleb has been into me since the first night we saw each other at The Jungle. It's romantic to think we had love at first sight. I know Caleb and Kris have a history, but it doesn't matter, the past is the past.

Except, Diablo's past looks me in the face every day.

"Here comes the whore," Ena says casually.

"Ena."

"What?" she asks with fake innocence. "She is a whore isn't she?"

"Cool it, kid," Caleb says. He strolls over to where we are standing.

"What?" she asks again. Batting her eyes at him trying to feign innocence.

"Those eyes won't work on me, kid," he chuckles. "Be good today, okay? No fighting."

"Come on, Diablo," she whines like a toddler.

"Ena, don't make Savy worry about you today."

"Fine, I won't," she says.

I don't believe a word she's saying. Ena may not start any trouble, but she sure as hell will finish it if it's started.

"McKena Marina."

"Geez! I said I wouldn't. Calm down."

Rolling my eyes, I turn my attention to the surrounding people. I've gotten to know several of the brothers and prospects over the last few weeks, and I like them all. They've taken Ena and me into their family. We are Havoc just like the rest of them. It's the first real family we've had since my mom died.

The brothers are standing around in small groups shooting the shit, drinking beer and from what I overheard, Wolf is telling dirty jokes. Everyone is more relaxed than I've ever seen them. This is the side of Havoc MC outsiders never get see. They are just like anyone else. They are hardworking, want their family taken care of, and will do anything they can to protect their own. They also know how to kick back and relax, and from what I hear, they can throw a killer party, too. We will definitely see tonight.

"Yo', Prez," a prospect named Tiny says. His name doesn't fit him at all. He's six foot six inches tall and has a massive frame. He looks like a giant. He also hates his name, but there isn't much a prospect can do about the road name he is bestowed.

"Yeah."

"There's a redhead at the gate asking for Savy."

"It's Joss," I interrupt. Looking to Caleb, I see the look that's exchanged between Tiny and Diablo. "What?"

"Uh, Prez. She is, uh," he stumbles. "She's–"

"Well spit it out already!" I shout.

Diablo turns his stormy, dark eyes to mine.

Shit.

I forgot. Women don't talk to any member of Havoc that way, even prospects. They're at the bottom of the totem pole, but they're still Havoc, and they're respected no matter what.

"I'm sorry, Tiny. I didn't mean that," I say. "Joss is my best friend. You can let her in."

"Prez?" he asks. Turning his attention to Diablo, Tiny basically ignores what just I said.

"She's cool, Tiny. Let her in. We'll meet her in the front."

Diablo pulls me with a little too much force around the side of the building. "You know better, Savy. We've talked about this. You can't talk to my guys the same way you talk to me."

"I know."

"Don't let it happen again," he says.

"I won't," I grit out. I may not be able to talk to the brothers how I want, but Diablo is another story. I can talk to him openly. That includes calling him a big stupid biker when I need to. I mean it's not like I called Tiny a name, I just told him to hurry up and say what needed to be said. I'll make my point clear to Diablo once we are alone. Now is not the time.

At the front of the Compound, I see Joss exiting her BMW, but something isn't right. Her eyes look funny, but she plasters on a fake smile. For my benefit, I assume. I'll get to the bottom of it before the night is over.

Running to hug my friend, "Joss," I say. I feel relief that my friend is here. "I'm so glad you're here."

"Me too," she whispers.

"Joss," Diablo says.

"Diablo," Joss replies.

Wait! Do they know each other?

"Uh? Do you know each other?"

"Yes."

"Kind of."

They say at the same time.

"Well, which is it? Yes or kind of?" I ask. My forehead wrinkles with a mixture of confusion and irritation. Why hasn't either of them said anything about knowing each other? Did they date? Have they slept together? How the hell do they know each other?

These questions assault me as I wait for their reply.

"We know each other, but not the way you're thinking," Joss says. Despite my best friend speaking, I'm looking at Diablo. I stare into his black eyes. They are clear, and I'm sure he's not hiding a secret love affair with my best friend from me, but I need to know for sure.

"Well, which way then?"

"I uh, I used to hang around the club," she says.

"What?"

"I was Wolf's sweetie for a while."

"What!?" I scream. I'm sure my eyes are bugging out of my head.

Joss was a sweetie.

Joss was a fucking sweetie!

"Don't talk MC to me, Joss," I say. I'm pissed, and I feel my anger rising. "I've been telling you about my life with Havoc since I've been here and you didn't think once to tell me you were once Wolf's *girlfriend?*" I scream.

By this time, Ena, Lexa and several brothers, including Wolf, have made their way to the front of the club.

"Savy–" she begins. An apology in her eyes, but I cut her off.

"Joss. What the fuck?"

"Joss?" Wolf asks.

Oh shit.

I know there will be a lot of questions about why Joss is here. And the look on Lexa's face guts me. She must have been around when Joss was here with Wolf, and she knows all about Joss and Wolf's relationship.

"Maybe I should leave," Joss says.

"No, you're not going anywhere. We're going to deal with this. You're always running," Wolf says.

"I seem to remember you were more interested in fucking sweetbutts instead of being faithful. Don't pretend I left for no reason, Jacob."

"Fuck woman, don't Jacob me," he groans.

"Not to interrupt or anything, but I haven't seen my girl in months. You know, the threat of death and all, I'd like to spend time with her, please."

Everyone within ear shot stares at me like I've lost my mind.

"What?" I ask.

"Shut it, woman," Caleb grumbles. "You ain't dyin'. I told you that."

Turning to Caleb, I wrap my arms around his waist and squeeze. "I know that, honey." I tilt my head back so I can look into his eyes. Eyes that mesmerize me. "Kiss me."

And he does. By the time we finish our sweet kiss, everyone has returned to the back lawn.

SAVY

THE DAY WAS PERFECT, EXCEPT FOR THE TENSION BETWEEN JOSS AND Lexa. They have been pretending to be nice to each other the entire night. I have to admit that I'm a little thankful that they didn't turn into catty bitches tonight. I want them to get along. They both mean something to me and I've had enough drama to last ten lifetimes, I don't need it from my friends, too.

Now that it's night, the picnic has turned into a full-blown Havoc MC party. The children have gone home, and the old ladies have mostly gone as well. Milly is still here though. She's Preacher's ol' lady. She has been helping me learn what is expected of an ol' lady, and life inside a motorcycle club. I like her a lot. She's has been supportive of Ena and I since we got to Havoc. She's not my mother, but nurtures us in a way I haven't experienced since my mom died.

We are outside around a huge bonfire, and there are sweetbutts in various states of dress. Sweetbutts are the property of the club, and are available for any brother's use, sexually or otherwise. And right now they are being used sexually.

I've never seen anyone have sex in front of dozens of people, but I've seen more sex positions tonight than I could imagine were possible. Sex is on full display and I'm having a hard time finding somewhere safe to look. To my right, Hazel is completely naked and sitting on Shadow's lap. Her fake breasts are pert and bouncing as Shadow pounds his dick into her. Her moans are loud as Shadow grunts his release.

I hope they use condoms with the sweetbutts.

I shiver at my thought. I hope the brothers aren't stupid enough not to use protection. That seems too risky. I'll have to ask Caleb later.

To my left, a new girl, Bonnie, is sitting on the lap of Tiny. It seems the prospect has the night off. He is talking to Axel, who also has a sweetbutt on his lap, too. I have had little interaction with Bonnie, but she seems nice. She's quiet and gets along with the other girls. She can't be much older than Ena, maybe nineteen. She looks like a college kid with her blonde hair and lean frame.

Tiny has one hand down the front of her shirt, fondling her breasts. Bonnie looks a little uncomfortable. I notice his other hand is under Bonnie's short black leather skirt. He's playing with her vagina, and she seems to be trying to prevent her moans from escaping. I tear my eyes away as Bonnie looks directly at me, flashing me a small smile.

Okay, enjoying it.

"Savy, I should go," Joss says.

"Sure, babe. Let me walk you out."

"I know my way. You relax."

"You sure?"

"Yep. Thanks for inviting me. It was nice to catch up with everyone. Sorry I didn't tell you."

"It's all right, babe," I say.

And it is. Joss doesn't owe me any explanations, although a warning would have been nice. At least then I wouldn't have had Lexa looking at me like I betrayed her all night. Lexa left about an hour ago. I guess she didn't want to deal with the tension. I don't blame her. I'll call her tomorrow to make sure she's all right.

As my best friend walks away, I watch Wolf as he watches Joss leave. After about two seconds, Wolf gets up and follows Joss to her car.

Looking to Caleb, he's watching Wolf follow Joss. And he doesn't look happy.

Glancing at me, I know he's not happy. He looks pissed and worried.

Oh shit.

CHAPTER SIXTEEN

SAVY

SIPPING MY BEER, I'M SITTING IN A PLASTIC LAWN CHAIR NEXT TO THE bonfire. The crackle of the fire serenades me as I zone out. It's the first time in a long time that I don't feel afraid. I feel nice and content. It's a novel feeling after so many years of running.

"You doin' okay, little bird?"

"Yes, Caleb. I'm good."

"Good."

"Can I ask you something?" I ask.

"Shoot."

"I'm glad you said that," I say. He raises an eyebrow in that sexy way of his. I hurry to continue before his sexiness distracts me.

"Can you teach me how to shoot better?" I ask.

A long pause dances between us. In the light of the fire, his tanned skin illuminates under its glow.

God, he's gorgeous.

It's still hard for me to believe he wants me, a battered and broken girl, who is still running from her demons.

"Yes," he says.

"What the hell took you so long to answer?"

"Well, I was trying to decide if you wanted to learn to shoot so you can shoot me when I piss you off again."

Punching him in his arm, he pulls me into his lap. "Of course not, baby. I'd only shoot you if you ever stick your dick in another woman," I say with a straight face.

I mean it too.

I would shoot his dick off if he cheats on me. I don't know what it is about Diablo, but I have raging jealously when I think about him touching another woman.

And we haven't even slept together yet. I'm totally screwed.

Grabbing my hips, Caleb lifts me from my seat on his lap and turns my body toward his front so I am now straddling him. His face looks pained. He isn't too happy by my confession of dick shooting.

Oh well.

"Listen little bird, and you listen good because I don't want to have this conversation ever again."

I shiver from the intensity in his eyes as he stares at me, despite the heat from the flames.

"I will never cheat on you, baby. Forget what you think you know about bikers. I'm a one-woman man when I'm committed. And I can say you are the only woman I have committed myself to since I was about twenty."

His admission that he had a former lover shouldn't have caused my chest to constrict, but it does. For the first time in weeks, the vice has returned, but this time it's because there is someone else that Caleb loved. What if he still has feelings for her?

Caleb must have felt my body tense because his grip on my hips tightens, and his eyes are now razor sharp and focused on my face.

"Don't."

"I'm not doing anything," I say.

"Bullshit, baby. You are pulling away. What is it? What did I say that caused you to tense?"

I don't reply to his words because it's stupid. How the hell can I get upset by his past when all he has done since the day we met was help me take care of mine?

"It's nothing." My attempt to avoid the confrontation is futile. He's way too smart for his own good.

"Katie was my first love," he says.

My neck becomes stiff and I try to jerk away, but his hold is steady. Him telling me about her shouldn't bother me, but it does. I don't want to think about a girl that had Caleb's heart before me.

"Come on," he says. His large hands tap both of my thighs and I swing my leg over and stand. Taking my hand, Caleb leads me toward the second large building on the Havoc property. I have not been inside this building, but it's large and sits off to the side of the main building. Stepping inside, I see it's a large garage where several bikes and cars are parked.

"In here no one will hear us talk," he says. "Katie was my first love. We met when we were in high school. Dumb kids. I had shit parents. Dad was a full-time drug dealer and part time drug user. He kept my mom high so he could sleep with anyone he wanted. When he wasn't fucking women in front of my mother, he was beating the shit out of her and us kids."

Tears pool in my eyes as Caleb tells me more about his childhood. He hasn't opened this much before, he only told me the basics, so I keep quiet, afraid that if I make a sound, Caleb will stop telling me his story.

"I got it worse than Nate. Being his older brother, it was my job to protect him. So when Dad got angry and beat Mom, I always stepped in. I knew if I could get his attention and anger directed at me, he would stop hitting them." Taking a deep breath, Caleb continues, "Katie was an escape from the pain and beatings. She never judged me and we spent each waking minute together. As we got older, she went off to college, and I prospected for Havoc. She was becoming this new independent person, and I was just a biker. I didn't want her to sacrifice her future for me, so I let her go."

This is difficult for Caleb to talk about, so I reach out and grab his hand to comfort him. A small squeeze from him lets me know he wants my comfort.

"Katie got caught up with the wrong people in college. She started dating this guy who supplied her with any and every drug you can imagine. She called me in the middle of the night and begged me to help her. Said she wanted to get clean and start over with me. I believed her. It turns out she was just setting me up. Her druggie boyfriend tried to rob and kill me."

I squeeze his hand tighter, unable to control my response to his words.

"I shot her boyfriend and then called my president, Chino. We took Katie back to the club, and I had one choice. Kill Katie for setting up a member of Havoc. Chino didn't give me any options. You never fuck with a member of Havoc, even a prospect." His beautiful black eyes are boring into mine as he delivers his final words.

"I killed Katie."

My breathing is loud in the quiet garage, and tears roll down my cheeks.

"Savannah, I don't feel sorry for killing her. She wasn't the girl I once knew, and she set me up to be murdered. The drugs were the most important part of her life. Nothing else mattered. All I ever did was love her. I let her go, let her have a normal life, and she repaid me with a death warrant from some son of a bitch she met in college.

"I was patched into Havoc a few months later and then I moved my way up to president."

Reaching out to wipe the tears from my face, Caleb continues, "I told you all of this to say I don't care about some bitch from my past. Her death still haunts me because it was my first kill, but I made it quick. Even though she deserved to suffer for what she did."

"Baby, it's okay," I say. Not knowing what else to say to the man I love. Not wanting to verbalize that she got what was coming to her.

"I'm not a good man, but I'd never hurt you, Savy," he says. The sincerity is clear in his tone. He's told me before, but now I can believe his words are true.

"You are a good man," I say.

"I'm not."

"You. Are," I grit out, daring him to challenge me. "Would a bad man take in a scared, broken women and her seventeen-year-old sister? Would a bad man work hard as hell to make that same girl feel safe and loved? Would a bad man vow to hunt down that girl's father and exact revenge for her?"

He busts out laughing and I follow, "Okay, maybe a bad man would do that last one, but you are a good man Caleb Masterson. Don't tell me you are a bad man. Are you perfect? No, of course not. None of us are. Are there things you do that I wouldn't agree with? Probably. But you are a wonderful, kind, caring, amazing, sexy man that I love."

I immediately stop talking. The words just popped out. I've been telling myself I love Caleb, but I've never said the words to him. I just told Caleb I loved him, and it's true. I love him and now he knows.

Caleb slams his mouth down on mine, and he thrusts his hands into my thick hair, gently pulling on my tresses. My sex gushes at the gentle forcefulness he displays.

"I love you too, baby," he says. His breath is coming in quickly. "I love you so fucking much, I didn't want to scare you off, so I never said the words."

Now it is my turn to slam my mouth down on his. Running my hands up his sides, under his cut and shirt. The feel of his bulging muscles, making me wetter.

"Caleb, I need you now," I say. "Please fuck me."

Lost in the moment, I don't think about what it would mean for Caleb to fuck me. I go with what I'm feeling. I want to follow my gut and it's telling me that it is time to make things official with Caleb Masterson.

Running his hands down my sides, he lifts the hem of my shirt, pulling it above my head.

"I want to see all of you, baby," he says. "I wanted our first time to be in a bed, but my cock is so hard, I can't wait to get inside that sweet pussy."

My pussy clenches at his words. "Yes. Take me right here. Fill me with your big cock."

"Take your pants off, baby, but leave your panties on. I want to fuck you with them on."

I quickly do as he says, unzipping my tight pants and slowly peel them off my hips and thighs. I'm standing in the middle of an industrial garage in only my bra and panties. It's the sexiest I've felt in my entire life.

"So sexy, baby. Come here."

Walking the few short steps to his embrace, Caleb kisses me again, though this time it is slow and sensual. Something I never would have expected from this rugged biker. Gently nibbling on my bottom lip, Caleb caresses my breast and slips his large hands inside the cup of my lace bra, caressing each mound. The gentle kneading, pulling a soft moan from my lips.

As his gentle caresses become firmer, he unhooks my bra and begins sucking my nipples, alternating between each breast. The wet, hot sensation of his mouth draws goose bumps across my almost naked body.

"You taste so fucking good, Savy," he says. Continuing his exploration of my breast, I explore his firm body as well.

"Take this off," I pant. "I want to see your body."

He quickly takes off his cut and lays it across the workbench. Then he removes his shirt and pants, allowing them to fall to the floor. I hold my breath as he removes his boxers, revealing his member. His cock is large and thick, much larger than anything I've ever seen. Let alone had inside me.

"Don't worry, baby. I'll be gentle, this time."

"I'm not worried."

"Good. Now get over here and let me make you feel good."

Running his hands all over my body leaves a tingling sensation in his hand's wake. I'm jittery and craving his huge cock to fill me, but he takes his time and my patience begins running out.

"Get up here," he says. Lifting me up onto the hood of a car. "I want to taste you."

Caleb licks my pussy from front to back, taking his time and getting his fill. He sucks in my clit and presses down with his tongue. My pussy gushes again.

"Mmm. You taste so good," he groans. Continuing his exploration with his tongue.

I have to admit it feels amazing; Caleb licking my pussy is one of the best feelings in the world. He's pro at this, combining his fingers and tongue, both gently stroking me. His tongue outside on my clit, and his fingers stroking deep inside my pussy, hitting the rough patch that brings me to climax almost as quickly as he started, but instead of letting me come, he pulls back, removing his fingers.

"Motherfucker!" I mutter.

"Not yet, little bird. I want you begging me before I let you come."

Letting out a frustrated cry, Caleb continues his exploration, inserting a finger into my ass. I tense from his entrance.

"Shh. I'm just preparing you. Trust me, little bird."

I've never had anal sex. My eyes pool with tears at the thought.

Diablo must have sensed the change in me and he immediately stops. "What's wrong, baby? Did I hurt you?"

"No," I choke out of my constricted throat.

"Then what is it? Do you want to stop?"

"No. It feels so good. It's just this is the first time I've ever had sex on my own terms. And I've never had anal. I was just thinking I'd be able to give you that gift. It's something I never thought I'd be comfortable enough to give."

"Oh, Savy. It's a beautiful gift. One I don't deserve, but I'm a selfish bastard and I'm going to take it when you're ready. For tonight, we're gonna take it slow."

"No please, take me anyway you want me. I like the idea of rough sex with you." It's the first time I ever admitted it to myself, let alone anyone else. I'd love for Caleb to grab my hair and tug. It can be something that I enjoy with a man I love and trust. "Please make me feel good, Caleb."

"I'm clean, baby, I haven't been with anyone since I met you. I want to feel you. Are you okay with no condom?"

"Yes," I whisper my reply.

And he does just what I need.

He lines up his shaft and slams home. Pausing to allow me to adjust to his length and size. Once I've adjusted, I begin moving my hips. Trying to force him to move. But he starts out slow and gradually increases his pace, slamming his dick into me while also rubbing my clit with his thumb. It doesn't take me long to feel my climax build.

"Oh god, please, please don't stop."

"Never." He continues to punish my pussy. His hips slamming into mine as a bead of sweat drips down his forehead.

"I'm close, baby, you better come with me," he says.

With the next few pumps, he lowers his head and sucks my nipple into his mouth, adding extra suction. As I begin to spasm, he bites down on my nipple as he catches my clit between his fingers and pinches. The sensation sets me off and I scream out as I gush all over his dick. He continues to slam home a few more times and then with one final slam, he comes too.

"Fuck!" he yells.

Pulling me to the surprisingly clean floor of the garage, he lays me across his broad chest as we catch our breath.

"Fuck, babe. You have the sweetest pussy I've ever had."

My cheeks flame at his words. "Thank you."

"Don't go being shy now," he teases.

"Oh hush," I say. "I'm just trying to catch my breath."

"Not so fast," he says. "I'm ready for round two."

"Ooh, me too," I squeal.

Taking control, I shimmy down his body and engulf this long thick member into my mouth. Tasting myself and his cum mixed together is exhilarating.

"Oh shit," he says.

Looking up toward the man I love, our eyes connect and he lets me take control as I bring him to pleasure.

I feel like a powerful goddess for the first time in my life.

CHAPTER SEVENTEEN

SAVY

I'VE BEEN ON LOCK DOWN SINCE TYLER TRIED TO BREAK INTO MY house. The farthest I've gone away from the club is the garage and the field we had our picnic in. Caleb doesn't want to take any chances that Tyler or my father catch up with Ena or me. My previous assumption about Tyler's demise was wrong. Tyler is still alive and still avoiding Havoc.

Needless to say, I've been climbing the walls with boredom and I'm sure I'm getting on Caleb's nerves, too. If he won't let me go to work, I'm going to annoy him until he gives in. Hopefully my plan works. So far, it hasn't.

Sitting in the main room of the Compound, I'm reading a romance novel Joker brought me. Poor guy. He's been on Savy duty for weeks and I haven't made it easy on him. I hate being cooped up inside knowing that Paul and Tyler are out there somewhere planning my demise.

Things inside the club aren't too terrible though. I've been eating regular meals and my curves have started to show. It's the first time in a long time I haven't had hunger pains. Caleb likes my new body, too. He can't keep his hands off me. Something I love.

Caleb has been trying to make my forced seclusion better. He surprised me with painting supplies. I asked for a note pad and pencils, but he went all out, having the prospects make me a small art studio in one of the empty bedrooms. I'm thankful for his sweet generosity. Taking on a psychopath for me hasn't been easy. I love getting to escape my worries and paint.

Ena and I have also been spending time with Preacher. He's the Chaplin and serves as the psychologist for the club. Preacher is an old sweet man that immediately accepted Ena and I into his family. Not just Havoc, but his actual family. His wife Milly is the mother Ena never had and Preacher is the father I've always dreamt of having. They both have introduced us as their daughters. The first time Milly called me her daughter, I broke down, something I'm much more comfortable doing. Preacher has helped me understand that emotions are normal, and that I shouldn't be embarrassed to express them. It's a piece of my existence I never realized I missed. I missed being a daughter and I'm thankful that Preacher and Milly have accepted us.

I'm normally in control of my actions, but it felt nice to have someone claim me as their child. To actually care about my wellbeing, other than Ena. Preacher has been giving me techniques I can use to get over my past.

"I'm bored," Ena says. Entering the main room with a book in her hand.

"Looks like you're about to get lost in a book," I say, "Sounds like a day well spent to me."

"It normally is, but I've already read this book, and I'm going to lose my damn mind."

"I know how you feel, but Caleb wants us to stay safe," I say. These are the words I know I should say, but I don't believe them myself.

"Oh bullshit, Sav," Ena says, "I know you're losing it too."

"Watch your damn mouth!" I say. Normally I let her get away with a little cussing, but right now I'm annoyed and taking it out on Ena. I'm tired of hiding. I need to live my fucking life. "Sorry," I say on a sigh. "You're right. I gotta get out of here, too."

Running my fingers through my hair. I need to think of a way to convince Caleb to let me go back to work and Ena to hang with her friends.

"Oh shit!" Ena says. She jumps off the chair she was sitting on.

"What did I just say?" I look toward Ena, and I see a real fear in her eyes. I stand.

"Don't move!" she says in a half whisper half scream. And I halt my ascent.

"There is a huge fucking snake right next to your head on the back of the couch."

"What!" I squeal.

Turning slowly, I come face to scale covered face with a huge, ugly black and green fucking snake. It slithers further along the back of the couch and it touches my neck. At that moment, I lose it. Screaming my head off, I knock the snake off the couch with my movement and Ena and I jump up on the chair together, both of us screaming bloody murder.

Several of the men come running at the sound of our screams.

"What the fuck is going on?" Caleb asks. His gun is drawn, and I'm pointing between the couch and the ground, where the snake was last seen. I don't answer him, I just keep screaming and pointing.

"Baby, what the fuck is it?" he asks again. Lowering his pistol now that he sees there is no immediate danger.

"A snake!" I yell. At my words, the rest of the men lower their guns. "It touched me!"

"Snake!" Caleb bellows for the biker with same name as the beast that just touched me. "Come find Basil so Ena and Savy can stop screaming."

"Basil? He named his fucking snake Basil? What kind of sick shit is that?"

Snake enters and pulls back the couch cushions, looking for his slithery friend. "You named your snake Basil?" I ask.

"Yep." I want to punch his stupid face. That's a cute fucking name for an ugly beast.

"You're twisted," I say.

"Yep," he says smiling.

Pulling the snake by the tail, he removes Basil from the couch. The couch I had been sitting on. The couch I will never sit on again.

"Come on, girl," Snake says. "I've been looking for you all morning."

Lifting the snake to his shoulders, he turns to face me. "Sorry, Savy."

"I hate snakes."

"She's actually sweet. Here pet her." He raises the snake like an offering.

"Are you crazy? I'm not touching that thing."

"Aww, come on. You're hurting her feelings."

"She hurt mine when she tried to kill me on the couch," I reply deadpan.

Chuckles sound around us and I notice that Ena and I are still standing on the chair. "Get that thing away from me so I can get down."

"Fine," he grumbles. "I'll take her to her enclosure, but you two will be friends one day."

"In your dreams."

Snake takes his nasty beast out of the room, and Caleb extends his hand toward me so I can get down off the chair. Hopping down, I look at him and he knows, like I know, that Basil and I will never be friends.

Ever.

Shivering again, I look at Ena as Caleb turns to help her off the couch.

"Take my hand, kid," he says, "I've got you."

"Thanks, Diablo."

"You're welcome, kiddo." The light in Ena's eyes clenches my heart. She's not used to affection from men. I'm glad she's been able to connect with Caleb. She often looks at him with stars in her eyes, like the big brother she's never had.

"Caleb, we need to talk," I say. My hands crossed over my chest. As soon as the words leave my mouth, the men disperse. They know I'm about to grill their president and they don't want to stick around for the blow out.

Smart men.

"Baby, I can't stay locked away forever. I want to get back to my life."

"No." After giving his answer, he turns to walk away, leaving me standing in the chair. My neck tenses and my anger rises.

"No?" I ask and lower myself to the ground. The steel in my voice surprises me.

He turns toward me, our eyes connect, and surprise registers in the black orbs I normally get lost in. Not today though. If my pissed off eyes didn't tell him I'm ready to argue him into submission, my hands on my hips and my tense body should. And Caleb is a smart man. He knows I'm pissed.

Let's just say weeks spent locked in the Havoc Compound has brought me out of my shell. Ena and I have been training with Joker, Skull, and Caleb in self-defense and I've been practicing shooting regularly. This has done wonders for my confidence because I have started speaking my mind more, much to Caleb's dismay.

"Not here, Savy," he says.

"Diablo, do not handle me right now. I'm losing my mind. I need to work. I have bills that need to be paid and my rent is due. I've depleted my savings, and I need to make sure I keep my house since we are staying in Sage."

"Savannah," he says.

"Don't Savannah me. God damn it, Diablo!" I say. "I have to get out of this place. I'm about to murder all the bitches in here."

"Stop." Staring at my face with his black eyes. The eyes I've seen compassion and adoration from are now soulless. Much like the eyes I saw when I first met him.

"You can let me out freely or I'm ramping up the crazy!" He doesn't budge. "I'm fucking serious, Diablo. Ena's miserable, I'm miserable, YOU are miserable!" I end on a yell.

When he lets out a heavy sigh, I know I'm right. I've made Diablo miserable by being here and the vice in my chest tightens. It's the first time I've felt this way in a while.

I hate it.

"Baby, you have to let us out or he wins."

"We'll talk about it tonight, Savy. I gotta get to church."

"You are always in church, *Diablo*. I know the drill," I say. "No questions. I get it, but I'm not a prisoner here. Don't make me take drastic measures. You know I will."

Grabbing my arm quicker than I could pull away he says, "Don't go making threats, girl."

The change in Diablo scares me, but I've been practicing my self-defense and instinctively, I raise the arm Diablo is holding and grab his hand with my free hand, rotating his wrist, and thrusting my hips toward him, I knock him off balance enough that he loses his grip on my arm.

I'm so stunned by my actions that I stare into his black orbs, mouth hanging open, unable to speak. I actually used the move he had been trying to teach me that I could never get quite right, and it worked.

Since we are standing in the middle of the main room, there are several people around and they just saw me essentially assault the president of their club. It doesn't matter that I have been sleeping with him for weeks. I've committed a crime against the club and I'm afraid of what the consequences of my actions will be.

I'm surprised to see the wide grin spread across Diablo's stony face. Shocked that I'm not being locked up and punished, I don't say a word.

"You did it, baby!" he laughs.

I still don't respond.

"Savy, baby you finally got it!" he says again. "I told you that you would get it. You kept practicing, and you got free. I'm so proud of you."

Realizing that Caleb isn't pissed that I used an escape move on him in front of all his brothers, I break out into a fit of excited giggles, and do a happy dance. I can't believe I was able to get myself free.

"You know I'd never hurt you, baby. I was just holding you to get your attention," he says.

Deep down, I know what he is saying is true. But with my experience with men, any action toward me that I can interpret as threatening, I usually do.

"I know, honey."

"I need to head to church, but we will talk about you going back to work when I get back, okay?" he says.

"Okay."

He leans down and captures my mouth. Searing me with a kiss so hot that I forget a beast named Basil attacked me.

"I'll be back."

"I'll be waiting."

And I will. I will always wait for Caleb to return.

SAVY

CALEB HAS BEEN IN CHURCH FOR THE BETTER PART OF TWO HOURS. I haven't seen Ena for a while. She was heading to her room to take a nap a while ago.

Teenagers.

She is constantly complaining that she's bored. I know Caleb and Nate want us both to be comfortable and safe, but Caleb has a soft spot for Ena, the little sister he's never had. I'm hoping when we talk, he will let us get back to life and stop hiding from Paul.

"He should have beat the shit out of you, bitch! What makes you think you can come in here and disrespect Diablo like that?" Kris asks.

"What?" My venom is crystal clear. I've been sitting at the bar, reading my book and minding my business. Of course someone has to fuck with me.

"You heard me," she says. You would think she had enough the first time we had a run in.

"You stole what's mine, and I always get what I want." She skitters away on her super high, clear stripper heels. Who the hell wears stripper shoes outside of a strip club?

Crazy people, that's who.

When I'm working at The Jungle, ignoring crazy girls usually works, but I know with Kris, I will have to face her head on. For now, it seems she just wants to get in my head. Something she has been trying to do more and more frequently. I hope she will find another brother to get under, so she can get over Caleb.

Wishful thinking.

Closing my book, I let out an audible sigh.

"What's wrong, Savy?"

"I'm tired of sitting around. I need to do something," I tell Lexa.

She's been avoiding me ever since the bonfire. I'm pretty sure she thinks I planned on throwing Joss and Wolf's relationship in her face. Instead of avoiding the situation, like I would have in the past, I need to make it right. Besides Ena and Milly, Lexa is the only other friend I have inside Havoc.

"Look, Lexa," I begin.

"Savy, you don't have to–"

"Yes I do." I hope my sincerity is written all over my face because I didn't mean for her to be hurt by Joss visiting the club. Hell, I know Joss didn't mean to hurt her either. She held information from me and it caused Lexa to suffer. I need to make it right. "I knew nothing about Wolf and Joss' past. She's my best friend, but she's also running from a past that she hasn't shared with me. Hell, I haven't shared my past with her either."

"I know," she says. Tears pool in her bright blue eyes. They look bluer from the tears she's trying to keep from spilling. "I know you didn't know, but I knew. As soon as you told me your best friend, Joss, was coming to the bonfire, I knew that it was Wolf's Joss."

Standing and walking behind the bar, I engulf Lexa in a tight hug. Something I would have never done before finding Caleb and Havoc.

"I'm sorry. I want us to be all right. It's been weird as hell since the bonfire."

"We're good, Savy. Promise."

Smiling at the beautiful blonde, I know my friend and I are good, but she's still hurting. I wish I could help her get through this, but it is something she will have to discuss with Wolf and probably Joss too.

"Okay," I say.

I'm letting it go for now, but I'm still worried about Lexa. She has a haunted look in her eyes. It's like a small part of her has died. For her sanity and healing, I hope she'll be able to let Wolf go.

CHAPTER EIGHTEEN

DIABLO

"FUCK THAT, DIABLO!"

Stone has been in a pissy mood since Savy and Ena moved into the Compound. It's understandable, but he needs to get the fuck over it. We have a lot of shit to deal with and we all need to be on the same page. We already voted to help Savy, there's no backing out now.

"Did you forget the vote?" I ask. "Stone, that was your chance to voice your opinion. Right now, we are doing what we need to do to protect Savy and Ena."

"And just fuck Zoie, huh? Leave her to rot in that hell hole?"

"No one said that, brother. You know we will get her back. We all love Zoie, too."

Zoie is Stone's kid sister. She is a sweet girl, in college and had a good life ahead of her. Then she got caught up with some Russian prick that got her hooked on drugs. Stone tried to get her to clean up her act, but she was hooked and fought treatment. She went back to her boyfriend, and he persuaded her to go on a trip to Russia with him. That was eight months ago. We haven't seen her since.

Stone got a letter from her saying she's all right and not to come looking for her because she's not coming back to the United States. That alone was a red flag, and we put out feelers to see if we could find out any information on Ivan Pavlov, Zoie's boyfriend. Turns out, the fucker is into some dangerous shit. He's the trusted nephew of Igor Pavlov, head of the Russian Mafia.

We sent in our enforcer, Ghost, and he's reported back some awful shit. We have Ghost working to get Zoie back from the Russians while we are cultivating relationships with them state side. The process is slow, but we are getting closer. I made a personal promise that we will get Zoie out, and I never break my promises.

Stone lowers his head, a sign of weakness he never shows. "I gotta get her back. She's all I have left."

"We'll get her back, brother. I made a promise."

With a small nod, Stone is back on board. He's still not happy with the slow progress, but it is progress.

"Speaking of Zoie and the Russians, we are expecting a communication from Ghost soon. He should have an update on the situation there."

Nods all around.

"Skull, I need you to go on a run for a few days," I say.

If looks could kill, I'd be dead right now, but I need my VP to deal with the Devils. It seems Ruger didn't like the way I handled Loco. I got word that Ruger has been talking about breaking off and establishing a club separate from Havoc. The Devils of Sin MC is our support club, and answers to me. I need to make sure he knows who he's fucking with. If Ruger doesn't get on board, I'll take his colors and send him to visit Loco.

"Mack's on Ena until I get back," he says.

I nod my head, affirming his request that sounds like a demand. He is frowning at me, but he knows what needs to be done.

Club first.

Always.

We spend more time discussing the various businesses, both legal and illegal that the club has. Our newest addition is The Jungle. Donny hasn't paid as promised so ownership of the club has transferred to Havoc permanently.

"Savy's been itching to get back to work. Now that we own the club, I think she can go back."

I get nods from some brothers, but others remain stone faced. I don't try to read their thoughts. If they wanted them to be known, they would speak up.

"Ena's also been asking to see her friends. We can't let them come to the club right now and it's not safe for her to be in public, but if she's at their house with two prospects guarding her, I'd feel comfortable with her going out. What do you think, Skull?"

"I don't like it."

"Can't keep her locked up forever, brother," Preacher says. "She ain't Rapunzel trapped in her tower."

"Fuck off, Preach."

"I'm just saying," Preacher replies. Not concerned by Skull's words. Preacher didn't even move.

"I need her protected. We all know Joker is the best prospect we have, and he's on Savy."

"Aero and Mack will protect Ena."

"I'm not happy about it, but I'll do what you say. I trust your judgment."

The rest of church goes as usual. Since it's Friday, tonight we party, and then Skull heads out on his run in the morning. Normally I wouldn't allow Ena to be at a Friday party because they get a little wild, but I know Skull will be raging for a week without seeing her, so I allow it.

Just this once.

SAVY

THIS IS THE FIRST TIME CALEB HAS ALLOWED ENA TO BE AT A FRIDAY night party. Skull is leaving for a week and despite how much I hate it, he and Ena like each other. Skull has claimed her and made himself her protector. Since he's leaving, Caleb wants them to spend some time together.

It's not that I don't like Skull, hell I do like him, he's charming and funny, but Ena is my responsibility and I need to make sure she's safe at all times. Even while inside Havoc.

"I'm soooo excited for this party tonight!" Ena says.

I laugh at her excitement as she riffles through Caleb's and my closet looking for something to wear tonight. She's eyeing my old beat up biker boots, and I nod my head as she turns to look at me over her shoulder.

"You can wear them," I say.

"Thank you, Savy. I'm going to be so hot tonight."

"Ena," I say. This girl will be the death of me.

"What?" Innocence written all over her face, but I don't believe it. She's plotting something.

"I don't want you to get too close to Skull. Please wait until you are old enough to make that kind of decision."

"I'm not going to do anything," she says. "I promise."

Her hands are behind her back. I'm sure she's crossing her fingers, but I don't want to fight tonight. I want her to spend time with Skull since they are so close, but I don't want her to *spend time with him.*

"I know you're crossing your fingers, but I trust you," I say.

"How do you do that?" she asks.

"Do what?"

"Know everything."

I smile at her words. Despite what she thinks, I don't know everything. If I did, we wouldn't be hiding out at the Havoc Compound like scared little mice. I would have known what to do about Jon and Paul and I would have saved Hope.

"It's a gift," I reply.

We both break out into a fit of laughter.

"What's so funny?" Caleb asks. He enters the room with a powerful stride.

"Oh, nothing," Ena and I say at the same time. Then we laugh again.

Caleb walks toward the bed, where I'm sitting, while mumbling, "Crazy women."

"Hey!" Ena says. "I'm a woman, but I sure ain't crazy."

"You are not a woman yet," Caleb says. "And you sure *are* crazy."

"I am. You'll see soon enough."

"What is she talking about, babe?" he asks. Leaning down to look at me at eye level.

"I don't know," I say. Pecking him on the lips I turn toward Ena and wink.

"I don't know what you have planned, kid, but it better be age appropriate."

"Age appropriate?" Ena and I ask.

"Did I stutter?" he asks.

"Nope."

And we both crumble into another fit of laughter. Caleb stalks out of the room, again mumbling to himself. I love when I get to spend time with Ena like this. We are just sisters hanging out. I don't have to be the mother figure in her life.

Time is limited, she'll be eighteen next week and off to college in less than a year. I love the woman she's becoming, but like Caleb said, she's no woman, yet. I want her to enjoy the childhood she has left. Because these are the times I will cherish forever, the memories I didn't get to have with my mother. I hope Ena cherishes the time we get to spend together, too.

CHAPTER NINETEEN

SAVY

PARTIES THROWN BY HAVOC ARE WILD, AND TONIGHT IS NO DIFFERENT. There are sweetbutts all around trying to entice a brother into sleeping with them. I'm sitting at the bar with Ena. We've been laughing all night, especially at Caleb. He nearly lost his mind when Ena came out of her room wearing skimpy shorts, a Havoc t-shirt and my black boots. She already looks older than seventeen. When she's wearing makeup, she looks even older. She's not wearing enough make up to look slutty, but enough to ensure that the brothers notice her. I wish she would stay my baby sister forever, but she's getting older. She'll be an adult soon, so I don't say anything. Thankfully, that didn't stop Caleb from threatening to lock her in her room if she didn't put on some more fucking clothes. I'll let him be the bad guy right now. I just get to be her older sister for once and it feels nice. I love just spending time with her and not having to worry about what kind of person she is becoming.

"Did you see how pissed he was?" Ena asks laughing.

"Ena, don't go pissing Caleb off."

"I won't, I won't," she says.

After being quiet for a while, she reveals, "I like having someone who cares about me, Savy. I mean, someone other than you." In an instant, unshed tears are brimming in her eyes. A look of pain flashes across her flawless face. And it hurts. The vice returns. It tightens so much that I clinch my hands into tight white fists. This is the first time Ena has expressed her pain. She's been having sessions with Preacher, but she's never told me how she feels about the life we've been living.

I feel guilty.

I made the choice to leave Georgia, but Ena didn't. For years I have been dragging her from place to place, running. And she never questioned me. She's been a trooper the entire time, but deep down she was hurting, too.

"I'm sorry, Ena," I say. "I never gave you a choice. I just ran, but I knew I couldn't leave you behind."

"Please, not tonight, Savy. I want tonight to be awesome. This is just going to spoil it. Can we talk about this tomorrow?"

"Of course, baby girl."

A hand touches my hair and I turn. It's not Caleb. I know his touch anywhere. I twist to see who is touching me.

Kris.

"Don't touch me," I say. Moving my head to the side causes her delicate hand to fall from my hair.

"What? I've never felt hair like yours. I wanted to see what it feels like."

"You see, Kris, that is a problem. You don't just go around touching people without their permission."

A sick smile slinks across her face, and a knot forms in the pit of my stomach. It's the same feeling I have had in the past. Something bad is about to happen, and I don't like it. But I'm ready.

Always ready.

"I just wanted to talk to our new ol' lady is all," Kris says.

Cocking my eyebrow, I don't say a word. I make sure my eyes are trained on Kris. I don't want to be caught off guard. With a crazy person that is the worst thing you can do. I feel Ena tense behind me.

She may be young, but she's been training with Caleb, Joker and I. She's good and fast. I know if I need her to help fight off this crazy bitch, she'll be there for me.

"Nothing to say, huh? It seems you always have something to say. I'm surprised at you, Sav."

"My name is Savy," I say evenly, "You're better off leaving right now, Kris. Don't start any more shit."

"I'm finishing the shit you started when you and that little whore you call a sister came around."

As quickly as the words leave her mouth, I'm moving. Throwing my body at her, I grab her by her thin throat and squeeze. As we fall to the ground, I'm on top of her still squeezing as Kris fights for breath. She is scratching and slapping, trying to free herself from my hold. Her fighting does nothing to loosen my grip though. Behind me, I hear pounding boots as several of the brothers make their way toward the commotion.

"Stay the fuck back, bitch!" Ena yells.

"She's going to kill her!" Hazel screams in return.

"Good! That bitch deserves it!"

I feel sharp nails scratching at my shoulders, but I ignore the pain. I want Kris to get the message. I'm tired of her coming around and starting trouble. Her calling Ena a whore was the last straw. I don't care how much she has to say about me, but when you attack a teenager, especially *my* teenager, you get dealt with.

"Oh no you don't!" Ena yells and I hear another loud commotion. "I told you to stay the fuck back!"

A sickening thud sounds as Ena knocks Hazel to the floor. They're rolling round in a heap of slaps and punches as I continue to choke Kris. I don't want her to die though so I loosen my hold before she passes out, but she's too stupid to realize she's lost. As I move to get off of her, she punches me in the face. The metallic taste of blood fills my mouth, and I see red. I kick and punch Kris where she is laying on the floor. I let all of my anger and rage go as I release it on this woman who has harassed me since I arrived.

"Diablo!" someone yells.

"Get the fuck out of the way!"

As I continue to punch Kris, I'm lifted off my feet and I tense, prepared to fight off the person grabbing me, but he pulls my head toward his face and says, "Stop, little bird."

I go limp in his arms.

"Are you hurt?" The chaos around me has ended and Preacher is helping Kris while Skull and Wolf are pulling apart Ena and Hazel.

"Ena," I say.

"She's all right. Can't say the same for Hazel though."

"My hand hurts." Hissing, as I speak, I feel my split lip, "And my lip."

Caleb carries me to his bathroom, and he sits me gingerly on the toilet. Looking down at my hand, I clinch and release my fist, testing it to see if it's broken. It'll be swollen tomorrow, but it's not broken. Thank goodness. The last thing I need is a cast.

"Savy, you can't go beating up the sweetbutts. I know Kris is a bitch, but you're my ol' lady and you need to set the example." Caleb takes my chin and lifts my face until I'm in a position where he can examine my face.

"She got you good," he says.

"Yeah. That won't happen again."

"You're right because you won't be fighting anymore," he reprimands.

"Sure, Caleb," I whisper.

"I know you're just saying that, but I'm serious. I can't have my ol' lady beating up the girls. Plus, Ena was fighting too. What the hell was that about?" he asks.

I explain how Kris touched me and what she said about Ena. His eyes intensify, but he says nothing. He just continues to check me over.

"You're all good. Ready to check on Ena?"

"Yes," I say. I'm glad I don't have to ask him to take me to check on Ena. He knows how much she means to me and takes me there without me having to ask.

Ena is in Skull's room, sitting on the bed. Skull is crouching in front of her, icing her left hand. She also has a split lip.

"Savy, are you all right?" Ena asks as we enter the room.

"Yes. Are you?"

"I'm great!" she squeals with excitement. "That was awesome."

"Ena."

"Kid."

"Ena."

Skull, Caleb, and I all say at the same time.

"What?" she asks. Her eyebrows are knitted in confusion, her lips pursed.

"No more fighting, kid," Caleb says.

"Sure, Diablo."

"What the hell is it with you two?" he asks. "I mean it, kid. There will be consequences."

"Oh like what? Being locked in the Compound?" she asks sarcastically.

"No, it will be worse," Caleb says. But not in a scary biker way. He speaks to Ena like a little sister. Right now, he's not Diablo, he is Caleb, my old man, and Ena's brother. If I think about it too long, it creeps me out. I'm sleeping with Caleb and Skull wants to sleep with Ena. It's like a big dysfunctional family, but we will make it work I'm sure.

"I didn't have time to tell you, but you can go back to work, Savy," Caleb says, changing the subject.

Turning toward him, with wide eyes I scream with excitement. "Really?" I ask in awe. I've been stuck inside these walls for so long, I was going crazy. I can't wait to get back to normal.

"Yes, really. And Ena, you can hang out with your friends again."

She jumps up and down in excitement, too.

"But," Caleb starts, "You both will have heavy protection and Ena you aren't to go anywhere without Aero and Mack. You got me?"

"Yeah, I got you." She doesn't care that two prospects will be there. She's just excited to be let out of the cage.

"Good," he says. "Now, can you two stop fighting Kris and Hazel?"

Ena looks at me and Caleb notices the look on her face.

"What kid?" he asks.

"Uh…" she starts and then stops.

I'm not sure what she is going to say, but I'm sure it can't be good. I begin shaking my head no, but Caleb sees me.

"What the fuck is going on?" he asks again. This time he is more impatient than before.

"Uh…" she starts and stops again.

"McKena, you better start talking," Caleb says again, but now he's using his president voice. Diablo is in full effect.

"Uh, hasn't Savy told you what Kris has been doing? She's been starting shit for weeks and Savy finally snapped."

I want to slap my hand over her mouth to keep her from talking, but it's too late. Caleb knows what's been going on.

"Savy, why didn't you say anything?" His voice is calm and goose flesh breaks out across my skin. He is still Diablo right now, he's not my sweet and caring Caleb.

"I didn't want to bother you, Caleb. You've been so nice with sheltering Ena and I and helping look for Tyler and Paul that I didn't want to bother you with another thing I couldn't handle."

"You always come to me when something is wrong, yeah?" he asked a question, but the command is clear. If I have trouble of any kind, I need to talk to him.

"This is my club and you're my ol' lady. Whatever you are going through is my problem," he says. "Now, tell me everything."

I spend the next few minutes telling him about Kris' antics and as I continue to speak, he becomes angrier and angrier. It's scary as fuck, but I tell him because I promised to be honest with him.

"Skull, bring Kris into the chapel."

As Skull leaves the room, he looks at Ena in the eyes and says, "You better tell me the next time someone fucks with you, got me?"

She nods her head, unable to force the words out of her constricted throat.

"Are you mad at me?" she asks.

"Of course not. It needed to be told." I needed to tell Caleb about Kris and Hazel's activities. I'm glad Ena wasn't too prideful to speak out. I'm a little torn though. I don't want to always have girls challenging my position in the club because they want what I have.

Diablo.

Little do they know, I love Diablo, but it's the man behind the cut, the man underneath it all that I truly love.

Caleb.

"Caleb, are you going to kick Kris out of the club?" I ask.

"Club business," he replies.

Letting out an audible sigh, I begin, "If you kick her out, I'll look weak."

He doesn't respond so I continue, "Please let me deal with it. I promise if it gets out of hand, I'll tell you."

Without saying a word, he nods his head, bends down and sears me with a kiss. Caleb exits the room, leaving me with a scared looking Ena.

CHAPTER TWENTY

DIABLO

STARING AT THE REDHEADED WOMAN I ONCE SPENT MY FREE TIME with, I don't know how I ever slept with her. It was never intimate for me. Kris was always a distraction to ease my thoughts away from Katie. It worked at the time, but now I have Savy. She's the woman that makes all the pain and shit in my life disappear. Skull is standing against the wall, arms crossed with a mean mug on his face. If he weren't my brother, he'd make a shiver run down my spine.

"Diablo, baby. I'm sorry for causing a scene, but she jumped on me," Kris says. Trying to show her innocence, but failing. I can see the lies lingering below the surface. Her eyes tell it all.

"You," I begin, "have been causing trouble for weeks I hear."

Kris sits up straighter, real fear shows on her bloody face.

"No–"

"Do not speak," I say. The timber of my voice is low and deadly.

Kris stops speaking immediately, and fidgets with her hands, the nervousness plastered across her face.

"You have been causing trouble for weeks. You know the rules,

Kris." I pause, and let her unease rise for several minutes. The silence is uncomfortable, but just what I need. This bitch has been crossing lines. And I need to make sure she doesn't cross them again. "You are a sweetbutt. You are the club's property and nothing more. Do not think you are anything special because I let you suck my dick."

She inhales deeply, but she doesn't move, doesn't speak. Silent tears roll from her green eyes. She knew what being a sweetbutt meant when she came to Havoc. Just because I slept with her, doesn't change her position in the club. We all know that is every sweetbutts' goal, and some do find the old man they desire. But Kris would never be my ol' lady. She doesn't have what it takes to be the president's property. She has no loyalty, no heart.

"You are lucky," again I pause. Leaving her to imagine why she is lucky. Skull is still leaning against the wall. He hasn't moved an inch. He's seen me expel sweetbutts for less. Hell, he's done it himself.

"Savy is my ol' lady. She's *my* property. And she has appealed for you."

Kris' head turns to the side, looking away from the devil standing in front of her.

"You better fucking look at me when I'm talking to you," I say.

She snaps her head back toward me, and stares directly in my eyes. She shifts her eyes toward Skull, pleading in silence for him to help her.

"Oh no, he won't help you. If it were up to him, you and Hazel would be dead. You'll get no sympathy from him."

She looks back toward me, realizing Skull will not help her.

"Savy has asked me not to kick you out of the club." I pause to let my words sink in. "You better fucking stay away from her and Ena. You hear me?" I ask.

Nodding her head, she doesn't say a word. And I smile.

"If you fuck with either of them again, I will kill you. Now get the fuck out of here and don't come back until you get your head out of your ass."

She scrambles to get out of the room, closing the door without a sound.

"What the fuck was that?" Skull asks. He's moved away from the wall, but his body is still tense.

"Savy asked me not to kick her out. She thinks it will make her look weak and I agree. She's gotta deal with this shit on her own."

"Is she hurt?" Concern wrinkled in his forehead and gray eyes.

"No," I say, finally laughing. "She has a swollen hand and a split lip, but nothing is broken. She's tough and, she can defend herself if she needs to."

"I'm glad she beat the shit out of Kris. I told you not to fuck with her, the bitch is crazy."

"Yeah, well, hopefully she's gotten the hint. I don't want to have to kill another woman."

"Well, from the way Ena was talking, Savy tried to smooth things over and Kris kept going. Once she called Ena a whore, she flipped and dove straight at her."

"Yeah. That's what Savy told me, too."

"I hope you never piss her off, brother, I'd hate to see what she would do to you," Skull laughs.

"Fuck, me either."

KRIS

I HATE THAT BITCH. SHE TOOK WHAT WAS MINE AND I'M GOING TO GET him back. I don't care what I have to do to get Diablo. I can't believe some country bumpkin came into Havoc and took Diablo right from under me. I've been with him since coming to Havoc and I can't let her get away with stealing from me. I need to learn more about her. She can't be as perfect as she seems. Sitting around the Compound all day and never leaving at all. There's something up and I will find out what it is.

I know Donny from the club Savy works at. She's hiding from something, but I need to find out what that is. Once I find out, I'll make Hazel help me take Savy down. Savy attacks me and expects me to feel grateful that Diablo didn't kick me out of Havoc? No one gets away with fucking with me.

Fuck her!

"Hazel, let's go," I say. I need to leave the club for a few days. I can't walk around with the bruises I'm sure she left behind. None of the brothers will want anything to do with me if I look like a rag doll.

"Coming," Hazel says. She patters over on her slut heels.

"I need your help." I explain my plan to Hazel, but I can see the fear on her face. Honestly I don't blame her, hell I'm a little afraid too. Diablo wasn't lying when he said he would kill me. He absolutely will. And now that he has that little curly haired slut hanging all over him all the time, he will follow through with his promise.

"I don't think I can help you with that, Kris," Hazel says and it pisses me off.

"Fuck yes you can! Don't forget what I know about you," I say. "I will tell the entire club you are a homeless whore from Minnesota. Don't fuck with me, Hazel, I'll tell them everything!"

"I don't care! I'm not helping you," she says. Her reluctance to help me take down Savy pisses me off. I'm surprised by Hazel's insistence that she won't help me. I know she doesn't want her secret out. Usually I can get her to do whatever I tell her to do. She used to do anything to protect against others from finding out about her sordid past. It looks like that's changed.

"It's okay, Hazel, I'll take care of the little bitch myself." I turn and walk away from my former minion. She'll pay for telling me no. Hazel doesn't know what I'm capable of, none of them do.

I need to talk to Donny. He's Savy's boss. I have to find out as much as I can, and fast. This bitch is going down and I will get my man again.

Savy

I haven't seen Kris around the club for several days. It's nice to not have someone trying to stab me in the back. I know if she could, Kris would take me out. Unfortunately, I went from constantly looking over my shoulder and running from Paul, to constantly looking over my shoulder because Caleb has so many sweetbutts after him. The difference between them and myself is I don't give a shit about being with Diablo the President of Havoc Motorcycle Club. I only care about Caleb. I also understand that Caleb and Diablo are one and the same. Diablo is the outer shell. The tough exterior he shows to the world. Fortunately, he has a family of brothers he is able to be himself with. Even better, we have found each other. With me, he can be who he truly is because I don't give a shit about him being the scary biker he has to be in front of the rest of the world.

I contemplate these thoughts as I'm getting ready for my first shift back at The Jungle. I'm so excited to get out of the Compound. I miss Cherry and the rest of the girls.

I never thought I'd say that.

It's amazing how much I have changed since becoming Caleb's ol' lady. Tonight will show me how much I have grown. In the past, I used to hide behind the tough exterior I showed the world. The only person I was comfortable with at the club was Cherry so I kept my distance from all the other girls. I hope that changes.

Fuck. I really have changed.

"You ready?" Caleb asks.

"Yep," I say. Popping the "p" and flashing my dazzling white smile.

"Let's go," he says.

We walk out of the front doors of the club and walk toward Diablo's bike. The bike is beautiful. Once he is seated, I throw my leg over the seat and slide as close to his body as I can. Leaning in, I rest my head on his back as I wrap my arms around his stomach. Inhaling the scent of oil, leather and Caleb, I let the feel of the bike beneath me settle me. I'm not afraid of the road any more. I got over that fear on our first date. I may love riding more than Caleb now.

Who am I kidding? That man loves riding more than anything in this world.

Riding allows me to be free, freer than I've ever been before. What makes this ride sweeter is this is the first time I've left Havoc grounds in weeks. The wind blowing in my face is a feeling I cherish.

We pull into the front parking lot of The Jungle and I see that things have changed. The parking lot is clean and there is a row of bikes parked close to the entrance. Before Paul's reentry into my life, we had a lot of bikers coming into the club, but it seems there are many more than I remember.

"Come on, babe, let's get you clocked in."

A chorus of greetings ring out as I enter the threshold of the club. There are several familiar faces, Joker, Wolf, and Preacher. What I notice most are the small changes like the waitresses' uniforms and the new coat of paint on the once shabby walls. It's still the same old Jungle I remember though. And for that I'm thankful. I'm just happy to get back to what I'm familiar with.

"Come with me to the office," Caleb says. He is still in a defensive mode, standing guard even though we are inside the club and safe. Paul is after me, but I don't think he's stupid enough to enter The Jungle and think he will get out alive. Closing the door behind us, Caleb rounds the desk and sits in the large leather chair.

What's going on here?

Where's Donny?

"Where's Donny?" I ask aloud.

"Donny doesn't own this club anymore," Caleb says with a straight face. "He forfeited ownership."

Staring with my mouth open, I wait for him to tell me more, but of course he doesn't.

Stupid club rules.

"So," I begin, "What does that mean for me?"

"It means I own this club, little bird. You work for me and I want to give you a new position."

"You want me shaking my ass out on a stage?" Mirth dances in my eyes.

"Fuck no! No one sees you shake your ass, but me."

Laughing at his reply, "So what's this new job, boss?"

"Club manager." My eyes bug out of my head.

What?

I couldn't have heard him right. I can't be the manager. I don't know shit about managing anything, plus I don't have my high school diploma.

I don't know shit.

I can't do it.

"You can do it," he says. Reading my mind.

"I can't." Lowering my eyes. I'm embarrassed. I can't let Caleb know I didn't finish high school. I haven't told him because I feel stupid, and I'm sure he has figured it out by now. I've been running for ten years, there was no time to go to school every day. Plus, Paul would have found us in an instant if I had enrolled in school during those first few years on the run. I couldn't risk it, so I haven't taken the time to complete school.

"Baby, you can." His words are gentle and encouraging.

A tear rolls down my cheek. I can do it, but it will be hard. I've been doing hard my entire life. I just want something to be easy for once.

"I can," I say out loud. In my head, I repeat the words.

I can.

I can.

I can.

The voice in my head wants to say I can't, but the voice in my heart is repeating I can like a mantra to convince myself.

"What do I need to do?"

Caleb spends the next two hours going over all of my duties and responsibilities. My head is spinning by the end of it, but I'm teeming with excitement. This will give me a chance to prove to myself that I can do something I thought was hard and succeed at it. I'm ready to get down to business. I walk through the club and check in with the girls, bouncers, waitresses and bartenders, announcing my new position. They all seem excited to have me as a manager. I hope I do well. I'd hate to fail and embarrass Caleb in the process. I feel like this is the first time in my life where I have something I can look forward to.

———————

PAUL

RING.

Ring.

Ring.

I look at the bright screen of my phone to see who the hell is calling me so late.

Tyler.

"What?" I answer.

"Uh, a girl contacted me about Savy. She's asking a lot of questions and seems to have an inside connection to the bikers Savy's been hanging with."

I sit up and swing my legs off the side of the bed. I need to meet this girl and see how I can make her work for me. I don't care what I need to do, but this needs to end fast. I've been waiting for over a year to get my daughter back and Savy is not getting away again. And I'm tired of chasing her.

"Bring her to the meet point," I say. I need to get my plan moving forward now.

"Okay, boss," Tyler says. "I'll bring her over right now."

Hanging up, I get dressed in my finest clothes. I need to make her desire me so I can control her. And if that doesn't work, I'll find out everything I can about her and use it against her. Less than an hour later, a beautiful redhead walks through the door with Tyler in toe. She's stunning. Her thin frame supports large, fake breasts, but she wears them well.

"Hello, beautiful," I say.

She smiles and extends her hand in greeting.

"Hello, Paul. It's nice to meet you. My name is Kris."

I shift my eyes toward Tyler and he cowers back. This little fucker told her my name.

"Please, sit down. I understand you have an inside connection to the biker scum that has my precious little girl locked away." I'm surprised when she tenses. She came to give me information about the bikers, so it's not the reaction I expected. I had assumed she hates the bikers, too. My assumptions may be wrong.

"Um, yes. I've been an integral part of the club for years," she says.

"Good. I think we can do each other a favor. I assume you are reaching out to me because you want my help with something, yes?"

"Yes."

"I know you have been looking for your daughters for months."

I turn to glare at Tyler. The fucking idiot has revealed too much already.

I will deal with him later.

"I have," I confirm.

"Well, Savy has taken something that belongs to me and I want it back. I don't care what I need to do to get that done."

"Well Kris, it appears we have something in common."

We continue our conversation and make plans to take Savy and the bikers down, and ultimately, get my sweet Ena back where she belongs.

CHAPTER TWENTY-ONE

SAVY

JUST WHEN I THINK LIFE IS GETTING BETTER AND EASIER, REALITY slams into me like a semi hitting a Prius. Today is no different. I mean, what the hell could I have done in a previous life that warrants so much fucked up shit happening to me? Whatever it is, I pray that I'm forgiven and allowed to live a simple and normal life.

I've been working as the manager of The Jungle for a few days and things have been going well. Caleb lets me decide how to deal with problems and doesn't step in. I'm thankful for his restraint because I don't think I could handle him trying to control my work life, too.

I'm sitting in the office when I hear a soft knock on the door.

"Come in!"

"Hey, Savy, there's a girl up front asking for you," she says.

Stella has a funny look on her face, but I don't ask who it is. It could be anyone. Some other strip clubs around town have been losing their dancers because word has spread fast that The Jungle has a fair, female manager now. We've been getting new dancers like crazy.

"I'm coming."

Leaving my office, I walk down the back hallway as the bass of the music fills my ears. Rounding the corner, I see Kris and Tyler standing at the opening of the hallway.

What the fuck is going on?

I look around to see where the hell my bouncers are. I know I asked Caleb to let Kris stay, but I don't like that she's here with Tyler. He's been ducking Havoc for weeks and suddenly he reappears with the woman that has been trying to get rid of me.

They're up to no good and not very good at it. They could at least stealthy.

Instead of staying at the opening of the hall where I'm mostly hidden from view, I move further into the main room of the club. I need as many witnesses as possible though I know Caleb will believe me when I tell him about Kris showing up with Tyler.

"What do you want, Kris?"

"I see Diablo has let you off your leash."

I don't reply to her insult. She wants me to lose my cool, and it's not something I am going to do, especially at the club.

"I'm just here to watch some beautiful girls dance with my new man."

Turning to address Tyler, I say, "You know Diablo has been looking for you." Not a question, just a simple statement.

A true statement.

Where the fuck is Caleb?

He was here earlier and said nothing to me about leaving. It's really shit timing for him to disappear. I look around and get nervous because the club is full of regular customers. A normal night at The Jungle has so many bikers present you can hardly find a citizen and not a single one is here right now. Where the fuck are they?

"You do that," I say to Kris, and I turn away from her, moving toward the bar. Normally I would never turn my back on an enemy, but I need to show Kris, and Tyler for that matter, that I'm not afraid of either of them. Their threats mean nothing.

They sit in the seats at the center of the main stage and watch Misty as she performs her routine. I'm at the bar, pretending I'm checking stock on the glasses and ice, but I'm really keeping my eye on the couple.

Bo, comes to the bar and hands me a cell phone. I'm relieved to see him. Since being back at the club, Caleb has appointed Bo, head bouncer and my personal bodyguard when he and Joker are not around. "I need you to act like nothing is up," he says.

"What?"

"Just look at the screen." He hands me a cellphone. It's a message from Caleb.

You're not alone. We saw them pull in. We are in the back.

I'm not alone.

The vice loosens. I hadn't realized it had tightened until I read Caleb's message. He's watching me, but from where? I'll need to make sure I find out if there are cameras in the club. I'm sure there are. Axel takes Havoc's security seriously.

Okay. What do I need to do? I reply.

Send a waitress to check on them. Act as normal as possible.

Okay.

Angel goes over to check on Kris and Tyler, and she comes back a little shaken. Whatever they said to her has upset her. I don't mess around when customers are disrespectful to the girls, but today I need to follow Caleb's lead.

"Are you all right?"

"Yeah," she says. "That guy is a real asshole."

"Tell me about it." Looking toward the pair, I shake my head. What did I ever see in Tyler? He's nice to look at, but he has no real personality at all. Plus, he's a dick.

"Look, Angel, I need you to watch that table. I'll make sure you're taken care of as far as tips go, but that is your only table until they leave."

"Whatever you say, Savy," she says.

I hate that she's has to serve Tyler, but she'll do it because she's a great employee. She's always been a hard worker, even when Donny was the owner. I make a mental note to propose she be promoted to my new assistant manager.

"Thanks, Angel."

The couple spends a few hours in the club. Often laughing louder than the music and glance toward the bar. Their feeble attempts to draw my attention to their public display fall on deaf ears. I just want them gone.

When they realize I don't care about them being together, they stand and walk toward the exit. Kris raises her hand and does a finger wave toward me. Tyler's hand is at the small of her back and he glides her out of the door. Once they are gone, I let out a large breath and see Caleb, Skull, and Joker come from the back of the club.

Caleb sees me and strides toward me. I hate to admit it, but I'm shaking. Seeing Tyler after he has been in hiding is strange. I don't like the way I feel, but something about the whole situation just doesn't sit well with me. I'm not sure what those two are up to, but I'm sure I will find out soon enough.

"You all right?" Caleb asks. He wraps his hand around my waist and his eyes scan my face.

I nod my head, but don't speak. Staring into those black orbs, I feel a sense of peace that I didn't feel just a moment before. I can't believe this complicated, sexy man, makes me feel at peace. Something I haven't had since my mother was alive.

Turning to Skull, Diablo says, "Get someone to close up tonight. I'm taking Savy home."

Without saying a word, Skull turns to do his bidding. Then he suddenly stops in his tracks and turns back around to face us. Skull looks at his brother and they have a silent conversation between themselves. Then Skull addresses me.

"We are gonna kill that son of a bitch." The viciousness of his words strike me. Skull hasn't always been the warmest toward me, partly because I stood in the way of him and Ena in the beginning. After learning about Katie, I had assumed he was trying to protect his brother from another betrayal. I wasn't sure Skull liked me at all, or even approved of me as an ol' lady for his brother, but now I know for sure. He would never make this declaration if he didn't care about me.

I smile as my eyes fill with tears. I like Skull too. He has become another brother I never had. It's nice to have such a large extended family. Nodding my head, Skull nods once and turns to continue toward the back office.

I stare after him because, Skull is the type of man I would want for Ena. Strong, caring, protective, and he's cute, too. If it comes to that, I will definitely give my blessing.

DIABLO

I WAS PISSED WHEN WE SAW THAT LITTLE FUCKER STROLL INTO THE Jungle like he owned the place. I don't know what the fuck Kris is thinking, but that bitch is out of Havoc for good now. I don't care what I promised Savy. She's fucking involved with Havoc's enemies. That cannot be accepted. As soon as we catch up with them, Kris is out and Tyler is dead.

"Let's go," I say. Extending my hand to Savy, I let her clasp her tiny hand in mine and I feel her shaking. I give a little squeeze for assurance and we head toward the front parking lot where my bike is parked. I need to take care of my girl, but we are not going back to the Compound.

As we ride by the moonlight, I think about what I'm about to do. I've never taken anyone back to my house. It's the one place I have that is all my own. Most of the brothers don't even know I own it since I spend so much time at the Compound. Skull knows where I am and that's all that matters.

Turning onto the long lane, I feel Savy raise her head from my back where it was resting. Her arms tighten around my waist. I'm not sure if that's from fear or something else. I'll find out soon. Pulling up to my two-story farm house, I feel her quick breathing. Turning off the switch, the rumble of the bike stops and I wait for Savy to let go.

This is the moment of truth.

She lets go and slides off the back of the bike. I dismount and grab her hand, leading her onto the wraparound porch. Unlocking the door, I lead her into the large foyer. She looks terrified, but I see a defiant gleam in her eyes as she looks around the space with curiosity.

"This is my house," I say.

She snaps her head toward me, our eyes connecting. "Why'd you bring me here?"

"I want you to be here, Savy. Permanently," I say.

My message is clear, but I need to make sure it's crystal clear. She has a history of running so I need to make sure she never tries to leave me again.

"I want you to get my ink, baby. I've been calling you my ol' lady, but we need to make it official."

Silence.

She stares at me with her big brown eyes filling with tears. As they spill out on to her speckled cheeks, I reach out and wipe a tear with the pad of my thumb. But that tear is replaced with many more as they continue to spill over her black lined eyes. I say nothing, giving her a chance to register my words. Just as the silence gets uncomfortable, she launches herself at me and peppers my rough face with sweet kisses. Wrapping her legs around my waist, I feel the heat of her pussy as it presses against my dick; despite the jeans we are both wearing.

Carrying her, I walk toward the bedroom. At the bed, I toss her on it and she lets out a shriek of excitement as she bounces on the soft surface. She lays back, propping herself on her elbows and invites me over to her in a come hither motion. Her hair is wild from the wind. She's the sexiest woman I have ever seen. I need to sink my dick into her sweet body before I come all over my pants like a fucking kid.

"Strip," I say. She begins to remove her shirt. "Slowly." Her pace slows, and she slides her black shirt over her head revealing her plain black bra. Reaching out, I unbutton her pants and slide them down her thighs. She has on purple panties. Laying across my bed, she's the sexiest woman I've ever been with.

"Get up on your knees." She shifts her position and we are once again eye level. Kissing her with a passion I've never felt before, I reach behind her and unsnap her bra, causing her breast to spill from their confinement. I massage each large breast and pinch each light brown nipple, testing her pain threshold. I like control in the bedroom and I want to make sure she can handle my intensity. Increasing the pain, she lets out a throaty moan.

"Does my baby like when I pinch her nipples?" I ask.

"Yes," she says, her moan is longer, raspier.

Pushing her back into a laying position, I slide off her panties, revealing her perfect shaved pussy, just like I like it. I can smell her sex. She wants me just as much as I want her. But first, I lap at her clit, tasting her essence. It's sweet and my dick gets harder as I continue to pleasure her with my mouth. I wasn't sure I could be any harder than I was five seconds ago, but I am and it's painful.

"You taste so fucking good, little bird," I say. I begin to fuck her with my fingers and bring her to the brink. Just before she releases, I withdraw my fingers, and she lets out a strangled cry.

"Taste." I place my fingers inside her mouth and she hungrily licks them clean. "Do you like that, little bird? Do you like the way your pussy tastes?" I ask.

"Yes, please, Caleb."

"Please what?" I ask. Teasing her with my fingers again. This time I lick them clean and her eyes dilate.

Fuck. What did I do to deserve her?

"Please fuck me."

"I will, baby," I say. "Trust me, I will fuck every hole you have on this luscious body, then I'm going to lay down my ink on you. Got me?" I ask.

"Got you."

"Good," I say as I lick her pussy again. Between licks, I insert my fingers in her pussy again, drawing out her pleasure. Moving toward her nether hole, she tenses. "Shhh. I won't hurt you. I'll never hurt you," I say.

I stick the tip of my finger in her puckered hole and hold it in place, allowing her body to adjust to the feel of having something in her ass. I won't fuck her ass today, but I will fuck every hole she has, eventually. She begins pumping her hips, trying to force me to move and I remove my finger. Her protest is loud. Maybe I will fuck her ass today after all, but first I need to fuck her pussy before my dick falls off. Positioning her on the bed, I pump in and out, increasing my pace as my balls slap against her ass, my pelvis rubs against her clit and intensifies her pleasure. Varying my rhythm allows me to last longer.

"Whose pussy is this?" I ask.

She doesn't reply, her eyes are closed, and she's moaning so loud, I'm not sure she heard me.

I pinch her clit and her eyes fly open. "I said, whose pussy is this?"

"Yours," she says, closing her eyes again.

I'm not satisfied with her answer, so I give another pleasurable pinch, this time her nipple and clit at the same time. I maintain a constant pressure, increasing her pleasure.

"Yours, baby. My pussy is yours. Only yours. Always yours. Please. Please, Caleb. Let me come. Please," she begs.

And I do. I increase my pace and apply more pressure to her clit, kicking her over the edge. I keep the pressure on her clit as I continue pumping, and wave after wave washes over her.

I continue thrusting into her beautiful body, and I quickly fall off the cliff with her, collapsing on top of her, I roll over and take her with me, positioning her on my chest. We rest for a bit, and I taste her again, then I lay my ink on her, claiming Savy as my ol' lady forever.

CHAPTER TWENTY-TWO

DIABLO

THE LITTLE FUCKER WASN'T SMART ENOUGH TO BE HIDING WHEN WE rolled into his neighborhood. He was sitting on his porch in his wealthy neighborhood. Being on this side of town makes my skin itch. We don't fit in here. But right now, I don't give a fuck about fitting in. I have some questions that need answers.

Thirty bikes rolling into the quiet upscale neighborhood would scare the baddest motherfucker, so we took cages. No need to draw unnecessary attention to ourselves. The little fucker wasn't even hiding when we pulled in. He's not too smart. Or he thinks he's a genius.

Stupid fuck.

He's sitting on his front porch drinking coffee like he's waiting for a friend to visit when we pull into his driveway.

"Hey man. Good seeing you again," he says.

What the fuck is wrong with this guy?

"Get the fuck up!" I bark. He doesn't move. "Get him up, Skull."

"Oh, Skull is it?" he says as Skull moves to pull him up by his shirt collar. If I weren't so pissed, I'd laugh at his stupidity. He looks like a wayward child being scolded. "Hey man, no need to get physical," he whines. "Would you like to come inside?"

"No," I say. Just as the word leaves my lips, the prospect pulls in his driveway with the cage. I look him in the eyes, and stare him down, showing him I have no soul. He knows he's fucked and begins to struggle.

"Wait, man. I have information that can help you!" The confident asshole is replaced with a little whining bitch. "I know about Savy's dad. He's after her man. He says he's going to kill her and take that brat back." Skull punches Tyler in the right temple as soon as the words leave his lip. Knocking him out.

"Get him in the fuckin' cage!" My blood is boiling. How the fuck does he know about Paul? Savy said she has told no one. "Joker, be thorough," I say waving a thumb in the direction of the house.

"Right, Prez." He goes inside to check every inch of the house for information.

"Let's get the fuck out of here," I say. Wanting to leave before any neighbors decide to be good citizens and call the cops.

KRIS

I'M LAYING IN BED AT TYLER'S HOUSE THINKING ABOUT HOW HE CAN change my life forever. He's rich and just the man I need to change my life. That was until I hear Diablo's voice. He's pissed. I'm sure it's because I showed up to The Jungle with Tyler. I knew that bitch would tell him. In this life, snitches die.

You are going to die too.

Shaking my head, I quietly, but quickly slide from the covers and snatch up my clothes. Hastily pulling them on, I enter the bathroom and look for an exit. The window is small, but large enough for me to fit through. I stand on the counter and lift myself to the sill, peeking out. I see no one so I lift myself up to the window and crawl through.

Ungraceful, I drop to the dirt below and lay flat against the earth, attempting to listen for approaching footsteps. I hear none, so I spring up and dash to the line of trees, out of sight. How the hell am I supposed to get out of this one? Reaching for my phone, it's gone.

Fuck! I left it in Tyler's house.

Diablo will find it and know I have been working with Tyler and Paul. They already know though. At least they know about Tyler. Maybe I can feign innocence and act like I know nothing about the plans Tyler and Paul have for Savy. This should work as long as Tyler keeps his mouth shut.

He will. He's afraid of Paul, too.

Paul!

I need to get to Paul and tell him that Havoc was here. I move to the other side of the trees to see when they leave. Once the trucks and vans leave the subdivision and the coast is clear, I go back to Tyler's house and climb back through the window. The house has been trashed, but my cell phone is still laying on the floor where it fell the night before. Tyler and I made love on the couch, and I remember hearing my phone hit the hardwood floor. Dialing the number programmed in my phone. I wait as it rings several times.

"What?" Paul answers.

"Uh, Paul. It's Kris. Havoc just took Tyler."

"Fuck!" he screams into the phone.

"Where are you?"

"At Tyler's house. I ran when I heard them outside talking. I came back when they left."

"Is Tyler's car still there?"

I look outside and see the black Mercedes sitting in the driveway. "Yes."

"Get in Tyler's car and come to the house. We need to kick this plan into high gear."

DIABLO

"LET ME SHOW YOU WHY THEY CALL ME THE DEVIL," I SAY. Typically, Wolf handles this part of the job, but this is personal, so I'm leading the interrogation.

"No! Please, I'll tell you anything you want." He's fucked, and he knows it.

"You are going to tell me everything I want to know, but first I need to show you who you fucked with." Turning to Wolf, he hands me a surgical blade, my tool of choice.

"You see, Tyler. Savy is *mine*," I say. My lip curls with so much menace, and some of my brothers start to fidget. I know I scare them when I get like this. I'm a scary motherfucker, hell if I ever had to face myself, I'd be afraid too.

I make the first slice down his chest. The incision is so thin that it doesn't bleed for a few seconds. Then it only beads blood. I plan to make thousands of incisions. He'll live for a long time, but will be in constant pain.

"Please man, I'll tell you everything."

"Start fuckin' talkin' then."

"Pa-Paul is planning to kill Savy. He wants her dead."

"You already said that, Tyler," I chastise. "Tell me something to save your life." We both know he's a dead man, but he tries to save his life, anyway.

"He is going to ambush her after work at the club. He's been watching her for over a year," he rushes out.

"How the fuck do you know, Paul?" I ask.

Tyler doesn't say a word. So I add ten more slices. This time, I cut deeper, making eleven straight lines in a row.

"How. The. Fuck. Do. You. Know. Paul?" I ask again, knowing Tyler is staring at the devil and afraid of how I will react to what he is about to tell me.

"He…" he stops.

"He?" I ask. He doesn't answer me fast enough so I twist the surgical knife in my hand and stab Tyler in the thigh, leaving the knife embedded in his flesh. His screams fill the dungeon. It's like music to my ears. The dungeon is the holding cell and torture chamber housed below the Compound. No one knows it's down here and no one will hear Tyler's screams.

"You better fucking tell me what I want to know, Tyler. If you do, I'll make sure your death is painless."

"He hired me," he rasps out.

"Hired you to do what?" I growl.

"To, to date Savy. He wanted me to have sex with her and marry her. Then he would kill her so I could collect the insurance money. I was supposed to get half, but she found out I was fucking my secretary and she broke it off with me. He was pissed that I fucked it up. That's why I wanted to meet her for dinner. I needed to get back with her. He said he would put me in jail and tell my father. I can't go to jail," he says all in one breath.

"What else?" I ask. My voice so low it's almost inaudible. I fight to control the anger rising within me. My neck is tight and my body feels hot. I want to snap his fucking neck. He plotted to kill Savy for insurance money. This shit is worse than I thought.

"That's it, man. I swear!"

"Bullshit!" I bellow. "You were outside her house that night. What did you want?"

"He wanted me to make sure the coast was clear. He knows you are helping her. He's a cop man. He said he will kill her and anyone else that tries to stop him."

I stand to my full height and pull the blade from his thigh, causing him to scream again. Handing the instrument off to Skull, I punch Tyler in the face and body. I work him over in a barrage of blows. For several minutes, I let all my frustration out on the man that tricked my ol' lady into dating him, just so he can fake a marriage and kill her. Despite my attempts, the rage within my body doesn't lessen. With one final strike, he topples over and the chair he is tied to crashes to the ground.

"Someone else can have fun with him. Make sure he disappears, forever," I say as I walk out of the dungeon.

"Wait! I have information on Kris!" I stop, but don't turn around.

"She's working for Paul, too. He had us go to The Jungle to scare Savy. He's crazy, man! Please! Please don't kill me! He also has that girl Hazel. He's fucking her up real good."

"Where is he?" I say one last time. He hesitates again so I continue walking out.

As the door closes, I hear his last cry, "Nooo!" Once the door shuts, his words are cut off, and he's dead.

Fuck!

How the fuck did I miss that Hazel is missing? I assumed she left when Kris left, they've always been close. I need to find this fucker. Now that he has Hazel, and he's still after Savy and Ena, it's as important as ever. Paul is getting more dangerous, and it's clear he doesn't care about taking innocent people to make his point clear.

Hazel's a good girl who never gave me any trouble like Kris did, but she's weak. Just the type of person Kris would attach herself to. Someone she can control. This bitch got Hazel mixed in with a psycho like Paul. We need to find her fast. Walking upstairs from the dungeon, I enter the main room and look around. I need to talk to Axel.

"Axel!" I yell.

He stands from the couch where he is talking to Misty and Molly. They are both sitting on his lap topless, but as soon as he sees it's me who called him, he taps their legs and stands up, almost dumping the women off of his lap to the floor.

"Yeah, Prez?" he asks.

"I need to talk to you, in my office," I say.

We walk to my office and I tell him what I need. He begins searching for Hazel's phone and looking for any new information we may have missed during our first search on Paul Riley. I need to know where this fucker is staying while he's in Sage, and I need to know fast.

We are going to find this fucker, and he will die a painful, slow death.

I smile at the thought.

CHAPTER TWENTY-THREE

SAVY

WALKING AROUND THE MALL ISN'T MY FAVORITE THING TO DO, BUT Ena is babbling along excitedly with her friends Ashleigh and Natalie. They're talking a mile a minute, being typical teenagers. Truth is, though, Ena is not a typical teenager. She's a teenager under Havoc's protection. That means she has a brother with her at all times. Even now, though hidden, we have four prospects with us. Apparently things with Tyler and my father are worse. Caleb wanted to lock Ena and me down again, but I begged Caleb to keep us out of seclusion. It worked, but we have four body guards with us.

Four.

It seems like overkill, but I don't argue. Caleb wants us protected, so we're protected. They stay far enough away that the people milling about don't notice them. They're in plain clothes so they blend in. I want today to be special for Ena. She loves shopping and I want to treat her for her birthday. Since becoming manager at The Jungle, my pay has increased, by a lot.

A.

Lot.

It's much more than I would have ever expected, but when I asked Caleb about it he said, "Club business." So in an unlike me move, I let it go. Now I can afford to get her some new things. Plus, her birthday is tomorrow and I want it to be amazing. She's turning eighteen so we are having a party at the Compound and I plan on giving her something special. I've been holding onto it for ten years.

We walk the entire mall, but I have had a weird feeling all day. The hair on the back of my neck is standing up and I feel like someone is following us. I don't want to scare the girls, but pay extra attention to everyone around us. Trying not to draw attention to myself, I pull out my phone and send a message to Joker.

I think someone is following us.

His reply isn't immediate and my stomach turns to knots. I move closer to Ena and her friends who are browsing inside a clothing store geared toward teenage girls. I want to be close in case something happens.

"Ena, honey," I say. My voice is tight as I try to keep my fear down. I don't want them knowing I think something is wrong.

"Yeah?" Her eyebrows raise and her eyes dart around the store.

Damnit! She knows something is up.

"I'm not feeling too well, let's head back to the house, okay."

"Sure, Savy," she says.

I'm impressed she's keeping her cool. Natalie and Ashleigh know a little about Havoc, so we both attempt to keep our cool. They are still considered outsiders, so we aren't supposed to share about Paul or Tyler or any of the crazy shit happening right now. Also, I don't want to scare the girls if I don't have to.

We pay for their clothes and step out of the store. I look side to side as we exit. There aren't many people in this section of the mall. Directly across from the store, Joker is standing with his hands inside his pockets. He looks like any other shopper, waiting outside of a store. I almost didn't recognize him. His hair is slicked back and his unruly beard is trimmed and straightened. He looks like a normal person, not the big scary biker I have become fond of.

Nodding my head, we walk toward the exit and Joker follows us. As we continue down the isle of stores, I see Bo. I'm surprised to see him, but I have the strange sensation of being watched again.

Someone *is* following us.

I look over my shoulder, but I see no one. I can't prove it, but I've learned to trust myself so we are getting the fuck out of here and back to the safety of Havoc. We continue walking and the other prospects appear, unrecognizable in their citizen clothes. Gunner and Tiny follow us as we exit the mall and walk down the lane of cars to where I parked my new sedan.

The girls pile into the back of the car, leaving me up front alone. I let out a sigh of relief as I see the black SUV driven by Bo, pull out of the parking space next to us. Once it's clear, I pull out and drive toward the exit. Joker pulls out of the space on the opposite side of my car and follows. As we pass the entrance of the mall, I see a man that looks like my father standing outside, staring. I stop the car and tighten my hands on the steering wheel, my fingers turning white from my grip, and we stare at each other. I press on the pedal and proceed out of the lot. The vice in my chest tightens. It's the first time I've seen my father face to face since Oklahoma and those old childhood feelings of helplessness slammed back into me like a sledgehammer to the chest.

I look in my rearview mirror and see that Joker has stopped his car and jumped out. Instead of stopping to see why, I keep driving home, while trying to maintain my composure for the girls in the backseat. I hope Joker is okay.

No matter what I do, he is going to keep pursuing us. Paul is never going to quit.

He won't stop until I make him stop. The problem is, I don't know how I'm going to make him stop. You would think aligning myself with a motorcycle club would stop him, but no. It didn't. I feel helpless as I'm surrounded by Havoc in the cars guiding me to Caleb's house. It's a feeling I haven't felt in a while and one I never want to feel again, but I know I will as long as Paul is around.

SAVY

CALEB WAS STANDING IN THE DRIVEWAY OF HIS HOUSE WHEN WE pulled in from our trip to the mall. He was pissed, but played it off well. Joker stopped by a little after we got home, but he didn't stay long. I think he just showed his face because I told Caleb I was worried about him. Of course, they didn't tell me what happened.

Now Caleb is hanging out with the girls in the living room watching TV and joking around. I love how he has made Ena and her friends feel welcome in his home.

He will be a great father one day.

I'm not sure where that thought came from so I ignore it. I can't deal with my wayward thoughts right now.

"Oh Savy," Ashleigh says. The excitement in her voice is hilarious. She hasn't taken her eyes off Caleb since getting to the house. It's adorable how she steals glances at him. He's kind enough to laugh at her puppy dog glances. "You're so lucky. Caleb is hot!"

I laugh with the girls as four loud knocks sound on the front door. Looking to Caleb, he nods once and stands, leaving the living room to answer the door. He didn't grab his gun that is stored inside the table in the foyer, so he must know who it is.

"Skull!" Ena says. Jumping up to run to him and jump in his arms.

Looking at Caleb with a frown, he shakes his head no. I say nothing, but I will be talking to Caleb about Skull and Ena's relationship. It's futile right now, I know, but I don't care. Skull is too old for Ena. Period.

"Hey, little bit," Skull says. Hugging Ena's small body against his large frame.

I sigh, knowing Ena and Skull are destined to be together. Why am I even trying to keep them apart? He puts her down, sliding her body against his on her descent. Ashleigh and Natalie are sitting next to each other on the couch, staring at Skull with wide, curious eyes.

Oh hell! Them too?

Their parents are going to be pissed if the men of Havoc corrupt them, too. There's not much they can say about it though. Both girls are already eighteen.

Fucking hell.

Running my hand through my curly hair, I bite my bottom lip. There's too much on my mind right now. I'm tired. All I want is to lay down and sleep, but I have too much to do. Tomorrow is Ena's party and we need to decorate tonight after the girls go to bed.

"I missed you," Ena says.

"I missed you too, babe."

Fucking hell.

All eyes turn toward me.

"Did I say that out loud?" I ask.

They all laugh. And eventually I laugh, too. Skull knows how I feel about his relationship with my sister, and Ena knows, too. There's not much I can do about it, but trust them to respect my wishes. I'll keep my mouth shut until they give me a reason to speak up.

SAVY

I WAKE UP WITH A START.

"Shit!" I hop out of bed. Well, I try to hop out of bed, but Caleb snags me around the waist and pulls me back onto the bed.

"Caleb! Let me go! I fell asleep last night. Fuck! I have so much to do today," I say. "God damn it, Caleb!"

"It's taken care of, Savy. Go back to sleep."

"Let me go! I need to make Ena breakfast and get to the club to decorate."

"Savannah," he says.

At the sound of my full name, I stop struggling. Caleb only calls me Savannah when he needs to get my attention. And it works.

"I said it's taken care of. Joss and Lexa decorated last night and Skull is bringing over breakfast for everyone in two hours. Now lay back down and go back to sleep. Fuck, woman, it's six in the damn morning."

"Joss and Lexa?" I ask. Those two worked together to decorate? God, I hope they didn't kill each other. Joss hasn't been back to the club since the night of the bonfire and Lexa has been avoiding Wolf like the plague. I hope they'll be able to get along at the party tonight.

"Yes. And I told them they better not fuck this up. They're getting along."

Turning to look into those dark eyes I love, I lean in and sear Caleb with a wet kiss. I love this man. He saw I was tired and let me sleep. And instead of leaving the work I needed to get done, left undone, he handled it for me.

"Caleb, I–" Unable to get the words out. I'm still uncomfortable saying them. What if I tell Caleb how I feel and he doesn't *really* feel the same way?

"I love you too, little bird," Caleb says.

My breath stops and my chest squeezes. It does every time he says those words. He *does* love me. I hate that I need so many reassurances, but I can't help it. It's the best feeling in the world to know that the man you love loves you back. Having a man that loves me with all of my craziness and drama. It's more than I ever imagined possible.

"I love you," I say. My voice cracks with my words. Leaning over to kiss me again, Caleb shows me how much he loves me, body, mind and soul.

CHAPTER TWENTY-FOUR

Savy

We are at the Compound getting dressed for Ena's party. She looks beautiful. She dressed in black jeans, a tight red low-cut shirt that shows her cleavage. Instead of wearing heels, she's opted for the black motorcycle boots we splurged on at the mall. They're badass and they look good on her. To top off her outfit, she's wearing a black leather moto jacket.

Her hair is down and the curly locks flow down her back in a black river, wearing a smoky eye and bright red lipstick, Ena looks amazing. This is the happiest I've ever seen her. I hope this happiness lasts for her. She deserves nothing but happiness in her life.

"Ena," I say. "I want to give you your present before things get crazy."

"You didn't have to get me anything, Savy. You already bought me new clothes. It's too much."

"It's not. And I've been waiting a long time to give this to you," I say. She looks surprised. "Sit down in that chair and close your eyes."

She moves toward the wood chair and lowers herself onto the seat.

Her breathing has increased, and I can feel her nerves radiating off her. I hope she likes it. Moving behind her, I open the small black box I've been saving for ten years. Pulling out the silver necklace, I open the clasp and place it on Ena's delicate neck. She reaches up and touches the thin chain, feeling the charm. Once I close the clasp, I step back and say, "You can open your eyes now."

She doesn't open her eyes right away, but when she does, the unshed tears are pooling in her eyes. She looks into the mirror sitting in front of her and our eyes meet. But we don't say a word.

The deafening silence dances between us until she speaks.

"You said you didn't have anything of hers." The awe of the moment shakes her voice.

"I lied," I say. Before running, I prepared our escape. I gathered not only money, but I also took and hid items of my mother's that I wanted to take with us. But the day it was time to run, I could only take two things, her silver bracelet, and a heart shaped necklace with two pearls on the charm. My mother always told me the pearls represented Ena and me. I wanted to give Ena something of my mother's so I've been holding onto the necklace until her eighteenth birthday.

"Savy," Ena says, "I don't understand."

"I took three things the day I ran. A bracelet, this necklace, and you." Emotion swells in my chest, making it hard to speak. My voice cracks, but I continue, "Ena, I took what I could the day we left, but you were the most important thing I needed to get out of there with. This necklace belonged to our mother, and I want you to have it."

"But," she says, "You don't wear a bracelet. Where is it?"

"I have it. I didn't want to wear something of our mother's without you having something too." Thinking about all I was able to get away with. "Ena, I have memories of a happier time. A time with Mom, which you don't get to have, and for that I'm so sorry. I'm sorry we had a shitty childhood that required us to run away. I'm sorry you never got to meet her, and I'm sorry you don't get wonderful, warm memories of a woman who literally gave her life for her child."

Ena's tears are streaming down her face now. I reach out and wipe her cheek, removing the tears that are quickly replaced with more tears.

"You are all that matters. You are all that ever mattered. Happy birthday, Pip. You are an amazing young woman that grew up in some pretty shitty circumstances, but you are stronger, braver and smarter for it. I love you with all my soul."

"Thank you, Savy. I love it. I couldn't have asked for a better birthday present."

"You're welcome. Now, let's fix your face and go have some fun," I say.

"All right, but first, I have one question," she says with a straight face.

Letting her ask her question, her face twists, her eyebrows rising, "When are you going to officially come out as Diablo's ol' lady?"

Of all the things floating around in my head, I didn't think that was what Ena wanted to ask.

"I know you got his ink already," she says.

This fucking kid is too smart for her own good.

"After your party," I say. Tonight is Ena's day. It's the first party she has had in ten years, and it has to be perfect.

"Savy, I want you to tell everyone tonight," she says. "What can be more perfect than gaining a big brother? I love Caleb like family and he loves you. What more can I ask for?"

God, I love her.

"If that's what you want, Pip, then that is what you get. I'll talk to Caleb."

"Good," she says. She has a smug ass look on her face.

Shaking my head, I smile at the woman I saved as a child, and I'm damn happy I did it.

SAVY

ENA HAS ENJOYED HER PARTY. SHE'S LOOKING GREAT, AND SPENDING time with her friends, Ashleigh and Natalie, who have been flirting a lot with some brothers. This isn't good, but they're old enough to make their own decisions. Caleb has been keeping an eye out too. I think he told the brothers to keep away from the girls because they aren't engaging with the girls as much as I expected they would. It's not stopping them from trying to get the attention of the older bikers, though.

Ena and Skull have been tied at the hip all night. She's not paying attention to her friend's antics. It's cute, but nothing keeps a biker away faster than a desperate woman. I'm not worried about them tonight. I'll talk to them about it after things from Ena's party settle down.

Sitting in Caleb's lap, I lay my head on his chest as he's talking to Wolf and Preacher. Again, Wolf is telling dirty jokes. It's hard not to like him, but I can't forget what he's done to Joss and Lexa. I haven't seen Lexa since we sang happy birthday to Ena. I'm sure she went home early, or she's hiding in her brother Axel's room. I don't think she wants to see the dance of Joss and Wolf. Wolf tries to talk to Joss and she b-lines to the other side of the room to avoid talking to him. I'm not sure what is going on with my friend. She won't talk about it. It seems she has secrets too. I'm all right with secrets. They're hers and she'll share with me once she's ready.

Hopefully.

And as with any part of my fucked up life, when things seem to go well, Paul crashes back into my life to fuck it all up. As we are all sitting around, laughing at Wolf's antics, Bo, the newest prospect, runs into the Compound and yells, "Pigs!" All the brothers rise and take various positions in the room. My heart is pounding, and my breaths are short. My whole life, cops have been the enemy. It seems that is no different with Havoc. I grab Ena's hand as Joker and Gunner move us toward the back of the club.

Just as we are about to exit the main room, the door flies off the hinge from a swift kick, and several heavily armed cops swarm the room. They shout commands, but I'm too afraid to move. I'm not sure why the cops are here, but I'm sure it has something to do with Paul. It takes all of my instincts not to run as fast as I can. Joker and Gunner both move into position, blocking Ena and me from view.

"Everyone get on the fucking floor!" We all lower ourselves to the floor.

"Put your fucking hands behind your head, fingers locked!" Again, we follow the cop with a buzz cut's commands.

"Who is Diablo?" another cop asks.

"I am!" Diablo bellows. I notice the change; he is no longer my sweet biker.

Tears form in my eyes as Ena and I stare at each other. I mouth, "I'm sorry." And she shakes her head no.

"Get the fuck up. We have a warrant."

"We didn't do shit," he spits. "We are having a nice family get-together on our own property."

"Shut the fuck up!" The cop punches Diablo in the jaw.

The sickening sound of a fist hitting flesh turns my stomach, and I squeeze my eyes shut. The awful thud reminds me of the blows I used to take regularly. Diablo spits out a mouth full of blood and flashes a sinister grin at the cop.

"Look around, officers, we have nothing to hide here."

"Yeah, I hear you store weapons and drugs here. And trust me, we will find them. Son of a bitches like you need to be off the street."

We continue to lay on the floor as more cops enter the room and split us into smaller groups to ask questions. I've never been happier to not know anything about Havoc's business. I can honestly tell the cops I know nothing about guns and drugs.

"I know your father," a redheaded pimply cop says. The name on his badge says Mills.

I sit straight up, but I don't speak. I have nothing to say to anyone who knows my father.

"He sent us here to find some shit on your boyfriend and get you and your sister out. It's okay, Savannah, you can trust me." His tone is sincere, but someone working for my father cannot be trusted. Giving up on questioning me, he turns his attention to Ena.

"McKena, you know you can trust the police. We can walk you out of here and you won't have to see these bastards again."

"You'll excuse me, Detective Mills, but I don't trust the cops. I'm sure my father forgot to mention how he beat the shit out of my sister and molested her best friend when we were kids. So you can fuck off! I'm eighteen. I don't want to leave Havoc. And for your information, these bastards are the best people to ever happen to Savy and I. They took care of us, when your kind left us abused." She turns her head and stares across the room at Skull, who winks at her in return. She lets a small smile cross her lips before it quickly leaves her face.

"Well, ladies. We will need to take Savannah in for questioning in the kidnapping of McKena Riley ten years ago. Please stand, Savannah. I need to put handcuffs on you."

I stand and turn around and feel the cold steel of the cuffs against my shaking wrists. I'm unable to look toward Caleb, instead I look toward the ceiling, just above his head.

"Yo! What the fuck are you doing? She's not going anywhere."

"Mr. Masterson, she is wanted for kidnapping. She has to come with us," Mills says. "Jones, come take Ms. Riley out to the cruiser."

"No problem, Detective." Jones grabs my upper arm and pulls me roughly toward the exit. He is digging his fingernails into my arm and drags me across the large room. He shifts his grip and grazes my breast, but it was no accident. Not only does he graze me, but he also squeezes my breast in a tight grip. I lose it and dig in my heels, snatching away from the officer. No man will ever touch me without my permission again.

"Don't you fucking rub and grab me, you son of a bitch!" I try to rip my arm from his grip. When I begin to struggle, he punches me in the face and openly gropes me in front of the whole room. He's obviously stupid. He grabs me again, but this time it's rougher than before. Every member of Havoc jumps up from where they are sitting and cuffed ready to charge over. Fortunately for me, and unfortunately for Jones, Joker is sitting close to where I'm struggling to free myself. He is only zip tied so with no real effort, he breaks his straps and picks Officer Jones up from behind. Officer Jones lets me go and I scramble away though ungracefully. You can only move so quickly with your hands cuffed behind your back and a sore face. The fucker hit me with his full force. I'm seeing stars.

"Put him down!" Detective Mills yells. He and every other officer in the room has their guns drawn and pointed at Joker, but they don't shoot. Doing so could mean they shoot and kill their bastard of a cop too.

"Joker!" Diablo says.

It's all it takes. Joker drops Officer Jones, and he slams into the floor in a heap of disgusting man.

"Now gentlemen, I cannot have you man handling my officers. Joker here will pay for that," Detective Mills says.

I lose it. Joker is going to pay? What about that fucking pervert that had his grubby hands all over me?

"Pardon me, Detective Mills, but I believe you are mistaken," I say. My words are slurred from the punch. I know I have blood dripping down my chin. I can feel it, but for now I ignore it. "Your officer, here was sexually assaulting me and my friend was merely defending me. There is a room full of people who saw him groping me and punching a handcuffed woman. And trust me there are cameras all around this fucking building that have recorded every fucking thing you have done here today. Don't try to find the tapes because they are wirelessly backed up, off site. McKena is safe. *You* can ask Paul why we ran ten years ago, but as far as what has gone on here, you should probably let it go. And, I know my rights, the statute of limitations for kidnapping in the state of Georgia is seven years. You yourself said ten years ago this apparent kidnapping happened. You have no grounds to arrest me."

"Ms. Riley, if these animals are threatening you, you can trust me to help you," Detective Mills says. He's trying and failing to sound sincere.

"Last time I trusted a cop, he raped me. No thank you."

His face pales at my words. He looks uncomfortable.

Good.

"Mr. Masterson, we're done here today, but you are on notice. One toe out of line and I will be back to arrest your ass."

The officers unlock our cuffs, and file out of the building. Once the door closes, I begin shaking. I don't know what came over me, but couldn't let him grope and hit me without fighting back.

"Come on, little bird, you're bleeding."

Looking up to Caleb's beautiful black eyes, tears fill mine. "He's never going to stop is he?"

"No," he says. An apology is written on his chiseled face. "He won't stop unless we stop him."

The only way to make him stop is to kill him. And given the opportunity that is exactly what I plan to do.

CHAPTER TWENTY-FIVE

Diablo

It almost killed me to see that fucking cop grab Savy and then punch her in the face. He's a dead man. I already have The Devils on it. They owe me some markers and I'm calling one in. Officer Jones is a dead man. I know the Compound is being watched, but I don't care. Cops harass us all the time. They are always looking for a reason to bring one of us in, trying to get information or just fucking with us in general. What they don't know is, Havoc never talks to cops. Ever.

This is something I didn't stress with Savy and Ena, but I'm proud of the way they handled themselves during the raid. Ena said what she needed to say and then kept her mouth shut. I'm damn proud of her. Savy, fought back. I'm fucking proud of her too. She's grown into an even stronger woman than when I met her. I made a mental note to teach her and Ena how to get out of cuffs and zip ties. They both need some work on the self-defense front, but they handled themselves like true women of Havoc.

"Are you all right, little bird?" I ask.

Savy has said little since getting out of the shower. We are staying at the Compound for a few days since I know the cops will watch our every move and I don't want them knowing where my house is.

"Hm," she says. "My face hurts. Can you get me more ice?"

"I'll be right back." I slide out of the bed and pull on a shirt. Closing the door behind me, I walk down the hall, decorated with pictures of Havoc's history, past and present. I always smile when I see the picture of Chino and I. I was a little young asshole when I met him, and he helped me become the man I am today.

I enter the main room, and I walk to the far side toward the kitchen. Axel is sitting on the couch, laptop on his lap, with his brows furrowed.

"What's up, Axel?"

"I got a ping on Hazel's phone. It says she's in the woods outside the club."

"Take Gunner with you. Let me know what you find."

"Right, Prez," he says while standing and walking down the hall to Gunner's room.

I get Savy's ice from the kitchen, and on my walk back to the room, Gunner and Axel are dressed in all black and heading out the back door, guns in hand. Hazel has been missing for a week and her phone has been off the entire time. It's a little strange that she shows back up right after the police raid. She's a sweet girl who took refuge in the Havoc Compound after a rough childhood. We took her in, and she's been in good standing ever since. When she got hooked up with Kris, she was still sweet, but easily manipulated by Kris. She was too innocent for this life, but she made the choice to live it. She also made the choice to go along with Kris, who still hasn't turned up, but she's out of the club after what that pussy Tyler told me. That bitch is as good as dead and as soon as someone from Havoc catches up with her, she will be.

I take the ice back to Savy, who is staring at the wall, not speaking. The gray pillowcase is dark and wet, she's been crying. I pull off my pants and shirt and slide into the bed with her, placing the ice on her cheek. It has already turned a dark purple. She will have a bruise for a while.

"I'm proud of you, little bird."

"Thank you," she says. Her voice is flat, but I press a little harder. I can't have her pulling away from me right now.

"Savy, what is it? You can ask me."

"Does the club deal drugs?" she asks quickly. It's almost as if she asked before I changed my mind.

"No," I say. "We don't deal drugs."

"Do you sell guns?"

"If I tell you anything, understand that you know too much. Just know it's a means to an end," I say. My words are cryptic, I know, but if I tell Savy too much about our gun running, she can take the whole club down or worse, she may get wrapped up in some shit with the Russians that she has nothing to do with.

"Are Ena and I safe here?" she asks, biting her lower lip.

"Yes, anytime you are on Havoc soil, you are safe." My eyes roam over her face, her beautiful, bruised face. "I can't promise that my enemies won't try to use you to get after me. You are my only weakness. Now that we're official, you are the only target they have to get back at me."

She nods her head. "I figured that much, Caleb. I'm not afraid of that."

"So what are you afraid of?" I ask.

"Paul getting his hands on Ena," she whispers. "I know she's protected inside these walls, but tonight, the outside came in, and we couldn't do anything about it."

"You listen to me. I love that kid like she's my own," I admit. I do. Ena is like the little sister I never had. It's fucked twisted because she's interested in Nate, but it's true. I love her too.

"Caleb," she says. Placing her small hand on my face, she leans in and gingerly kisses my lips. Her plump lips are soft and a small moan slips out of mouth. "Please, make it better. Take the feeling of his hands off me."

At her request, I lay Savy back on the mattress, and love her body properly, erasing the offending touches of a corrupt cop.

DIABLO

BANG.

Bang.

Bang.

Loud knocking wakes me, and I reach out to grab my gun from the night table next to my bed.

"Prez!" Axel yells from the other side of the door.

"Who is it?" Savy asks still half asleep.

"It's Axel, go back to sleep, little bird," I say. Laying a kiss on her forehead before I slip from bed to throw on clothes and leave the room. The door clicks closed behind me, and I look at Axel's face, he's in distress.

"What's wrong?"

"It's Hazel. She's lookin' real bad, Prez," he says. Worry is etched on his face. Running a hand through his blond hair, he looks like a man in suffering. I've known for a while that Axel has a thing for Hazel, but he never claimed her so he's had so sit back while the woman he wants fucks other men. It can't be easy, but he did it for his own reasons.

"Where is she?"

"Aero has her on the table," he says.

We walk toward the small clinic we have downstairs near the dungeon. The familiar scent of a hospital hits my nose and we enter the small exam room. Aero was a flight medic in the military. He keeps the clinic stocked with the necessary equipment and is capable of preforming minor surgery at the Compound.

"How bad is she?" I ask.

Aero looks up from his patient with a grim look on his face.

"It's not looking good, Prez," he says. "She's been starved, beaten, and from the looks of it raped. She won't let me examine her though so I don't know for sure."

I walk over to the table where a scared, wide-eyed Hazel is laying.

She turns her head slightly, but her movements are shaky. She's coming down from whatever drug was given to her. The signs of drug use are clear. Hazel is jittery and her eyes are hollow, like she hasn't slept in days.

"It's okay, Hazel," I say. "We need to see how bad it is." Soft is not my style. I try, but my words still come out gruff. Her eyes dart back and forth between Axel, Aero, and I. I'm afraid she may try to run and hurt herself more.

Axel is moving anxiously in the corner.

"Axel, give us a minute."

"No," Hazel says with a squeak. "Please Diablo, let him stay. Please."

Noted. Hazel likes Axel, too.

"Fine, but you have some explaining to do, girl. Were you raped?" I ask. We don't have time to bullshit. I need to know where the fuck she was for a week. Paul is getting riskier by the day.

"Yes," she whispers. Embarrassment shines in her eyes as tears form.

"Who raped you, Hazel?"

"P-Paul." Silent tears slide down her cheeks.

As the name leaves her lips, Axel lets out a series of curses.

"Shh, it will be all right, girl," I say. I'm unsure of what else should be said. She survived it. So she will eventually be all right. At least I hope so. This is uncharted territory for Havoc. I've never had to deal with a psychopath who rapes club property.

"Tell me what happened," I say.

"She asked me to help her get rid of Savy the night of the fight, but I told her no. Kris called last week and asked me to help her pack her things. She said she was going to leave Havoc for good since you made Savy your ol' lady. She said she couldn't be around and watch you be in love with someone that wasn't her." She pauses to catch her breath. Her ribs must be broken because her breathing is labored. Taking a shallow breath, she continues, "I went to her house and there were two men there, Tyler and Paul. I didn't know who they were, but I wanted to help Kris. When I asked Kris where the boxes were, she told me she wasn't leaving and that Tyler and Paul were going to help her get back at Savy."

She cries as the words spill from her mouth, "I told them I wouldn't help with that because Havoc has been good to me, but Kris said I didn't have a choice. She threatened to reveal the real reason I left Minnesota to the club. I told her I didn't care, but Paul grabbed me and told me I wasn't going anywhere. He hit me several times, and he must have knocked me out because the next thing I know I am tied to a bed down in a basement."

Turning to Aero, she asks, "Can I sit up? My back is hurting laying down like this."

"Of course," he replies. Raising the hospital bed into a sitting position. "Better?"

"Yes, much better, thank you."

Hazel continues her story, and Axel moves closer, taking a position next to her and grabbing her hand. He strokes the back of her hand, providing reassurance and comfort.

"He kept me tied up in that bed for days. He would come in at all hours and punch, choke and slap me. I wanted to die down in that basement, but I needed to get back to Havoc. This is the only place I feel safe."

"You are safe, Hazel," Axel says. "How did you get free?"

"He untied me so I could use the bathroom when Kris came down the stairs. She told me how stupid I was and how I deserved everything that Paul was doing to me. I don't know if she knew Paul was listening, but she told me she can never come back to Havoc because you all would kill her before she made it through the gates. Paul was pissed. He came in and started yelling at her. He choked her right there in front of me. He was yelling about how fucking stupid she was and how she ruined everything."

A small smile on her lips as she continues, "He didn't remember to lock me back to the bed when he dragged Kris' body up the stairs. I stayed in the bathroom and prayed that he wouldn't come back before I got my chance to escape. He didn't. Once I heard the car start and him pull out, I bolted toward the door as quickly as I could. Thankfully he left that unlocked too. I grabbed the clothes he discarded on the floor and ran. That was yesterday. I've been hiding in the woods since then." Her last word a whisper.

"How did you get your phone?"

"It was still in my pants pocket."

"Why were you hiding in the woods?"

"Because I didn't want you to kill me," she says. "Please don't kill me, Diablo! I didn't do anything. I tried to leave, but he kept hitting me. I was too weak." Her sobs are loud and a small tap of the clinic door has everyone turning toward it.

"Caleb," Savy says.

"I'll be out in a minute, Savy," I say. But it's too late; she is already pushing the heavy door open and walking in, a look of utter horror on her face.

"What happened to Hazel?" she asks.

"I'm sorry, Savy," Hazel cries. "I tried." Her unintelligible words muffled by the arm she has thrown out to covered her face.

"What the fuck is going on?" Savy is pissed and concerned.

I tell her what happened to Hazel. There is no sense in hiding it from her. She will find out eventually.

"Oh god. Hazel, I'm so sorry. This is all my fault," Savy says.

What the fuck?

"It ain't your fault, little bird."

"Isn't it? I brought Paul here. I brought a monster to Havoc and now Hazel has been hurt too." She cries and moves next to Hazel's bed. Making sure she is gentle, she grabs Hazel's other hand, as Axel still has the first.

"Aero, clean Hazel up, then Axel can take her to his room to rest."

"Got it, Prez."

I take Savy's hand and we go back through the Compound to our room. She's crying uncontrollably now and I don't try to stop it. I just wrap her in my arms and let her cry it all out. Once she calms down, she takes a shower. After getting dressed, she asks to go for a walk outside.

"I want to go sit in the grass. Please, honey?" Looking at the clock, it's almost six in the morning, so I allow her to walk the grounds alone. She's safe as long as she's on Havoc property.

"Take your gun," I say.

A peculiar look crosses her freckled face. "Babe, I don't need a gun. I'll be all right."

"At least take your knife. Give me some peace of mind, little bird," I say.

"All right honey," she says. Slipping the knife in her boot. She looks like a real badass biker chick. She was made for me, and this life, and I want to protect her at all costs. "I'll be back in a bit. I just need to clear my head."

She rises on her tiptoes and plants a chaste kiss on my lips. I send Tiny to watch Savy in the field. I don't care what she thinks, there's no way I'm letting her outside unprotected, even on Havoc soil.

SAVY

WALKING AROUND THE OPEN FIELD SURROUNDING THE HAVOC Compound, I'm thinking about all the things that led me to Havoc. The death of my mother, the beatings by my father, the molestation by Jon, and ultimately the kidnapping by me. I never thought I would find a man I love with all of my heart. Hell, I never thought I could tolerate being around a man for longer than five minutes, let alone wanting to be around one at all times.

I love him with all of my heart.

It's crazy really. A beaten, battered girl has grown into a beautiful, confident woman. I sit down in the middle of the field, on the backside of the brick building that houses the Havoc Compound. The sun has been up for only about twenty minutes and the dew on the grass is getting my pants wet, but I don't care. I love it out here, just nature and me.

I've always loved being outside, but was too afraid to enjoy it for fear of Paul finding me out in the open. As my thoughts drift back to my mother, I hear footsteps approaching. They are of heavy boots.

Caleb.

I turn with a huge smile stretching across my face, but it's not the sight I thought I would see.

Paul.

My heart stops. He has a rifle pointed at my head.

"Get the fuck up, bitch."

I stand. Making sure my movements are slow. I don't want to die in this field.

"What do you want, Paul?" I ask. "It's over, Ena is an adult now. You can't have her."

"Shut the fuck up!" Spit lands on my face as he screams his command. "You're coming with me."

"I'm not." The calm in my voice scares me. Here I am staring down the barrel of a gun and I'm not afraid.

Not anymore.

"You are." He hits me in the head with the muzzle of the gun. Dropping to the earth, I reach up and grab my temple as blood covers my fingers. "Now get the fuck up before I kill you right here."

I stand again, continuing to hold my head. He grabs me by both arms and locks a zip tie to my wrists, behind my back.

Fuck! I've been practicing and failing my escape from zip ties. What am I going to do now?

"Move," he says. Shoving the gun into my back as he walks me toward the trees. Once we are inside the tree line, he hits me again in the back of the head, knocking me out.

SAVY

I WAKE UP TO ARMS STINGING LIKE A THOUSAND NEEDLES HAVE BEEN pushed into my flesh. I'm swinging from my wrists above my head, tied to the ceiling. My shoulders are stretched almost to the point of dislocation and I'm barely standing on the balls of my feet. Instead of lifting my head and opening my eyes, I keep my head bowed, breathing shallow, and try to assess my surroundings. I hear water dripping and it's freezing in here. I can't tell if Paul is in the room with me, so I open my eyes to slits. It's dark in the room, but there is a sliver of light coming from underneath the door. I try not to move too much, I don't want to pull my arm out of the socket, if it's unnecessary.

"Oh good," Paul says as he opens the door and enters. "You're awake." He is carrying a bucket, but I'm unable to see what's inside it. I don't respond to his words. I remember as a child, Paul liked when I cried. I won't cry today. I'd rather die than give him the chance to get satisfaction out of my torture.

"Are you ready?" he asks with a sick smile stretches across his face. "It seems we have a lot of time to make up." He throws a pail full of freezing water on me. I shiver immediately, but I remain silent.

"Oh, are you not talking, you little bitch?" His face is red, his anger simmering beneath the surface of his eyes. "You don't need to talk, all you need to do is scream."

He pulls out a long crude knife. It looks like something you would see in a post-apocalyptic movie, or something a psychopath would use on his victims. I guess a psychopath is using it. It looks sharp. Paul presses the cold metal against my thigh and barely presses down as he drags it down my leg. It's definitely sharp. The pain is bearable. It feels like a mild paper cut, but he brings the knife back to the top of the red line he created and he cuts inside the same line again. This time it burns like hell, but I remain silent. I barely move, pissing Paul off more.

He creates several more lines down my thighs, trying to elicit a sound, but remaining unsuccessful. Moving back, he pulls out a sharp dagger. It looks like an icepick, but with a thicker blade. And instead of teasing, he plunges it into my other thigh.

The bastard laughs as he leaves the dagger where it has been thrust into my flesh and he quickly thrusts another in my other leg. Tears are running down my face as I endure the pain of the torture that Paul is inflicting, but I don't cry out. If he is going to kill me, it will be on my terms.

He is ranting about me killing my mother, as he continues to mutilate my legs, arms and torso. I'm losing blood fast. Just as I feel myself slipping into a black abyss, Paul places a tourniquet around my thighs to stop the bleeding from the deep wounds, keeping me alive, for now.

He's going to keep my alive until he gets what he wants. What Paul doesn't realize is, Caleb will never let Ena go without protection. If I never return, I know that Ena will always be protected and Paul will die for what he has done. Caleb will hunt Paul down and kill him to avenge my death. At the thought, I smile and Paul smashes his fist into my face, knocking me out again.

CHAPTER TWENTY-SIX

Past

PAUL

SITTING IN THE STERILE OFFICE, I REACH OVER TO SQUEEZE MARY'S hand. Dr. Raynott has called us to his office to discuss Mary's recent visit. Squeezing Mary's hand until the point of pain, she brings her free hand to stroke mine and I release my grasp.

The doctor enters his office and sits behind his large oak desk. As he sits, the knot in my stomach drops to my feet. The pained expression on his face tells me everything I need to know.

It tells Mary too.

She squeezes my hand as I had hers minutes before. Clearing his throat, the doctor speaks, but I hear nothing. I already know the lump we found is cancer. My best friend and the most important person in my life is sick. The rock that has been sitting on my chest for the last few days gets even heavier.

What am I going to do without the other half of my soul?

―――――――――

Savy

The next time I gain conciseness, I'm lying on the hard, cold concrete floor. My hands are tied to my front and my vision is blurry for a few minutes as my eyes adjust to the dim lighting in the damp room. With nothing to protect me from the cold, I'm shivering. I don't move because I don't know where Paul is. He has to be close and I'm surprised that he took me down from the hanging position I was in previously. I assumed he would leave me hanging until my arms ripped from their sockets. After all, his goal all along has been to inflict as much pain as possible.

I hear a chair scrape across the concrete and I close my eyes again, keeping my breath shallow. "Fucking bitch. She murdered Mary. It's all her fault my Mary is gone. She took her from me."

I don't dare move an inch. The punch to my head has caused it to pound so much that I can feel the blood rushing in both ears. As Paul continues ranting about my mother, his footsteps move from one side of the room to another. I count as he moves in one direction and then turns, and moves in the opposite direction.

One.

Two.

Three.

Four.

Five.

Six.

I focus on his steps. Only six steps from one side to the other. It's the only thing keeping me awake. I want to sleep, but I'm afraid if I close my eyes to sleep, I'll never open them again. But I've lost too much blood and even the counting of steps cannot keep me awake. I fall into blackness. I'm exhausted and I pray for death. Paul has finally gotten his hands on me, but at least he'll never get his hands on Ena.

"Get the fuck up, bitch!" Fire grows in my thighs as he snatches me up from my horizontal position. He is holding me up against a wall in the dank basement or dungeon. At this point I can't tell the difference. His eyes are black pits. No soul, no humanity left. His eyes are unlike the black soulful eyes I look into each night.

"Are you still keeping quiet, bitch?"

This time instead of remaining silent, I let loose all the words and emotions I've had since I was a little girl. It's bad enough I lost my mother in a tragic accident, but what's worse is the treatment I received from my father, the one man I was supposed be able to depend on. I'm going to die anyway, hell I might as well tell him what I really feel about him.

"He's going to kill you," I say. My voice is a deep rasp. I must have been down here a long time. I just noticed how thirsty I am. Clearing my throat, I continue, "Diablo will gut you, you motherfucker!" He backhands me, my head twisting to the side, but I keep speaking, "I'm not keeping quiet any more. I've done that my whole life and look where that's gotten me."

He slaps me across the cheek again. My head snaps to the other side, but it doesn't stop me from saying what I have to say. I've taken enough slaps in my life and at this point I don't give a fuck. He can kill me, but he *will* listen to what I have to say first.

"Does that make you feel better?" My eyebrows are knitted in disgust. "Does hitting a woman make you feel like a real man? What about hitting a little girl? Beating an eight-year-old girl that just watched her mother die in a car accident. Is that what gets you off, you son of a bitch?"

"She's dead because of you!"

"No!" Today is the first time I have yelled at my father, ever. He is shocked at my rage. He loosens his hold on my body, but continues to hold me pinned to the wall. "I did *not* kill her. It was an accident. A fucking tragic, horrible accident, but I was eight." I let my words sink in. I think I'm getting through to him, but then I see the shudders in his eyes fall into place and his rage comes full force.

"Shut up! Shut up! You killed her!"

"No, you idiot. YOU were driving. If anyone is at fault here, it's you."

He lets me go and I drop to the ground with a hard thud. I can feel the dampness of my blood against my pants, but I need to keep my attention on Paul. He scrambles backwards like touching me burns his skin. I continue my barrage of words, it's the first time I see hope that I might make it out of here alive. I don't know where I am, or how long he's had me locked up, but I have hope.

"You were the parent. The only parent I had left and instead of taking care of me and protecting me, you gave me to a rapist. Jon raped me every day for six years. And you knew." A statement. Paul knew I was being molested, and he did nothing to protect me. Any normal parent would have pressed charges or killed the bastard, but Paul kept handing me over like I didn't matter to him. I was nothing to him. "I was there the day mom died too. She fought you. She begged you to save me and what did you do?"

"I saved you when I should have saved her," he admits. It stings. Despite all the fucked up shit he has done, he is still my father and deep down I had hoped I could forgive him, but he has sealed his fate. He is dead to me.

Forever.

"Yes, you should have saved her. And what kind of life would you have lived after that? She would have resented you for saving her instead. You bastard. You were supposed to protect me!"

"Shut up!" He slaps me hard across the face, stopping my words in their tracks. My cheeks are already burning from the other blows so I don't feel the pain much, but the defiance is still in my eyes. He punches me over and over until I black out again.

I really wish this fucker would stop hitting me so I can think of a plan to get the fuck out of here.

DIABLO

Savy has been missing for six hours.

Six fucking hours!

We didn't find out she was missing until about ten minutes after she was gone. Tiny was sliced across the throat from behind when he was watching Savy in the field. Thankfully the fucker didn't hit Tiny's carotid arteries or his jugular vein. Paul did a shitty job of finishing the job. He was trying to get out of there fast and ambushed Tiny. Bo was doing a normal perimeter check when he found Tiny bleeding in the field. He's been in surgery since the attack, but Aero tells me he will survive.

Thank fuck.

I can't let this fucker get away with trying to kill my brother and kidnapping my ol' lady. I need to find out where she is. I can't lose her now. "Axel, I need everything you can find on Tyler, Kris and Paul. Fuck, put Hazel in there too. This motherfucker took Savy and I need to get her back."

"I've been looking, boss, but I got jack shit!" he yells in frustration.

I feel helpless. It's an emotion I'm not used to feeling. I'm Diablo, the devil and President of Havoc Motorcycle Club, but right now I feel like a scared little boy, much like I felt as a child. I need to do something, anything to get Savy back. I want to be out there searching for Savy, but if I become reckless, I will likely get her killed sooner. That is something I cannot live with so I sit and wait for Axel to find something.

Ena has been sitting in the main room on the couch the entire time Savy has been missing. Joss, Lexa, Hazel and the other sweetbutts are sitting around the Compound in silence. Every once in a while, Joss or Lexa tries to get Ena to go lay down or eat something. She just yells at them to leave her the fuck alone and she continues sitting, staring off into nothingness as tears roll down her cheeks.

Skull is sitting on her other side silently providing stability in an unsure situation. He doesn't speak, just holds her hand and squeezes it to reassure her. We are all on edge. It's a painful waiting game we must play. When I get my hands on Paul, I'm going to fucking kill him.

"I got something!" Axel yells as he enters the room.

"Church! Now!" I call.

"Kid, I'm gonna find her, you hear me?" I say. Looking Ena straight in the eyes I vow to find her sister and the woman I love.

"Yes," she says. I see a spark of defiance settle on her face and it's just what I need as I walk into the chapel.

"What did you find?"

"Two weeks ago, Kris called Donny. I ran her call records. I didn't see it before because she called him at his house. Then I ran Donny's records, and he called a Georgia phone number several times a few weeks ago."

"Savy and Ena are from Georgia. It's gotta be Paul."

"Yeah, that fucker didn't even use a burner. I have a ping on his phone right now. He's on the Southside of town, near the old railroad tracks. He must be keeping her in a different place than he kept Hazel. We found jack shit there," Axel says.

"Let's go get my girl."

We head out. We're strapped with every weapon we have available. This is a critical mission. If Savy dies, I won't be able to face Ena, let alone myself ever again. I hope she can hold on long enough for me to get to her.

CHAPTER TWENTY-SEVEN

SAVY

I'M SO WEAK. I WANT TO JUST DIE, BUT I NEED TO GET BACK TO ENA and Caleb. They are the two most important people in my life and I want to be around for them. I open my eyes, but it's still dark. I have no idea what time it is because it has been dark the entire time I've been in this room. I have to pee, but I don't think I can get myself up if I want to. I lay on the cold floor and just lay there. There are no thoughts floating through my head, other than escape.

Eventually my urge to pee is greater than my need to lay in one place. I take what seems like an hour to pull myself up into a sitting position. Paul is no longer in the room and I can't hear anything on the other side of the door. He was kind enough to leave me a dirty bucket to do my business in, but the asshole didn't leave any toilet paper. I do my business and shake as much as possible before slowly pulling my pants back up.

This shit hurts.

I sit in the darkest corner of the room and wait. My legs have pretty much lost all feeling, but I know they are still alive because I can wiggle my toes. As I'm flexing my foot, I feel the cold steel in my boot, and a new surge of hope fills my chest. I forgot all about the knife that Caleb forced me to take with me. I try to slide it from my boot as fast as my numb fingers will allow.

Dropping the metal to the concrete floor, I pause with an abated breath, waiting to see if Paul will burst back into the room and take it from me. After a few minutes of waiting, I slowly pick up the knife and cut my bindings. I take a while to cut through the thick rope, but when I cut myself free, tears cloud my vision. I hastily wipe the tears and slide the knife back into my boot. I need to keep it hidden. I will only get one chance to escape so I need to make it worth it. I drape the rope over my wrists, so when Paul returns he will think I'm still tied tight.

It doesn't take long for Paul to come back into my prison with a large roll of plastic. A shiver rolls down my back and the hair on my arms stand on end. He has come with supplies to clean up the mess he is about to create while killing me.

"Wake up!"

I slide from my corner, careful not to jostle the loose ropes. I will only have one chance at this. Paul leans in close and stares at me, like I'm an animal in the zoo. Just as I'm about to reach up, I hear a loud pounding sound kick in the heavy door.

"Stand the fuck up, mother fucker!"

Caleb.

His voice washes over me and I want to weep, but I don't. I can't lose focus now, I reach down and grab the knife tucked in my book and with the last of my strength, I thrust the blade into the side of Paul's neck. His eyes hold a surprised expression, but I don't let the knife go, I twist it in further, his warm blood flowing over my hands and forearms. I don't let go. I'm afraid if I do, he will get up and kill me. So I keep hold of the knife, ensuring he won't walk away from his injury.

Paul grabs my hand, but he is losing blood fast and his hold is weak.

"Burn in hell, motherfucker." My whispered words ring out loud and I collapse to the concrete. Before I hit the ground, I'm swooped into Caleb's arms and his face is scrunched with concern.

"Savannah, baby, where are you hurt?" This is the first time I've seen Caleb lose his calm exterior. He's genuinely worried. I'm having a hard time focusing on his face, my eyes are heavy and I just want to sleep.

"Everywhere," I whisper. "Sleep, I need to sleep."

"No baby, stay with me, little bird." He is whispering against my ear as he brings me out of the house, it is barely light outside. I can't tell if it's morning or still the same day.

"Savy, baby, you gotta stay awake for me."

"Aero! She's fading fast," he says.

They put me in the back of a van that looks like an ambulance from the inside and Aero gives me an IV. That is all I remember because again I slip into the abyss, but this time it's worried loving black eyes that I see before I go.

DIABLO

"HOW IS SHE, DOC?"

Savy has been under heavy sedation for the past week. We had to bring in Doctor Rothstein, a small man with kind eyes. He's a retired doctor that helps the club when someone needs serious medical attention without the heat coming down on us. We pay him a hell of a lot of money to keep quiet about anyone we bring him in to work on.

"She's getting better," he says.

"Why hasn't she woken up yet?"

"Sometimes it takes the mind longer to heal even when the body is on the way to a full recovery."

"And the babies?" My stomach flips every time I think about them. I found out when the doc came to evaluate Savy's condition.

She's pregnant, and she doesn't even know it yet. She's about eight weeks along and we are damn lucky they survived the hell Paul put Savy through. Once she wakes up, we will have a rough road ahead, but there isn't anything I want more than spending the rest of my life with the sweet, sassy curly haired spitfire that captured the heart of the devil.

"The babies are fine. They are fighters, those three. You take good care of them, you hear?" He moves toward the bedroom door and softly closes it on his way out for the night. He will be back to check on Savy in the morning.

"I will," I say.

Running my fingers through my hair, I look over at Ena who is sleeping on the couch we brought into the bedroom at our house. Ena hasn't left Savy's side since I brought her home. Every waking minute, she's at her sister's side reading to her, combing her hair and making sure she is taken care of.

The second day, I tried to get Ena to take a break and get some food, but she told me to fuck off because she wasn't going anywhere. So, I fucked off and let her stay where she was. Not my typical reaction to someone telling me to fuck off, but I know Ena is hurting. I can't imagine the anguish she's experiencing, knowing her sister dedicated her entire life to ensuring she was safe.

I climb into the bed next to the woman I love and reach into my pocket, pulling out the four-carat cushion cut diamond ring. It has been in my pocket for two weeks. I wanted to wait for the perfect moment to give it to her, but that moment never came. Taking the ring from its holder, I reach out to take Savy's hand and slide the ring on her finger. I barely sleep while lying next to her motionless body, every sound or movement from Ena on the couch wakes me.

God please don't take this woman from me before I get the chance to show her what a cherished life free from fear is like.

I close my eyes and try to sleep, but I don't. Instead I whisper, "Savy, baby. Wake up. Please, baby. You are so brave. Fight to get back to me."

DIABLO

IT HAS BEEN ALMOST TWO WEEKS SINCE SAVY HAS BEEN IN HER COMA. Doc has her on medication, but not enough to sustain a coma. We are beginning to worry she may be in a coma long-term. This is not something I'm prepared to deal with and when Ena heard Savy may never wake up, she became so inconsolable that Skull had to drag her kicking and screaming out of the room to calm her down.

Once Ena began crying, Savy's monitors started to beep. It was then that I knew she was still in there. She heard her sister in distress and she reacted, like she had been reacting her entire life. Since that day, we have been telling Savy it's time to wake up. Each time we do, her heart rate increases, but she doesn't move, doesn't wake. We have hope that she will come out on the other side of this. God isn't that cruel. I just got her. I can't lose her now.

You don't deserve her.

I'm a selfish bastard, so I'm never letting her go, even if I don't deserve her. She's the best thing to ever happen to me and the club isn't the same without her. I'm not the same without her.

"Savy, you need to wake up," I pause, "Baby, I *need* you."

"Her eyes are opening!" Ena says.

"Savy, baby. Open your eyes." It's the moment my world is all right. The most beautiful brown eyes stare into my black ones.

"Honey, don't move." Turning to Ena, I say, "Go get the doctor."

"No need I'm right here," he says. "I heard her yelling down the hall."

The short man moves to the side of the bed, with a small smile. "Well hello there, Savannah. You gave us all quite a scare. Are you in any pain?"

She nods her head and tries to speak. At first, nothing comes out, but then the sweetest sound I've ever heard rings loud, though not clear.

"Throat."

"Here," Ena says. Handing the doc a cup of cool water. He allows her to drink a small amount of liquid slowly.

"You've been in a coma for ten days. Other than your throat, dear, what else hurts?"

She moves her hand to her stomach and with tears pooling in her eyes, she says, "My babies, are they all right?"

Ena takes in an audible breath. It must be true. Savy knew everything that was happening around her. The doc has been telling us she can hear us, but I wasn't sure.

"They are fine, dear, perfectly healthy. Those two are fighters, just like their mother."

She visibly relaxes. Looking toward me, she says, "I heard everything." And then her eyes close again. "I'm so tired."

"It's all right, dear, you need to rest. You've been through a great deal and we need you strong so you can get back to normal."

She is asleep before the doctor finishes his sentence.

"This is good news, Diablo. Don't look so worried. She was tortured, and she's pregnant. She will need lots of rest. I'm going back to the living room. I will be back to check on her when she wakes up again."

Ena and I look at each other and she lets out a happy squeal. Savy is back, and she's going to have my babies.

SAVY

IT'S STRANGE BEING IN A COMA. I'M SO TIRED, BUT I'M OFTEN AWARE of what is being said or done around me. The only problem is I can't open my eyes, speak, or move for that matter.

The shit sucks.

I've heard Ena reading to me, and Caleb whispering sweetly. I also know I'm pregnant with twins. Thank goodness I'm knocked out or I would freak the fuck out.

Twins.

Holy shit.

Twins.

If I could, I would do a happy dance, but alas a coma. I'm exhausted from laying in this damn bed too. I've been trying to force myself to wake since I got here, but I haven't been able to wake up. I'm not sure how long it has been, but I know it's been longer than a week and the doctor is getting worried about me never waking up again.

I think today is my day. No more lying around letting life happen to me. I will determine what happens to me from here on out. Caleb is near me and talking in hushed tones. I can feel his scratchy beard on my neck.

"Savy, you need to wake up." He pauses and then continues, "Baby, I *need* you."

"Her eyes are opening!" Ena yells.

I'm so tired, but I needed to make sure my babies are all right. I needed to hear for myself, not from the haze of a coma.

After I woke up a second time, it seems my family has relaxed a bit. Ena has left the room to sleep in her own bed for the first time in ten days and Caleb is still right by my side. He's a stubborn man. Nothing I say will get him out of the room.

Now that he knows I'm on the road to recovery, I begin getting visitors. Joss, Lexa, and the brothers come to visit. When I heard about what Paul did to Tiny, I felt terrible, but thank goodness he's not dead. A sliced throat is usually a surefire way to kill someone. Lucky for all of us, Paul is the only one dead.

It has been three weeks since my kidnapping. Every night I dream of the time in the basement with Paul and every night, Caleb consoles me by wrapping me in his arms and telling me each day how much he loves me. Preacher has been by the house more times than I can count too. He's definitely the father I never had. Milly and Preacher have taken Ena and me into their family even more than before, and I'm happy to have them as grandparents to my children.

We don't know what we are having yet, but we all have a lot of fun arguing about the gender of the twins. Ena, Joss, and Lexa are team girl all the way. Caleb, Nate, and the rest of the brothers are team boy. I don't care either way. I just want them to be healthy and happy. Each night before I close my eyes to go to bed, I vow to my children that I will always protect them and if god forbid, I'm no longer here to protect them myself, I know they have a whole club of crazy, rowdy uncles that will protect them from any harm.

Laying down to rest, I place my hands on my still flat stomach then I move to the scarred, but healing skin on each thigh. It's a tender reminder of the horrible past I fled and eventually caught up with me in Sage. It's a reminder of The Monster that terrorized me since I was a child. Then I look to the pink line on the palm of my hand. It's the scar I look at often. The only evidence I vanquished The Monster of my childhood. A scar I received when I plunged the knife into Paul's neck.

It's a constant reminder that I'm strong. Once I stopped running and faced the past I was so eager to flee, I could face the pain and humiliation of my past. It's a reminder that I needed no one else to save me, a reminder that the only person I needed, was me.

My scars are a reminder that running gets you nowhere. I tried to run and ended up in the same place I was before. You have to be brave enough to face all the demons and be brave enough to save yourself.

EPILOGUE

SAVY

LOOKING OUT THE BACK WINDOW OF OUR KITCHEN TO MY HUSBAND and kids playing in the back yard, I revel in the realization this is a life I never imagined I would be blessed enough to have. It has been two years since I killed my father. I'm mostly over the trauma his torture caused, but some days are worse than others. Hearing the twins playing with their father is the best cure for my tortured soul.

"Again, Daddy!" Kylie squeals. Her wild hair flying as Caleb tosses her in the air and catches her while planting a kiss on her forehead before she repeats her squeal, and he tosses her again.

Kane is pulling on Caleb's leg. "Me now!"

I can't help the smile that crosses my face. I have to admit that soon after recovering from the torture, I felt guilty. I was ready to give up when Paul had me tied up in that basement. If I had allowed Paul to complete his plan, two beautiful souls would have never made it to this Earth. It's something I'm still dealing with.

"Knock, knock!" Preacher says. He and Milly are coming over for a family barbecue today. As always, they are the first to arrive.

"Hey, honey," Preacher says. "How are you feeling?"

My heart swells with love for this man who is continually concerned about Ena and I. "I'm good, Pop."

"Move, Hank," Milly says while pushing Preacher out of her way. "I need a hug from my girl."

Preacher moves out of Milly's way and she wraps her arms around me and whispers, "I love you."

"I love you, too," I whisper back. My eyes fill with tears, but instead of being embarrassed like in the past, I embrace them. It means I'm alive.

I'm feeling.

And I'm all right with that.

"I talked to Ena today. She's doing so well at school I can't wait for her to come home to visit," Milly says.

"Me either!" Ena yells. She moves from behind Milly and wraps me in a tight hug.

I'm shocked to see my sister standing in my kitchen. She's been in college for a year now. Since she is going to UCLA, she doesn't get home often enough.

"Ena!" I scream and we jump up and down as we always do when we see each other after an extended period apart. "What the hell? You can't do that to me!" I chide her with a smile on my face. Turning to Skull, who walked in behind her, I say, "You asshole, I told you yesterday she's been ducking my phone calls."

"Sorry, Savy. I was threatened by those two," Skull says pointing to Ena and Milly.

I've been calling her for two days and she's been dodging me. Now I know why.

"Aunt Ena!"

"Aunt Ena!"

The twins say in unison, and we all laugh as they run to my sister and attach themselves to her legs. Caleb comes behind me and wraps his hand around my swollen belly. Leaning in to whisper in my ear, "I can't wait for everyone to leave so we can make baby number four."

"Baby number three is still cooking, honey."

"I can't wait for everyone to leave so we can *practice* making baby number four."

Turning around to face the man I love, the father of my children, I say, "Me either honey." I plant a wet kiss on the man I love.

"Eww!"

"Eww!"

And we all burst out laughing at the twins. Here in this moment, is where I was destined to be. It has been a long road, but I'm thankful for the lessons I have learned and I'm glad to be standing here with the people I love most in the world.

ACKNOWLEDGMENTS

There are so many people I need to thank for all their love and encouragement as I wrote Uncaged.

Mom & Dad - Thank you for everything you've taught me, and your unwavering love & encouragement.

To my baby sister Jade, I see so much of you in Ena. Thank you for being you, and loving me, in spite of my flaws. I'm grateful to have you as a sister.

Mallory, if it weren't for you, Uncaged would still be sitting in a file buried on my computer. Your "just write the damn book" was the push I needed. Thank you for being my ear to vent, rant and whine, and always just being there to tell me to get back to writing. I'm so thankful to have you as a best friend!

My sweet Halee, thank you for all you've helped me with: reading the very first draft of the book, naming Basil over pizza, beta reading, and providing feedback on the cover. I'm blessed to have a friend like you.

Danica, Brenda, and Maryanne - I love you all! Thank you for spitballing names for Dr. Rothstein and encouraging me through this whole process.

Jennifer, my friend, your feedback, and help through this process has been fantastic! Thank you for reading an early version of the book. I'm so thankful to have a friend like you.

To my beta and ARC team, thank you for everything! I am so thankful that you chose to spend your valuable time to read a new, unknown author. I'm grateful to have you on my team. I can't do this without you.

To my tribe, Emily & Christina, you both know how much I adore you. I'm blessed to have your love and support. You are fierce writers, and I can't wait to read the amazing things you put out into the world.

And to my glitter sisters, you all inspire me to keep writing. Thank you all for your kindness, your friendship, and your help crafting this book! Debbie, you know I love you, and I definitely couldn't have done it without you. Keep throwing glitter around, you know it's one of my favorite colors!

ABOUT THE AUTHOR

L.A. is a Sin City girl, living in a Georgia Peach world. She lives in Sugar Hill, Georgia with her two pups, Bella and Willow. Raised in Las Vegas, Nevada, she grew up playing in the desert and riding bikes with her older brothers and younger sister. She loves the color pink, coffee, romance and all things nerdy. In her free time, she enjoys reading, painting and spending time with her family. With experience as a Sexual Health and Wellness consultant, L.A. focuses on positive self-talk and body image. These are strong themes, weaved throughout her novels.

For more books and updates:
www.laboles.com

f facebook.com/laboleswrites

🐦 twitter.com/laboleswrites

a amazon.com/author/laboles

𝓟 pinterest.com/authorlaboles

g goodreads.com/authorlaboles

Printed in Great Britain
by Amazon